How to be a
Terrible Teenager

BEX PLENDERLEITH

DEDICATION

To my legions of fans.

CONTENTS

1 FAMILY

How to Refine Your Dining Etiquette
(So That No-One Will Eat With You Ever Again)

It is scientifically proven that there is **nothing worse** than having to sit at a table with your family to eat. Not even being run over by a Skoda when you're playing "chicken", getting skin cancer at 19 (life's so unfair - you're still in your best decade) due to your sun bed addiction, becoming pregnant under-age (maternity clothes are so gross), or even getting a pube trapped in your zip because you're a bloater, or a scissor-shy hippie. Eating with your family - particularly at a table (yep, that means no TV!!!) not only means an inane interrogation about your fabulous life, but you'll also have to actually **look at your parents** which forces you to somewhat acknowledge that your dad isn't really a multi-millionaire rock star and your mum aint no supermodel. And, by association, neither are you.

Incidentally, parents *only* insist on the family eating together for a very simple reason - not because they do want to find out about your very private lives (they couldn't care less) but because they actually want the dreadful mealtime experience to drive the other parent so nuts that they'll finally give in to granting the divorce.

How To Guarantee You'll Never Eat Together Again

WARNING: you may well find the following information highly offensive. It goes against everything you've never believed in. However, if you put this advice into practise - however traumatic - it *will* result in you NEVER having to eat at the table with your family EVER AGAIN. Furthermore, if you perfect these techniques **now**, you will ALSO never have to eat formally with your future husband/wife or children either. So, really, it's worth the short-term sacrifice.

1. Instead of traditionally being last to the table, *be the first*, telling subsequent latecomers to show more respect and gratitude to the meal-maker. If at all possible, say this without any swearing or emotion as this will have a most chilling impact. (The bonus side-effect of this behaviour is that your Mum'll give you the least burnt burger).

2. Pull the chair out for your Mum - remembering to reassure her you're just being polite because her first reaction will be to suspect you're going to pull the chair out

hilariously from under her. (Save that joke for elderly relatives).

3. Don't make any comedy vomiting noises when the "meal" is dumped on the table (even if it kills you not to)... instead say, "Mmm, broccoli, my favourite. Spiffing". (Broccoli, due to its greeniness, can actually easily be hidden up your nose for disposal later. Indeed, if left to harden, it makes perfect flicking material - your victim won't know it's bogus).

4. Before the family begins slurping, take the hands of those next to you and say a prayer. F o r   e x a m p l e : "Dear Lord,

Thank you for the food we eat,

Thank you to the farmers,

Thank you to the non-organic animals who gave their life,

Thank you to the GM soil,

Thank you to the planes for bringing the produce thousands   of miles,

Thank you to the life-giving water from the radio-active sky,

Thank you to the ozone layer for letting in more sun,

Thank you to the check out girl who dropped and bruised   e v e r y t h i n g   s h e could,

Thank you to the 1,637 non-handwashing people who   handled this food first,

Thank you… (blah blah – continue thanking who/whatever until the food's gone cold)

Amen".

To avoid disgusting physical contact and very possible contamination from your supposed family, discreetly (or not so discreetly) - wrap your hands in protective cling film first. You can burn this later in your room… the smell is dead funny. Almost as good as stink bombs.

5. This is time-wasting madness, but actually cut the food into actual *mouth-sized* pieces, and put only a small amount of food into your mouth at a time - instead of your usual seeing how far your cheeks can stretch before they burst messily.

6. Chew your food. (Translation: *chewing* is the action of using your teeth to break the food down into a pulp before swallowing).

7. Under NO circumstances speak with your gob full. Reprimand those who do (without even so much as raising your voice because this will sound most demonic). Instead, introduce stimulating topics for good-natured debate. Helpful suggestions include:

    i. Should the government provide incentives for supermarkets to buy British first, before importing?

    ii. Was Harold the Great correct in moving his third battalion to the left flank in the Battle of Agincourt?

iii. Would you describe yourself as a happy and content member of this family?

8. As spoilsport as this is, swallow <u>all</u> your belches (with any luck, they'll reappear with a vengeance later on, and this time with an extra stench from being trapped in your belly for so long).

9. After the meal is gulped, thank your Mum out loud. It'll make everyone else at the table look really ungrateful - even if they *were* going to say "Thanks", it's *only* the person who says it first who counts since any further "Thank yous" sound fake. Also, under EU law, saying "thanks" entitles you to kick a sibling under the table.

10. Finally, to guarantee **never** having to sit at the table again,   smile like you've never smiled before (to help you achieve this, imagine your family members are mirrors) and ask if every meal can be taken at the table… you'll be met by a resounding chorus of "NOOO!"

If all the above clever tactics fail - clearly only because your parents are really desperate to terrorise each other with future family mealtimes, just sing "Come By Ya" (ask someone ugly to teach you it). This'll result in Post-Traumatic Stress Disorder for anyone present and they'll never be able to so much as look at the table again. LONG LIVE TV DINNERS. In your cesspit, of course.

How To Accidentally Do Your Bit For Charity
In fact, by putting your blood, sweat and tears into making sure your family never shares a mealtime again, you'll actually be unintentionally contributing to the preservation of an endangered species, The Family. It's a well-known guess that 87% of parents whose families eat, and *therefore argue*, at the dining table once a year or more get divorced - it's got nothing whatsoever to do with adultery, money troubles, or becoming physically repulsive as was previously believed.

How To Wash Up Like a Teenager
Your selfish lazy Mum constantly (e.g. once every 147th day) takes out her anger caused by your Dad being a lazy good-for-nothing *on you* by trying to make you do the washing up. Cheek - it's not as if you ate anything anyway. Talk about exploitative child slave labour. More to the point, doesn't she care that she's ruining your chances of becoming a famous hand model? It's absolutely irrelevant that a recent national survey revealed that a typical teenager is *only* ever asked to do the washing up three and a half times - that's still enough times to get sprout fingers.

Fortunately, Mums' soon learn their lesson. You see, just by *being* a teenager, you are genetically programmed to be crap at it.

1. You'll break stuff, or, more annoyingly to your Mum, just *slightly* chip everything so she can't decide whether to keep or chuck it.
2. You'll stack the washing up like Kerplunk on the draining board so if your Mum tries to put anything away it'll collapse like a Bovis home as soon as the warranty expires.
3. The washing up will actually be *dirtier* than before you started. Therefore, save yourself the trouble of putting your hands in hygienic water by putting the dirty plates directly on the drainer.
4. Your Mum will eventually discover that the real reason you wanted a pet/to befriend a homeless person is because they lick the plates clean.
5. You can't *actually* see what you're doing: either due to the ridiculous amounts of mascara you wear, or because you've accidentally glued your eyes shut after sticking on your clearly fake nails; or being *so* lazy that you've simply forgotten to open your eyelids.

How To 'Load' A Dishwasher

Nowadays, most decent families have dish-washers - any woman without one of these modern-day miracles actually prefers to be chained to the kitchen sink because this is the only time she ever gets to herself. Plus, she's hoping that her hands become so wet and soggy that they drop off and she'll be banished to a leper colony by her embarrassed family. Traditionally, the father of the house is psychotically obsessive about how to load the dishwasher correctly, to increase maximum efficiency. If only he put as much effort into being a Dad. So, why not have hours of fun messing up his anal preparations:

- Crawl inside the back of the dishwasher and every time he meticulous places an item, move it to somewhere wrong when he's fetching the next item. Remember to get back out before the door is shut or you could end up horribly sparkly.
- For some insane reason, many people rinse their dirty crockery before it goes in the dishwasher!!! Teach them not to waste water by sticking picture of thirst-dying children on the taps.
- When the rinse cycle is complete, beat your Mum to unloading   (Dads never unload as this would mean putting things away and they haven't got a lazy clue where anything goes) and throw a bucket of manure over the pristine crockery. Not only will this cause hilarious arguments between your Parents, they'll spend a fortune calling out the man to check the machine. This tactic will stop them frittering away your inheritance on selfish, expensive relationship counselling.

How To Eat Socially With Non-Family People
Occasionally you may be invited to dine at your friends' houses - this isn't because they actually like you, but because your friend's depressed parents

secretly want to see if you are as nasty as their teenage offspring. Now, your sneaky friend will quietly be banking on you being your usual charmless, foul self, because this will make *them* look not as completely hateful as their parents originally thought. Doesn't your friend know you at all?! How good at evil you can be?!! Your mission in life is to make your friends look as rubbish as possible in front of their parents - they might end up wanting to adopt you, or better, buy you The World's Best Bogey Catapult.

How To Show Up Your Stupid Friend

1. Prior to eating, make a big deal about washing your hands first - don't panic, you can easily make them putrid again afterwards by simply touching your hair or face.
2. Sit up *straight* - to achieve this you'll have to have your spine fused with metal plates by a top Harley Street surgeon. Or an actor from "E.R" - they basically know as much as a real doctor, and they're better-looking.
3. Use the knife as well as your usual shovel fork - although as a typically unfit teenager you'll possess no actual physical strength and won't even be able to cut through gravy.
4. *Don't* speak with your mouth full - to be on the safe side, better not speak at all.
5. Once you've eaten *absolutely everything* (this is most easy for bulimics), engage the parents in delightful small talk. For example: "Tell me, how did you two cool cats meet?", "Where, oh where, do you get those fabulous

hair cuts", "I wish my parents were as splendid as you", "I say, let's play 'Scrabble'?"

6. Offer to do the washing up - of course, you already know that they've got a dishwasher and the Dad's O.C.D. about loading it.

7. Play footsie with the parent of the opposite sex.

Of course, your friend will temporarily hate you for being so charming in front of their parents, but they'll soon be forced to forgive you when they remember that they have no other 'friends'. They will, however, wish to get their own back. Amateur. Invite them for tea *even before* you've barfed up that dreadful meal over their front step.

How To Have A Friend Over For Tea

Before you have your friend over for tea, you need to lay the ground-work with your parents *first* as this will negate any Dream Teen behaviour your pal may try to throw at your parents. Your aim is to make your parents so terrified of your pal that they pay absolutely no attention whatsoever to your friend's delightful behaviour.

1. Tell your parents that your friend has recently been diagnosed with a really high IQ - your folks'll be too busy concentrating on not showing off their stupidness to notice your friend *not* eating with their hands.

2. Say "I love you" to your parents moments before your friend arrives, not only will they be massively disorientated, they'll be frantic

with worrying whatever evil you have done that has warranted this huge suck-up. They won't even see that your friend is pretending to drink plain water.

3. Make curly-wurly mental gestures behind your friend's back as your friend tries to engage your parents in inane conversation; *and* if you add in a wacky-baccy puffing motion, your parents'll believe that your pal is drug-induced paranoid schiz.

-o-

How To Survive Divorce (A.K.A. What's In It For You)

Sadly, today, two out of three marriages end in divorce. This is sad because the statistic is so *low* - if Teenagers were allowed to divorce *their parents*, the success rate would be an impressive 100%. Who says Teenagers today can't apply themselves. Mind you, it's a miracle that more parents' *don't* divorce... after all, parents are so naff, crap, annoying, wrong, viscosey, degrading, stupid, cringe-worthy, boring, petty, childish, irritating, disgusting, nit-picking, stinky, judgemental, cleverer, mean, argumentative, negative, dull, humourless, humiliating and mega embarrassing...

Top Seven Shameful Mother Boobs
1. Her selfish panicky hot flushes in public: these are annoying for you because people think she's

having a heart attack and are really nice to her. What about you - you'd be the one left motherless, for crocodile tearing out loud!?!

2. Her insistence on getting blonde highlights even though her fading skin tone can't take it… she looks like an albino - and you wouldn't want people thinking you were from Eastern Europe. Plus, that's *your* housekeeping money she's frittering away.

3. Her humiliating refusal to accept that she's now too old to wear knee-length skirts. Even ankle length is still a bit short.

4. Her degrading attempts to walk alongside you on the street or at home.

5. Speaking to your friends.

6. Speaking. Full stop… not that there ever is at the end of her sentence, she just goes on and on and on and on and

7. Breathing.

But these cringing blunders pale into insignificance compared to the horrors of your Dad's midlife crisis.

Top Seventy Four Mortifying Dad Cock-Ups

1. Wearing his shirts tucked into his high-waisted chinos… or worse, leaving his shirt flapping *outside* his fat bloated belly.

2. His failure to accept that he's balder than an anorexic celebrity after their hair extensions have been removed.

3. Listening to the same radio stations as you when he's legally required to listen to Radio 2 (preferably Radio 4).

4. Dropping you off in front of your friends when you distinctly asked to be dropped off round the corner from the bench.

5. Saying "Wotcha", or "How's it hanging?" to your pals.

5. Hooting hot babes in the car when your mum or step-mum isn't there.

6. Ruffling your hair in a too-late attempt to demonstrate physical affection (actually the slaphead's trying to steal hair follicles for his transplant from you).

7. Trying to "get in" with you by farting out loud.

8-74. Flicking his fingers and saying "Booshakakaka"?!

How To Survive The Crime of the Millennium (A Crime Worse than Accidentally Knocking Off the Head of a Zit)

Currently, in the UK teenagers are **unable to divorce their parents**. Ahhh, the bittersour irony… how are you *ever* supposed to grow up if you have to stay at home with them cooking, cleaning and washing for you???! It's clearly *their* fault you're a Spoilt User; in fact, due to their domestic smothering of you, why would you ever want to leave your kingdom?! Oh yes… the only reason you will *ever* have for leaving home is the endless, terminal worry it will give your parents.

HOWEVER, should either parent commit the following indecent act of gross parental intrusion, you are morally, ethically, spiritually and blinking well hormonally entitled to immediately seek parental divorce:

They slither over to you when you're pretending to do your homework or your face is hilariously stuck to the mirror following zit detonation (ooh, kiss yourself) and "casually" ask you whether you "like" anyone at the moment, and do you know about condoms and sexy stuff; and worse still, do you want to bring them home for tea!!!!!! C-C-C-C-RINGE.

How To Divorce Your Creepy Parents
If you live in America, obtaining a divorce from your parents is as easy as getting morbidly obese. Yes, *that* easy. Therefore, why not caterpult your pimply butt over there pronto… the possible risk of dying mid-journey is definitely worth it because, once in the U.S., you'll look and feel positively anorexic compared to those porky Yanks.

How To Travel To America
Obviously, for 98% of Teens, caterpulting yourself will probably only get you as far as the ground immediately below you, so you'll need to make alternative travel arrangements… unfortunately, you can't really ask your Dad to give you a ride as he'll realise - once he's driven though the Atlantic Sea - that you're up to something dodgy.

Now, you *could* buy an airline ticket to the Land of the Free (that's the Land of the Free Heart Attack) but that'll cost you, like, over £22.86. And, quite frankly, why should you spend your own hard-earned/pinched pocket money on a ticket, when there's still lots of sweeties or under-age alcohol, fags or knives to be bought from your local corner shop. Fortunately, you can easily travel to the USA (and prove just how enterprising and independent you can be) by using someone else's ideas:

- *Stowing away on a ship*: try distracting the Captain by throwing a mermaid (they've got them in the frozen fish freezers in 'Iceland') on the deck and then leg it aboard, trying not to slip over as that's très uncool. Then, hide by pretending to be the woman strapped to the front of the ship because no-one'll think to look for you there. What this hiding place lacks in dryness and warmth it more than makes up for with a great view; plus, when you're seasick you can just vom there and then without having to clear up; you can also catch fresh dolphin to eat with your mouth when they jump up to say hello; and salt water is very good for exfoliation - so by the time you arrive in America your skin will be really smooth. Or raw. Plus, ooh ooh, you can easily pass the endless time by pretending to be Celine Dion and singing the theme tune to Titanic under your breath.

- *By plane*: DON'T hide in one of those exterior enginey things - it's too chuffing cold. Besides, you could get oily. Instead, dress up as a gay airplane attendant (ask to borrow *that* boy's clothes from school) and simply mince on board. No-one'll question your right to be there because you'll look like you truly belong, especially if you smile like a maddie and walk with a hand on your hip. Indeed, everyone will be *too afraid* to question your legitimacy in case you sue them for gay discrimination. The advantages of choosing this mode of transport include eating lots of free nuts; you can play wee-wee darts on the loo (even girls can play this fun game because - despite their claims - no girl actually pees straight); and really bad air turbulence is way more fun than a theme park ride. Plus, when passengers are asleep you can balance the refreshment trolley on their heads.

- *By private plane*: only poor, no-hoper, non-famous people travel by charter plane. Really, you deserve to be travelling on your own aircraft, you (undiscovered) star you. So, cut out two wings from cereal boxes - paint them with pretend feathers if you're artistic (e.g. you've never really had any friends to actually play with and have become good at art because you had nothing else to do), and attach to your arms. Flap, repeat. Flap, repeat etc. About 14, 58273659142 times. You need to have quite strong arms to pull this one off, but if you do, you'll be famous. And rich - on the TV freak-show circuit. That's if you don't die first.

- *By post*: this method is best employed by thin teens, probably the self-obsessed female variety. Just slip into an A4 envelope - remembering the address "To America, and make it snappy Mr. Postman" - and putting a £2,837 stamp on it (obviously, you're not going to buy this expensive stamp, just apprehend a 2nd class stamp from your Mum's purse (might as well take a fiver whilst you're there) and scribble this price on it biro. She doesn't buy first class stamps because she pockets the difference for her future secret life transplant). You won't need to pack any food as delivery only takes approximately 5 days... that's not nearly long enough to get hungry.

- *By reality TV*: apply to any reality TV show and win. You'll automatically become famous and your agent will send you state-side to be loved and adored and hounded by the paparazzi.

How To Legally Finalise Your Divorce From Your Parents

Once you arrive safely in Americashire, you can obtain your divorce simply by asking an immigrant taxi driver to crash you to the Whitehouse and meet with the President of the United Steaks. Mr. Bush'll be delighted to take the time out to grant you your divorce because invading countries without U.N. permission is very tiring and he'll need a break.

-o-

How To Retaliate If Your Parents Divorce *Each Other**

Now, should your parents be selfish, self-seeking, self-centred, self-interested, stinky, mean, childish, pig-faced, smelly, and naive enough to actually divorce *each other* (as if anyone else'd want them), you should behave - you may be surprised and pleased to know - just like your usual vile and obnoxious Teen self. In fact, ***even more so***. How else can you see them through this difficult time but by being an absolute git... they need continuity, reassuring familiarity. By being an absolute arsehole, you can help them take their miserable mind off their own me-me-me excruciating woe.

How To Help With Bonus Disgraceful Behaviour
1. Whenever you deliberately catch one of the embarrassing drips blubbing in private, mimic the parent theatrically, then they'll see just how ugly they look and stop. (It's a scientific fact that only people under 19 look good after crying due to the skin's youthful elasticity and ability to snap back into place without causing permanent wrinkling).
2. When they begin having their nervous breakdown about their pending financial meltdown, steal even more money from them and then leave two pence pieces on every alternate stair every 37 minutes. They'll think they're going mad and start worrying about this instead.
3. When they start trying to change their image to make themselves attractive enough to be able to start sleeping around again, you should: draw wrinkles on the mirror; pluck some of your own hairs and colour them grey, then glue them to their head when sleeping; and take all their new "trendy"

clothes to a seamstress to be massively taken in so they'll never be able to wear them (and look better than you).

4. Destroy anything of value in the home - whether electrical or sentimental - because this'll stop them warring over who has what. Of course, this won't affect the quality of your lifestyle one iota because you have a few grand of gear in your room that they wouldn't dare trying sneaking off with. Besides, it's all glued to the spot with bogies.

5. Spread rumours amongst your friends' parents that *both* of your parents have 'come out'... traditionally, newly-divorced parents are well up for it and targeted by your peers still-married parents to have a dodgy affair with, but now they'll be shunned socially, giving your folks something new to be neurotic about.

Ahhhh imagine, once your parents finally divorce and you get stuck living with the loser, you'll have their undivided attention *all to yourself...* for cooking, cleaning, washing. You don't even need to worry about being so unbelievably hideous that both your parents secretly decide that it'd be better to stay in a loveless, hateful marriage than run the risk of getting sole custody of you... they *do* actually hate their spouse *more than you*. Wow. In fact, parents divorcing could easily be the best, most fun thing that ever happens to you, apart from - obviously - when you become a part-time movie star supermodel singer.

How To Milk Your Parents Divorce

1. Now they no longer have each other to play twisted mind games with, it's your immoral responsibility to take up the slack. E.g. agree with everything they say, offer to clean the car, tell them they look nice.

2. Similarly, now your custodial parent is missing their spouse to bicker with, you are morally obliged to quadruple your efforts at being argumentative. Easy.

3. Birthdays, Easter, Xmas, Sundays when you're returned home… they all take on a whole new meaning after a bitter divorce because your parents will buy you *huge* presents to show each other up. They won't even notice when you don't say "Thankyou" because they'll be too busy relishing their ex's bulging annoyed eyeballs.

4. With one less pair of eyes watching you, boring into your skull, it's much easier to chuck your vegetables out the window at dinner.

5. If you get into <u>real</u> trouble at school, home or on the street, simply burst into tears and blame your bad behaviour on your parents' divorce and your need for attention. Boohoo. There, there, there. Scot-free.

6. There's more wardrobe space to hang your clothes. Especially if you chuck out your custodial parent's clobber too. They'll be too busy lying in bed for months to notice anyway.

7. Unless your parent hits the bottle, they'll be *much* more booze to secretly glug from the drinks cupboard.
8. When they finally hit rock bottom and beg you to stay in one evening because they're afraid of what they may do, grudgingly oblige. They'll be *forever* in your debt.

How To Behave If A Miracle Happens And A Parent Re-marries

Such miracles *do* happen: should your parents find themselves new partners - there are always blind people or needy psychos looking for love/someone to stop them dying alone - it can actually be a very positive, rewarding experience for you. Firstly, the very obvious benefit of your desperate parent meeting a new partner is that they'll go all silly and *forget you even exist so you can do whatever you bloody like*. Secondly, this new Step-Prat is a virgin adult on which you can inflict all your best Teenager moves on; they're fresh meat. Terrorising this new idiot will *just about* make up for the fact that you will probably have to listen to your divorced parent trying to have sex again.

How To Terrorise Your New Step-Parent

This new adult invader will be *expecting* you to be a typical Step-Teenager: moody, violent and hysterical. They'll *think* they've prepared themselves for dealing with this kind of behaviour by watching "Oprah" and "Biker Grove" repeats. So, luckily then, you'll need to take your nightmarish performance up a notch (or hundred) in order to send them packing:

a) Cuddle them frequently, even when they're peeing.

b) Bring them cups of arsenic-free tea or champagne every 6.66 minutes.

c) Clean and valet their squalid car every Sunday, leaving a Ferrero Rocher on the windscreen. Do this blindfolded to eliminate the possibility of seeing their discarded 'sexy' underwear.

d) Having had them under surveillance, don't grass on them when you catch them cheating on your parent with someone else's newly-divorced parent. Merrily show them the evidence... and their cheque book.

e) Nightly, clean their shoes properly with brush and polish - absolutely no shoe shines. Freakish.

f) Call them "Mummy" or "Daddy" the very first day you meet them.

*WAKE UP. They don't actually want to divorce EACH OTHER. One of them is SO SICK OF YOU that they'd rather divorce and live out their lives horribly alone than stay in the family home with you! Parents become stressed in divorce proceedings, not because of the solicitor's fees or adultery turmoil, but because they're living in fear of winning custody of YOU.

-o-

How To Find Your Christmas Presents

You *already* have the greatest Christmas present you could possibly ever want... your amazing parents. Your folks are the finest, kindest, funniest, cleverest, coolest, wisest, hippest, best-looking, sweetest, loving, cuddliest, generous, bestest parents in the whole wide world. They already give you *more* than you could ever dream of, so you know you have no need for endless materialistic presents at Crimbo. It's just amazing and rewarding enough sharing all Christmas day with them... playing charades and that Seasonal classic, 'Guess The Farter'.

But, aw shucks, your generous parents are so ridiculously perfect that they probably *have* got you something truly fabulous - like slipper socks or a novelty item of clothing - so you're hardly going to disrespect their generosity and thoughtfulness by going looking for your pressies. Gosh, you really love them...

Bah Humbug, that's just a load of old twoddle to throw your parents' off your devious scent. You see, at some point your amateurishly sneaky parents will steal this book of genius from your booby-trapped room in a feeble attempt to try and outsmart you. Ha. What they don't know is that the publishers of this mighty book have secretly **weighted** the paper in this book to fall open at exactly this page; now, having read the introductory nonsense at the top of this page they'll be racked with guilt for snooping, idiotically believe this entire book to be just incredibly ironic, and that you're actually a great kid. Ha.

The "How To Find Your Christmas Presents" title will con your oldies into thinking, "Ahhhh, how sweet, they still want to look for their pressies." Pish. Hunting Christmas pressies is for toddlers and lonely spinster women in their early twenties. This article is dedicated to finding far more important, and *wanted* things…

Finding Your Parents'* Will

Now, regardless of how vile a teenager you are (congrats), your parents are morally obliged to make provision for you in their wills. But you'd better check it out, just in case they *really* hate you. The obvious places to look are:

- The secrct panel in their bedroom (it's this thing called drawers - it's where clothes mysteriously get put away).
- If you're working-class and don't have built in clothes storage, try that kitchen drawer where *everything* gets stuffed (including their car keys - handy if you need to pop out joy-riding).
- Or, if you're middle-class and find that the drawers are only stuffed with gimp costumes, the document can be found at their solicitor (simply put on their iffy clothes, a fake, fake posh voice and visit their dodgy brief to blag the will - the solicitor will be

too busy counting their exorbitant fees to notice).

- If you're upper class, there is *no* will - your parents know that they're made you into a spoiled twit and intend to spend every last penny before they die in order so there's bugger all to inherit... forcing you into finally standing on your own two feet. Kill them**.

How To Seek Revenge If You've Been Cut Out Of The Will
If you discover that your thieving pair-runts *have* left you nothing whatsoever to blow on 5* holidays, illiterate tattoos and spacedust, then retribution is easy... simply fart in their bed and slip out *without* disturbing the covers.

* Remember, when it's in *your* interests, you will *always* be their child, so no matter how old you are, get hunting (even if you're reading this work of literary genius in your advancing years like 20+)... their money *is* your only way on to the property ladder.

How To Unearth The Life Insurance Policy
You need to know the whereabouts of this get-rich-quick policy in case your parents have a "mysterious accident" - especially if your parents are clearly on the brink of an expensive divorce. This document is also particularly crucial if your folks are over forty. Luckily, you don't even need to get off your cellulite to find out where this

policy is stashed - just start bawling when one of those soppy adverts comes on the telly about Dad (the breadwinner) dying and leaving his young family destitute because Mum is too useless to provide her own income. Selfish dead Dad.

Your parents'll be embarrassed, confused and disgusted by your emotional outburst, making them putty in your greedy, grabbing hands. Tell them the only way to calm you down and stop blubbing is for you to see the aforementioned life policy. If they don't actually possess this policy (197% of them), insist the only way you'll stop hugging them is if they buy one immediately.

WARNING: LOCATING THE ABOVE TWO DOCUMENTS WILL BE YOUR ONLY WAY ON TO THE PROPERTY LADDER.

** Best not.

How To Locate Their Birth Control

Of course, imagining your parents having rumpy plumpy is disturbingly creepy and verging on child abuse, but hunting out their dusty contraception can have many loving, touching, and wicked advantages:

  1) For blackmail - parents get *so* embarrassed at the mere mention of sexy stuff that holding their contraception ransom can be used as bartering for many things like DVDs, holidays, cars and Pick and Mix.

2) For *your* personal use… well, buying your own from the chemist is just way too embarrassing.
3) If you find their contraception is covered in asthma-inducing *dust,* you can stop living in fear that you'll hear them having sex. Also, why not snort the dust to have a days-off-school asthma attack.
4) If you find *cobweb-free, in-date* contraception, you can relax knowing that they're NOT planning to have another brat who will steal their time and, more importantly, money from you…

But where to look for the contraception? If you're a transvestite you'll already know the answer… your mum's underwear drawer. She naively assumes that you'll be too repulsed to look in here. As if - you shop in 'Primark' - you've seen worse. Just wear rubber gloves, protective goggles and hold your breath. Hopefully, you'll also discover the piles of cash that your Mum has been siphoning off from their joint account and *your* child benefit. Finders keepers, loser can't say a word.

How To Survive The Annoying Arrival Of A New Sibling
Some parents bizarrely decide to have a child long after their bodies are sexy enough to make it worth their while. The unexpected arrival of another brother or sister is traditionally called the parents' last-ditched attempts at saving their relationship, or trying to have a nice child to cancel out the fact

they had you. Your (entitled) reaction to this infantile impostor should be one of jealously and hate. But, think smarter, and remember that a new baby in the family can have many benefits - largely because your past-it folks will be too knackered from trying to look after It to bother harassing you. Indeed, sleep deprivation and exhaustion as a result of broken nights with a screaming infant will accelerate your parents inevitable divorce, giving you the chance to live with - and, therefore, manipulate - the weaker parent (A.K.A. Mum). Plus:

- Another sibling will give your parents someone else to moan and whinge at, taking some of the heat from you.
- If you're a girl, having a baby at your disposal means you can pretend to your mates that you've had a secret baby and are going to get loads of welfare benefits and a free mansion.
- If you're a boy, having a baby at your disposal is a great chick magnet.
- Nappy poo is really funny.

So, it's almost in your interests to get yourself a baby stooge: if you find The Pill, try replacing some of the tablets with Smarties or dried bogies. Or if you find condoms that *don't* have a use-by-date from 20 years ago (tip: try not to look at the size, shiver), make small holes using the teeth of a cute vampire bat (ask your neighbourhood goth - if they try and palm you off with a silly mouse with stuck-on homemade wings, throw some glitter at them. Hee hee, they'll be twinkling for years).

How To Hunt Out Your Birth Certificate

Don't go looking for this document if you suspect you won't be able to stomach the fact that, in fact, you **AREN'T** adopted. Discovering that your Mum and Dad *really are* your blood Mum and Dad may ruin the rest of your life. Not only will you have to accept that you aren't the offspring of really beautiful, wealthy, famous folk who only gave you up because you were more perfect than them and were too jealous to keep you, but you'll have to accept the likelihood that, one day, you'll grow up to be just like your sodding boring, dumpy parents.

So, why bother looking for this soul-destroying document? There is a platinum lining in this dark cloud of discovering that you're NOT adopted… *if you ever need to have an organ transplant* (which is highly   likely because of your unhealthy lifestyle*) you'll be able to force your parents into being the donor*. They won't be able to claim that you're adopted. Actually, they'll only agree to the operation to make themselves look good in public - they couldn't care less if you snuffed it.

You'll find your birth certificate in the one place your parents' think you will never look - the vegetable rack.

How To Celebrate If You _Do_ Actually Find Adoption Papers

Who says there isn't justice in the world. Discovering adoption documents gives you moral permission to truly start messing with your "parents" heads... start asking them about your actual birth, what you were like as a newborn, who do they think you take most after... Eventually, they'll crack under the hideous strain of their terrible secret and admit that they found you in a church doorway. This "catastrophic, emotionally devastating news" is your domestic passport to:

- staying out late - you can always claim you were looking for your real parents,
- bringing weirdos "home",
- getting really expensive presents you can flog on Ebay,
- going on bankrupting shopping sprees with Mommie dearest,
- getting a rat as a pet and not being made to eat your sprouts.

In fact, if you're nifty on computers it's defo worth knocking up bogus adoption papers. Then, you can storm in to your parents as they're pretend to watch the late News in the futile belief that it'll send you off to bed, and scream that you've just discovered you're adopted. The chances are that they'll either be so brain-damaged by alcohol and burgers that they'll believe you; or, because you're such a vile piece of work, they'll have blocked out the memory of your actual birth to try and forget that you _are_ theirs and be quite happy to agree you're adopted. Ker-ching.

-o-

How To Watch TV With Your Parents And Get A State Of The Art Media Centre In Your Bedroom Pronto

Watching excessive, brain-numbing amounts of TV as a family is really good for you:

- It helps distract families from bitter, unforgivable fights - as funny as these bitchfests are, you should save some of your nastiness for your friends.
- It stops you having to look at the mingers (although be very careful during sunny weather as you may accidentally catch a glimpse of their mutant reflections in the telly. Therefore, insist that the curtains always remain drawn - other family members will surprisingly hastily agree... they don't want to look at your ugly mug either).
- It helps you forget that you have no life, or friends.
- The TV stops you going outside and running the risk of being hit by alien poo that is jettisoned from their spaceships.
- Your soap-addict Mum won't be arsed to do any nutritious home cooking, preferring to

serve up life-shortening yummy convenience meals instead.
- TV is the 21st century's Teen primary form of education - where else could you learn about what it's like to be filmed by a film crew 24/7?
- It keeps you from street corners and dodgy woods where you could get murdered. Sadly, getting murdered would somewhat prevent you from being able to annoy your parents... although the rancid memory of you *would* continue to rankle them.

But occasionally, just occasionally, what's on the telly is so diabolical (e.g. you've already seen it 362 times) that you *may* grow bored, providing you with the perfect opportunity to *really* get on your family's frayed nerves... And get your private bedroom cinema.

How To Destroy Your Family's Only Source Of Pleasure

1. Hide the remote control in places your Dad'll never think to look (e.g. places he doesn't know exist): the washing machine, the cleaning equipment cupboard, the salad box or your stomach (douse with ketchup, salt and vinegar first). If you're hiding the remote to irritate your Mum, try the tool box, or her sexy underwear drawer. Alternatively, if you're the creative type (e.g. not clever)

then why not make a fake remote control unit! Tee hee hee hee hee. Here's how:

a) Take a cereal box (eat the contents first in a cereal eating competition with yourself - timing how long each bowl takes. The winner receives tooth decay, A.D.D., and a deadly dose of the RDA of vitamins and minerals.)

b) You *could* cut the box to the right size but, firstly, that requires effort, and secondly, your comotosed parents won't notice anyway. So don't bother.

c) Paint with your Mum's make-up, or those aerosols you use for graffiti, and stick on lots of delicious sweeties for pretend buttons. Blue Peter badge for you, and you're not even disabled. Much.

When you've replaced the real remote control for this huge box of a one, remember to hide your face with an invisible-making cushion to conceal your hysterics.

2. During I.T. lessons, use your time profitably on the computers by scanning, cutting and pasting the TV guide and rearranging the programming scheduling so it's mucked up. For those of you not at school and therefore unemployed, you'll find a computer at the library (to enter without being seen by your peers try hiding in the billowy skirt of an old lady - of course, you'll probably get shat on. Ho hum). Then, sit back and admire your extra-curricular homework as you parents

truly fight (even more than usual) about who mis-set the DVD recorder (this is the second largest cause of divorce after getting ugly). What a hoot.

3. If something sexy comes on the telly like, say, a late night film, car advert, music video or 'Newsround' (hey, you're a teenager, anything's sexy), increase your parents already huge embarrassment by putting your hands over your eyes and shouting "La-la-la, la-la-la". Alternatively, start making your own sexy noises. This'll have them going to bed faster then a politician in a bordello. Result. Now you're free to play trampoline on the sofa.

4. Pretend you're a born-again religiousy person and demand to watch "Songs of Praise". When your parents scoff at the possibility of your goody-two-shoes conversion, bang on about religious freedom and oppression and they'll be so scared of karmic repercussions they'll go off and do parenty things (Mum'll go and spend Dad's money whilst Dad will go and try on her underwear)... allowing you to get on with stress-relieving slaughtering on your games console.

5. When the news/films/soaps/documentaries/ cartoons/music shows/light entertainment/ drivel comes on, ask "Why?" to *everything*

that happens. Your stumped, stupid parents will soon give you lots of money to go out. (Remember not to get carried away with the "Whys" when they give you the cash - just take the money and slouch).

6. Bribe a member (tee hee) of the opposite sex (preferably one you actually fancy) with stickers, stink bombs, or letting them rub a balloon on your hair to come round and pretend to be your date. Then, when your parents start barraging them with naff questions (parents do this knowing that the majority of Teens will just go out and leave them in peace) get 'your date' to start flirting with one (or both) of your parents. They'll be so confused and embarrassed they'll go to the kitchen to make the longest cup of tea. Later, when they bring it up, insist *they* started the flirting. You'll be grounded for a month, giving you many a romantic night for the accused (naturally, they'll have fallen for you) to climb in through your bedroom window - using the outside Stannah lift you've secretly had installed for years.

7. Every time someone good-looking of the *same sex* comes on the telly, rush up to the screen and snog it. Your parents will then lavish expensive clothes, haircuts and bodily products to make you more attractive to the opposite, correct sex. And if this behaviour

actually makes you gay, who cares, a date's a date, right?

8. With your hands rigid by your side, *watch* your parents *watching* TV out of the corner of your eye, for no other reason than it will creep them out. To prevent yourself from actually seeing your parents, glue milk tops over your retinas.

9. Sit right next to them, your leg touching theirs. They won't be able to handle the blatant show of affection. But, if you just *can't* bring yourself to make physical contact, then simply sitting on the same sofa as your parent will also have them on the internet for 'Curry's' or 'Dixons' faster than you can say "It's got to be a plasma".

10. Laugh - happily - at the telly. This is the most *disturbing* thing any Teenager can do, ever.

Of course, once you've got your debt-inducing media centre installed in your festering pit, you'll need to get it replaced - continuously - with the latest model. You can achieve this by breaking your current model by peeing on it (naturally, the toilet is just too far), smashing the screen by detonating your zits on it or sticking a screwdriver or your teddy down the back (you'll need to earth yourself with something wooden - try eating a ryvita).

How To Translate Parents' Traditional Yawn-Yawn Catchphrases

At any one moment in the world, 3,763,976 parents' are performing one of their many famous clichéd catchprases in front of their misunderstood Teenager. Now, don't be misled by the angry, seething tone of their voice... parents', too, are much misunderstood. They're not mad at you *at all*. They don't really hate you, just each other; in fact, they're just too scared to admit it because they're both afraid they'll get custody of you. The Teenager is the parental punchbag. And sometimes, they just simply have difficulty in expressing how they *really* feel - due to being blottoed. So here's a guide to translating what they say into what they *actually* mean...

What they say...   **What they mean...**

Go to your room now!   M   e
                                     a n d
                                     y o u r
                                     o t h e r
                                     parent
                                     w a n t
                                     to get
                                     jiggy!

You're not going out in that!   It'll
                                     look
                                     better on me.

Don't you dare speak to me like that.

I don't unders tand - u s e simple r words.

You're grounded for a week!

W h y should y o u h a v e a n y fun? I don't.

You're grounded for a month!!

E v e n y o u r compa n y ' s better t h a n m y lesser half's.

Tidy your room.

L e t ' s see if y o u detect t h a t I ' v e found

and
read
your
diary.

GET A JOB.

I
know
you'v
e been
in my
purse,
I just
can't
prove
it. Yet.

Eat your dinner or you don't get dessert.

There
is no
desser
t.

You're going to your Nan's and that's that.

She
still
loves
you,
makc
the
most
of it.

I love you.

I'm on
t   o
you.

Who the hell do you think you are?

Is this a good t i m e to tell y o u you're adopted?

Have you been in the drinks' cupboard?

Or is it my spouse who's turned t o alcohol?

PUT YOUR DIRTY CLOTHES IN THE

It'll stop m e compulsively

LAUNDRY BIN!!!

looking for signs o f sexual activity.

It's against the LAW!!!!

I
should
know,
I got
caught
a   t
y o u r
age.

You treat this place like a hotel!

I can't
r e m e
m b e r
t h e
l a s t
time I
h a d
sex in
a
hotel.

I'm not a taxi.

L e t
m   e
t a k e
y o u
s o m e
where
—   I
n e e d
t   o
G E T
O U T
O   F
HERE

!!!!!!!!
!

My
life
sucks.

F!?*!$?*! C*!?

I'm
jealou
s ... I
had to
g r o w
up to
T h e
Beetle
s.

Turn that racket down!

W h a t
a
bargai
n .
H a v e
s o m e
m o r e
money
, you
clever
shopp
e r
you.

It was how much!?!

I ' l l
blame

They're a bad influence on you.

your friends for my failing as a parent.

For the **last** time, NO!

We both know I don't mean it. I never do.

I wish I was dead.

I wish I was dead.

How To Achieve Saint Status
Of course, if you really want to improve communication with your parents (e.g. get exactly what you want 24/7), when they do bother to speak to you, say exactly what you know they want to hear, then *do exactly what you were going to do all along*. It's called the art of compromise. Everyone's happy!

-o-

How To Learn To Drive And Become A Responsible Young Adult (Or, How to Drive Your Dad Bonkers)

One of the greatest joys of reaching your late teens is that the government actually encourages you to destroy your parents' will to live by legally allowing you to learn to drive (17 years old normally, but 12 years old in inner cities because they grow up faster). Foolishly, many parents offer to help their Teen learn to drive, *not* because they stupidly hope that learning to drive may give their annoying Teen a sudden growth spurt in maturity and responsibility, but because they desperately need to believe that this new-found independence driving gives will encourage their Teen to leave home. Tcha. The naïve parents also deludedly think that providing parental lessons will *save* them money since you won't need so many proper lessons. Double Tcha. You'll need **loads more** expensive tuition to correct all the duff instruction your Dad gives you. They'll happily cough up too - because it'll start dawning on them that you're getting ever nearer to eventually passing your test and being able to legally drive in *their* car *alone...* which, of course, will result in you ruining it. Or worse - that you'll force them to haemorrhage up for a car of your own... to ruin.

How To Give Your Parents A Crash Course In Emotional Break-Downs

Amazingly, you're already inherently, fully qualified to freak your parents out when they take you out for lessons - without even trying. This is because just by virtue of being a Teenager you will suck at driving:

i. You've never concentrated on anything for more than thirty seconds (apart from farting).

ii. You've never had to use your hands and legs simultaneously before (apart from farting-obviously, arms are used for wafting).

iii. As a learner driver, you're not supposed to scream abuse at other (better) drivers... but holding it in takes all your physical effort, so you really can't be expected to hold the wheel as well. You have to sit on your hands to stop them making 'involuntary' rude hand signals.

iv. It's nigh on impossible for you to not use the rear view mirror for preening and loving yourself for hours on end. Who cares about the pile up behind. Mingers. And definitely mingers after.

How To Make Your Dad Instantly Car Sick

But there are many **additional manoeuvres** you can perform to force your parents to stump up for endless, extra professional driving lessons so they don't have to take you out ever again. Luckily, this enables you to get on with failing your first test sooner, rather than later.

Advanced Driving Techniques

    a) Each time you go driving with your reluctant parent, fill the backseat ledge with hundreds of toys (yes, even if you're male - just take out the cuddly bears that you hide under your bed). If the parent tries to remove them "in the interests of safety" (that's a manipulative exaggeration, they're just jealous cos they didn't have as many toys when they were growing up) throw a tantrum, screaming "You don't love me anymore. I'm just trying to be like the little me that you used to love". That'll shut 'em up as they try to figure a way out of that one.

    b) Insist on playing distracting CDs or the radio at full volume. When they object (yawn - it's just because they don't know the words), remind them it's far better for you to learn in the conditions you will actually be driving in. They won't be able to fault your warped logic. If they carry on nagging, ask them if they're still *in love* with the other parent, as opposed to just *loving them*. Tumbleweeds. Carry on Car-eoke!

c) At traffic lights, zebra crossings, rubbernecking at car accidents, nay, at any opportunity whatsoever, practise your nose-picking and bogey-wiping manoeuvres. The best places to park the bogey are... if quite moist:

> i. The steering wheel - which also, over time, conveniently hardens to help with grip.
>
> ii. On the seat - this also gives extra cushioning to help you see over the wheel.
>
> iii. On the sound system - if your dad's a tightwad and owns an old-fashioned car with just a crappy radio, this'll help you mark out your favourite radio stations.

But if the bogey is *crispy*, flicking the asteroid is not recommended as it may ricochet off the windscreen and hit you in the eye. However, this is worth the risk because it may also hit your parent.

d) The next manoeuvre is quite tricky and only pays off if you're good looking. If you're a minger, you'll only receive rude hand gestures in return... but at least you'll be able to practise your own signals back - stupidly, this isn't covered by most driving schools!!?! The manoeuvre is called 'Hooting the Hottie'. Finely tune the manoeuvre by ducking when the Hottie turns to look (they always do - in case you're a millionaire and driving a Jag) so it looks like it was your parent. If taking lessons with your *Dad* he'll secretly enjoy this manoeuvre but he won't admit it. If taking lessons with your Mum, she'll either secretly love it, or kick you out of the moving vehicle, regardless of her own pending death.

e) If a police car should slime by, flick your tongue out at them like a sexy lizard. If the fuzz humourlessly pull you over, remind your cursing parent that this is good practise for when you pass, but if the parent remains irate, whisper that you know about their secret unpaid speeding ticket. (Of course, this is just a guess but it's probably true).

f) A tried and tested technique for getting hundreds of extra professional lessons is to eat masses of beans, egg sarnies and cabbage before the parental lesson. Usually, these farts are silent and manga violent, but if not, hide the noise by asking the parent how they are - it's the ultimate distraction technique. By the way, remember to use the child lock so your parent can't escape the stench by leaping out in to oncoming vehicles. Then again...

g) This manoeuvre is *sooo* easy: wave at your friends as they slouch on street corners. In fact, it's *too* easy so make it harder - and therefore all the more rewarding - by doing the double handed wave. Or even harder, by waving your feet too. Cooey.

h) Ask the parent difficult, relevant driving questions from the Highway Code like: "Do you *have* to stop if you hit someone and they get back up quite quickly?", "Who has right of way at this roundaboaaaght?", or "Zzzzzzzzzzz" (this works a treat if you throw in the nodding head manoeuvre).

How To Make *Both* Parents Suffer - You Believe In Equality, After All

Now, traditionally, it'll most likely be your Dad who takes you out for these driving lessons; this is because it is scientifically proven that although women have fewer accidents than men, men are simply the better drivers because they can handle driving faster. But what about your poor, neglected Mum? You don't want her to feel left out... of the misery. Therefore, when you're being ferried round by your Mum, treat her just like a taxi:

- Completely ignore her - talking only to your friends, passers by or the police after they've pulled you over for making sexy lizard tongue faces at them.
- Annoyingly open and shut the window to secret tunes you're playing in your head. This may, alas, result in you getting some fresh air, but that's the price you've got to pay.
- If at all possible, leave a huge pile of steaming sick: you don't even need booze to pull it off - sweeties or reading will have the same effect.

How To Behave In A Car If You're *Under* 17

If you're too young to legally drive (what a stupid law - suppose there was a terrible emergency like your Mum and Dad selfishly refused to drive and get you some fags or sherbert, you'd *have* to be able to drive yourself, durr!!) there are still plenty of other ways to get at your parents. Whining "Are we there yet?" every three minutes is for toddlers. (Still, good fun though).

- Make retching noises, preferably whilst sitting behind the driver, adding spasmodic convulsing for extra authenticity.
- Recite your three times table over and over (if you can), when they finally snap, inform them they can't lawfully stop you as this is *your* education and y*our* future they're messing with.
- Excitedly initiate a game of "I spy" but when it's their turn shout out random words, beginning with any letter. They'll soon stop at a service station to shut you up with a burger. However if *they* attempt to start a game, refuse to join in, reminding them that, according to TV car advertising, today's children are supposed to have DVDs in the back of the front car seats for entertainment.
- Sing any song by The Venga Boys, Cheeky Girls or Duran Duran – this last one will particularly bug them because it'll remind them of their long-lost youth and when they

were last happy. (Tip: look up this band in a historical encyclopaedia).

- Knock the back of their seats just enough to be annoying but not so hard that they definitely know it's you - deny responsibility and blame it on the bumpy roads or claim it's the old, blind people they keep running over.
- If visiting **rubbish** relatives*, make a high-pitched whine as soon as you set off. Your Dad'll think there is something seriously wrong with the car and instantly refuse to go (he doesn't want to go either). *Surprisingly, *not all* relatives suck: grandparents ply you with fluffy sweeties and secretly give you money (even if it is loose change) in the hope that you won't leave them to rot in an evil nursing home; whilst Aunties make great homemade cakes in an attempt to show up their lazy sibling.
- Make rude words out of number plates. Your parents may appear annoyed, but secretly they'll be most impressed at your precocious "Countdown" like genius.

Finally, once you arrive at your destination, your parents will be praying that you skulk off moodily without so much as a thankyou - as far as they're concerned, the fewer exchanges they have with you the better. Therefore, kiss cuddle and thank them until they start begging for mercy and promise that they'll pay for your own limo and private chauffeur. Having your own limo will guarantee that you'll have a few friends. At the weekends.

-o-

How To Whinge Pets Out Of Your Loveless Parents

Fortunately, it's quite likely that by the time you're a Teenager you'll *already* have had numerous pets which you've mercilessly used for dressing up, catapulting and various science experiments. This is because a pet is mercilessly used by the average dysfunctional family as a substitute for love and affection. *Un*fortunately, by the time you reach your Teens your parents will be quite reluctant to buy you any more pets because they're already secretly squabbling over who gets lumbered with *you* when they divorce, never mind any animals. Plus, your Mum has long since twigged on that - despite your seemingly heart-felt promises - you'll never actually clean up any pet shit. Oh, what a Shakespearian dilemma: this is *precisely* the only reason why you ever want a pet... because you absolutely love watching your quietly cursing Mum cleaning up animal excrement.

However, you can *easily* manipulate your parents into buying you tons of new pets if you display some weirdo, psychopathic tendencies: they'll be convinced that if you don't have some form of affection in your life you'll definitely turn into a loonie and they'll be forced to visit you at a scary secure unit - they'll be terrified that someone will flick jism at them like in 'Silence of the Lambs'.

How To Appear Like A Love-Starved Potential Sociopath

- Stand facing the corner, for hours - to make this marginally less boring pretend that you're a triangular spy.
- Grow an unruly beard. If female, simply convince your local transgender assignment surgeon that you want to be a bloke, they'll slip you enough progesterone hormones to start sprouting a 5 0'clock shadow. This facial fungus is also handy for creating friction and sticking balloons to walls.
- Start keeping a diary full of loathing and hate (shouldn't be too difficult then) - and leave it in places your mum may 'accidentally' find it, like on her head.
- Write "I love Ted B*" over and over using a black pen somewhere your Dad may 'accidentally' see it, like his head (incidentally, biros are a much cheaper option than tattoos, *and* stops you having to only ever go out with 'Sharons' and 'Duanes'). *Only the cleverest and widest read, or sickest of you will actually know who 'Ted B' is.

Now, once this easy part of your scheming plan is achieved, you'll still need to convince your wearisomely sceptical parents that you are genuinely responsible enough to look after a pet, and be a right proper Dr Doolittle... Dr Doolittle To Actually Look After The Pet Apart From Stroke It Once In A Blue Moon, that is.

How To Prove You're A Regular Little Johny Morris

- Show your new-found caring attitude towards animals by practising digging lots of little graves in the back garden. Don't forget to shed a few tears to add authenticity - your Mum'll get all emotional at seeing you actually cry and'll get you the pet to make you feel better. When this pet does prematurely snuff it due to your ineptitude, crying really hard at their funeral will guarantee that your soft-touch Mum'll get you a much bigger, better pet next time - ad infinitum. Eventually, she'll give you an elephant: this is when it's time to *stop* - elephant craps are so huge and stinky that they're not even funny.
- Every time you see road kill, absolutely *don't* laugh hysterically like normal, but cry your heart out. (To achieve this, imagine Jade Goody has been assassinated - who else can you look to now, to make yourself feel superior?).
- Pretend you've realised that you love so animals so much that you need to turn vegetarian - this is easier to pull off than you may think because it's not as if you eat at home anyway. Just remember to remove the telltale kebab intestines from between your teeth before returning home.

But your Mum isn't (always) as stupid as she looks and she may realise that all your animal loving behaviour is a sham - if she starts bringing takeaway burgers home all the time, she's on to you... So, you'll need to resort to traditional vile Teenager blackmail tactics to simply screw the pets out of your parents.

How To Blackmail Pets Out Of Your Stingy Parents

- Tell all your friends' Mums that your parents won't let you have a pet in case they divorce and have to fight for custody of the creature. This'll soon get back to your parents via the Mums Chardonnay Grapevine, and they'll pronto cough up the pet to quell those rumours of marital strife - regardless of the truth.
- When in the car, stick your head out of the (open!) window like a suffocating slobbery doggie. To stop themselves getting into trouble for you probably getting your head cut off, your parents'll hastily promise to get you a pooch. Get this in writing as parents have a tendency to lie... on that pre-printed contract you always carry with you.
- When asked to write a story at school about what you did in the summer holidays, or an analysis of the language of metaphor in Shakespeare's texts, or street graffiti, write "I

want a doggie/cat/rabbit/hamster/goldfish/
llama/rat/tiger" (delete as appropriate) a
zillion times - you'll probably actually enjoy
the mindlessness of it. When your parents
are summoned to school/copshop for a
caning by your teacher/policeman, they'll
wimpily agree to their insistence that a pet
will aid your emotional well-being, (that's a
grown-ups way of saying stopping you being
an effing pain in the arse). To achieve a D for
effort, add little drawings of your preferred
pet choice in the margins; to get an
impressive D+, colour them in without going
over the lines.

- When it's your Mum's time of the month, or
if she's going through "The Change" (no, not
a sex change), she's hilariously emotional
and very easy to manipulate. So tape one of
those RSPCA TV adverts and play it
whenever she's around. Or sing the theme
tune from 'The Littlest Hobo'... she'll be on
the phone to the dog home faster than you
can say "rabies" - if the hormonal witch is
wavering, hum the theme tune from 'Lassie'.
That'll clinch it.

How To Adapt Your Blackmail Tactics To Acquiring Specific Pets

Dog - If you want a pooch (dogs are terrific at
farting), simply chew everyone's slippers (you'll
grow quite fond of the repulsive taste - it's tastier

than your Mum's cooking), slobber on the newspaper, gnaw on all available wooden chair legs, bark at strangers, leave skid-marks on cream carpets, and the piece de resistance, when your parents are entertaining, jump on a guest's leg and start making sexy-sexy movements. Having a *real* dog will suddenly seem a much more attractive option to your Mum and Dad.

Cat - Easy-peasy. Simply ignore your parents, sticking your nose up in the air whenever they pass by (this actually may be harder than you imagine as you'll have to resist making your usual witty, rude comments), then jump over your neighbour's fence and crap in their garden. Your neighbours will be so angry with your parents that you're fuming parents will retaliate by *getting you* the cat (who *will* also poop their stinking craps on the moanie neighbour's lawn). If you're cunning, you don't have to give up crapping on next door's lawn either - just blame the cat. In fact, blame everything on the cat - it can't stick up for itself).

Hamster - Now you *could* drive your Mum mad by unravelling hundreds of loo rolls and attempting to crawl through the tubes but, truth be know, it's far easier just to sneak off with your pocket money (e.g. the contents of your Mum's purse) and buy *yourself* a hammie from "Pets Bred For Profits R Us". Then, keep the hairy boring blob stashed in your room, hidden by your maths text books - your Mum won't dare go near these because she still has hideous flashbacks about fancying the maths teacher when she was at school. A hamster only makes a good pet because it looks like a poo that's been rolled in pubic hairs.

Goldfish - This'll be second nature to you... no matter what your parents say or tell you to do, forget it immediately. If this irritating behaviour fails to net you a goldfish in return for stopping (this is more likely to work on Mum than dad who also has a tendency to also 'forget' to do what Mum tells him), then simply float on your belly face-down in the bath. They'll be so relieved that you're not actually dead that not only will you get a poxy goldfish, you'll also get an entire aquarium. They'll *only* be relieved because they won't have to have the forensics team round to examine their filthy bathroom.

Rabbit - By far the easiest pet to con out of your parents. *ALL* parents **hate** mowing the lawn, so just remind them that rabbits **love** to eat grass. It's called killing two birds with one moan. Also, when the rabbit dies, you can hack off its paw for a good luck charm; plus, the turds make the most excellent trick chocolates.

Tarantula - Go outside (yes, this *is* a tall order - 'outside' is that place where your computer and TV *aren't*) and collect lots of itsy bitsy spiders. If you've inherited your Mum's fear of arachnids, you can lure the spiders into a box with a mini leg waxing kit (hopefully, you'll inherit better stuff from your Mum when she snuffs it). Then, deposit the spiders where your Mum - and Dad if he's a wimp - will see them, i.e. their mouths. Promptly inform your hysterical parent(s) that if you owned a Tarantula, then *all* spiders - *nay all insects* - would be too scared to come in your house. Silly scaredy cats will believe you. Also, drippy "friends", Aunties and Jehovas won't want to come in your house either. Triple whammy.

Tiger - Dress up as a policeman - stand on your friend's shoulders to add convincing height - and call on your parents when they've had a few (pick a night, any night). Notify them that break-ins are rapidly on the increase in your area, and that the only proven deterrent to burglars is a Siberian tiger like that one that mauled that creepy magician (that tiger so knew he was dodgy). To seal the deal, inform your now terrified parents that if you adopt one of these endangered species, your parents will be entitled to massive tax benefits. And non-stop, seeping bleeding back scratches that'll convince their friends and colleagues that they're getting hot sex. Hello Kitty!

How To Enjoy Owning A Pet

Erm, this is a tall order. Pets are almost as needy and annoying as you:
1. They have to have their meals bought to them. And they won't do the washing up either.

2. When they do a poo and leave a dangleberry, they won't wipe it off and expect a gagging human to do it for them.
3. They hate having a bath, yet think nothing of grooming themselves for hours and hours on end.
4. The average dog costs £20,000 in their pointless lifetime; yet, if you asked to be treated equally and requested this lump sum you'd be locked in the kennel.
5. Pets have a tendency to die and steal the attention of your grief-stricken family from you; plus, if the pet spitefully chooses to snuff it in your room it could be *months* before the smell is even detected.
6. They're allowed to wee and poop wherever they fancy. You're not. And your poo doesn't even contain the toxocara canis worm virus. In fact, a single gram of dog dirt contains an average of 23 million fecal coliform bacteria like parvo virus, whipworms, hookworms, roundworms, giardia and coccidian. Cats make pathetic pets as they only harbour *one* nasty disease to humans - and merely pregnant ones at that - toxoplasmosis. Sack. Canal.

Mind you, pets have their moments (unlike you):
1. It's funny when they lick their private parts.
2. It's blinking hilarious when they get a piece of poo stuck on their arse so you can place bets on when and where it'll flick off, or

which gagging parent caves in first and cleans it.

3. They ruin your Mum's furniture and don't really get into trouble for it - you'd get sent to your room. Therefore, you can secretly encourage your pet to treat the lounge like an obstacle course using your Dad's secret steak stash as bait.

4. Their farts are baaaaaaaaaaaad. So, feed your pet human food to *really* upset their digestive system.

5. You can use them to create static and stick balloons to the walls - yes, even goldfish. Did you know that the coldness of water in a toilet bowl is scientifically proven to revive many a dead goldfish. It's just such a shame that all that toxic bleach your Mum flushes down there forces their brains to squeeze out of their gills.

6. The average dog costs a whopping £20k in their lifetime... Consequently many parents prefer to stay miserably married than get sole responsibility for footing the bill, which enables you to watch and marvel at their hilarious marital breakdown.

7. When no-one else will listen to your self-induced, self-indulgent, self-pitying wailings, a pet makes a perfect companion: it's just sheer coincidence that this is when 97% of pets hang themselves. Even goldfish have been known to commit suicide - you know that poo that often hangs from their

bum-hole, well, this is actually rope they're growing to top themselves.

But **best of all**, if you fail to look after your pet adequately you may be lucky enough to be the recipient of pet revenge... it may scratch you excessively. You can then pass these 'scars' off as self-harming prowess, a poltergeist attack or the result of a nasty incident involving a Zorro-wannabe goldfish.

-o-

How To Throw Trashing Parties Whilst Your Parents are Away (Probably Futilely Trying To Save Their Marriage)

Your parents have been psyching themselves up for this catastrophic rite of passage since the day you were born. That nano-moment of sheer joy as you entered the world was quickly replaced by the overwhelming sense of doom they felt at what you'd do, one day, to their home. So, really, it's *not* even a terrible shock when they come back from a weekend away to try and rekindle their relationship to find the house trashed after you've thrown a buy-some-friends house party. They've known they had it coming - they've spent getting on for two decades preparing for this... In fact, their anger and rage is practically *a put-on, part of the overall family experience.* So, take their seething rage with a pinch of salt (but you may need that for the red wine stain.

How To Help Your Repressed Parents Finally Express Themselves
Indeed, they've almost been *looking forward* to this family meltdown because it gives them the opportunity to finally truly scream and shout - feelings they normally repress for fear of actually killing you. Fortunately, they probably *won't* because they won't want to go to prison since cell décor is a bit worse than the state of your house after the party.

How To Diffuse Your Parents Wrath In A Jiffy
However, if your parents' anger appears really O.T.T. it could be genuine and they may change the will (or worse, the locks), so just call your grandparents and ask them for ammunition on the parties *your parents threw when they were teens*. Touché. Actually, it's a fact that they caused **far more damage** at *their* house parties back in the olden days because there were fewer effective cleaning products available, less home cleaning services operating, and not as many cowboy builders working. Hypocrites!!!!! But, if your parents *really* won't get off your back, tell them you've found a stash of child porn.

How to Throw the Most Reckless Party, Ever!

The Booze - If you're clever (a.k.a. sneaky), preparations for this crucial part of any successful party should begin *several years in advance.* Start by siphoning off alcohol from your parents booze cupboard a little at a time so they don't notice. Mind you, if your parents are unhappy in their relationship you can afford to siphon off *much* more as each will believe the other spouse has hit the bottle. Store the booze in empty fizzy pop bottles, throwing your tipsy mum off the scent by telling her they are for a recycling project at school (as if). After a few years, or weeks, you'll soon have enough alcohol to open a pub in an inner city, never mind for your party.

The Water - You what?!? Surely not. Aha, apparently, drinking lots of water helps you avoid a hangover in the morning (and hangovers are to be avoided at all costs because they make you look like (more) crap)... it's got something sciencey to do with water helping you *pee the alcohol out in your sleep.* Therefore, make sure your irresponsible lazy parents have paid their water rates bill so your water supply isn't cut off as your paralytic guests down their sobering *whole mouthful* of water before staggering off home to puke in their own home. Or on the pavement. Or their girl or boyfriend's mouth.

The Buckets - Most normal families only possess one bucket for cleaning the car once a year... if you have actually have more than one bucket it's highly likely that your Dad's a window cleaner, car thief or planning to dismember your Mum. Consequently, to be the hostess with the mostess, you need to provide *alternative* puking arrangements:

1. The **bath** is your best option as it is just about big enough - it'll hold an average of 124 good pukes. Be warned, though, corner baths only hold an average of 63 pukes (however, if your naff enough to have a corner bath you may want to consider not holding your party at your home and, instead, break in to someone else's home and hold the party there instead - it's best to do this when the real homeowners aren't in). Baths are also easy to rinse afterwards... rinse!?! What's that, you cry. It's what your Mum does with the shower head to remove the scummy residue after you've been in the bathroom.

2. However, if there are too many pukers and your bath looks hilariously in danger of overflowing, you should politely offer your guests the **sink**. Sick is too lumpy to pass through the drainy hole thing at the top of the bath, and in your drunken stupor you may mistakenly think it's a great game to try and bash the sick through the hole with the shit- sticky bog brush. This 'lark' will *only* result in you chucking up all that precious alcohol you've downed.

3. When these puke-holders are full, other options include the kitchen bin (bribe your younger sibling into emptying it with hollow promises of bringing round your good-looking friends).
4. Shoes - ironically, walking in puke filled shoes is just as therapeutic as having expensive reflexology. However, still don't let your guests vom in *your* shoes.
5. Plant pots - many plants are known to thrive on a good puke as they're full of nutrients from all those burgers and chips. But should the plants die, then good, because they provide oxygen for the earth through photosynthesis and, quite frankly, you'd rather the air was thinner because being dizzy is well funny.

The Food - Absolutely not necessary. You don't want to spoil your guests' appetites for that dodgy kebab on the way home that they'll keep down for approximately 11 metres.

The Neighbours - A.K.A. Killjoy Pigfaces. Neighbours can be a real bore when you're throwing a noisy all-nighter... What with banging *out of time* to the music on the wall, calling the spoilsport police or trying to cut off your electricity supply. To prevent this selfish inconvenience put them under surveillance in the run-up to the social gathering, recording things they shouldn't be doing for blackmail purposes. For example:

- Flicking slugs and cat poo over their fence into your parents' garden (not that your parents actually care that their garden resembles a Palestinian territory... your neighbours don't know that).
- Sticking fingers up at your Mum and Dad when their backs are turned - though secretly you admire them for it.
- Or putting bird seed on your Dad's (better) car so that birds crap on it. Your neighbours'll be begging to be your bouncers.

The Music - It doesn't matter what brand your sound system is, or whether you have a DJ or live band, all that matters is that so long as the bass is LOUD enough to make your female guests' jiggle... this will spiritually bring your male and female guests together. (Alas, and unavoidably, with the current trend in rising youth obesity, you may also be witness to male boob jiggle too).

The Cleaning Up - As with the booze preparation, you can pre-plan the clean up operation several years in advance by dedicating a mere 1% of the money redistributed from your Mum's purse and/or your sibling's piggy bank to hiring a professional cleaning contractor (Yellow Pages - the Teen's Bible). However, if you can't be arsed with picking up the phone (who can blame you) then it's your legal right as the host to make your guests who stayed over because they were "too tired" to go home to clean up for you. That way you can also use that 1% of your savings for ill-fitting underwear.

How To Clean Up Specific Scene of Grimes

    a) *Removing Burns* (not the facial variety - these tend to be annoyingly permanent): you can't actually disguise a fag burn so your best bet is to *cut out the entire burn* from the carpet or sofa. Your parents will be so confused and perplexed as to the blatant obviousness of the hole that they'll put it down to their own hangovers, or going blissfully senile.

    b) *Wall skids*: usually caused by people amusingly falling down the stairs, or getting jiggy against the paintwork, and rarely by your guests smearing their botties on the wall (unfortunately just 3% of cases). These marks are easily removed by using Tipp-Ex; but if the offending wall *is not actually white to begin with* and your parents notice the strange white area, simply inform them that they *were* once white. Then, tell them that you've been watching The Boffin Channel and have discovered that their/ your smoking, bad breath and farting has caused chronic discolouration, and you've merely used a solution of 1/10th turps to water to reveal the walls' true colour. (The potential drawback to this almost plausible load of nonsense is that smoking, bad breath and farting may be outlawed to prevent further discolouration and house price devaluation. Leave home).

c) *Smashed ornament*: just get out all your sticky-backed plastic and double-sided sticky tape that you made your Mum go searching for hours for when you were a kid and never used, and *really badly* stick back the naff ornament back together. Immediately realise you have no future in antique restoration (goody goody bumdrops) and bury the offending article in a landfill site/neighbour's garden (if you're lucky, you'll unearth a skeleton). To get away with the vandalism, simply clean away all the dust surroundeding the naff object - this way your Mum'll never even notice it's gone. Twelve years later when she suddenly realises it's missing, admit the truth immediately because your Dad'll give you some money there and then for getting rid of that bit of tat.

d) *Stench*: to remove the vague, yet not unpleasant, deadly waft of booze, puke, fags, cheap aftershave and adolescent hormones just get out your old Play Doh and make crazy rude shapes with it. Upon returning, your parents will be so distracted by the smell of Play Doh, they'll not even notice the stench because they'll be too worried that you're regressing to childhood and that they'll have to live through your puberty again.

TOP TIP: if your house is trashed beyond recognition, the solution is obvious. Just swap house numbers with a similar house in your street.

How Parents Try To Punish And How To Punish Them Right Back

Your parents may attempt to punish you for your wicked party by grounding you. Your genetic reaction to this will be to scream and shout and create even more damage to the house. DON'T. Let them ground you willingly. A couple of days with you round the house will soon see your parents coughing up loads of cash and endless taxi rides to get you out of their sight.

2 SEX

Sex Education for Teenagers

Huh. Like you need any sex education. You're a veritable professor of porn moves. A scholar of stroking. A lecturer in lovin'. A boffin in bonking. A tutor in tickling. Er, where's the clitoris?

So, you *could* get your sex education from what's written on the school's toilet walls, but the cubicles will be too full of pupils doing their "biology homework", shooting up, or compulsory bulimia-practise. Besides, the graffiti will probably be full of illiterate mistakes that may lead you to make an idiot of yourself… e.g. "put your pen's in the funny hole" may cause you to stick a biro in the clown's face of a visiting circus.

Or, you *could* get your sex education from your school or college's "Personal Development" class but your embarrassed, burning cheeks would quickly reveal that you're either a virgin, or in love with the naff teacher, or, worse still, that you like Enya as this will be the soothing music the teacher will play to stop you all mucking around - you won't be able to stop yourself la-la-ing along. How degrading.

You *could* perhaps get your sex education from the telly, for example, like on a saucy movie or Grange Hill but you're usually far too busy pretending to those present in the room that you're *not* in the slightest bit embarrassed by hugging yourself and making snoggy noises - even when you're only audience is the dog.

Maybe you *could* sneak into a bookshop or library and take a peek at the Korma Sutra, but it's Sod's Law that one of your peers will see you entering this place of literary worship and you'd never live it down, you hippie square - you'd end up getting stoned with organic flapjack. Alternatively, you *could* use the internet to surf for sex education tips but this can seriously erode into the time you've set aside for eating crisps, burgers, nuts, toast, sweets, scabs, chips, pizza, battered anything, bogies, biscuits, chocolate, sugar, and lard.

You *could* even let your very reluctant parents give you the hilarious Birds and the Bees talk but, then again, they *accidentally* had you, so instead of telling you how to get the stupid bra contraption off in less than thirteen minutes, all they'll bang on about is that you should get a hysterectomy or vasectomy *right now.* (Incidentally, if you're female it's worthwhile considering *not developing* breasts as removing a fiddly bra is a complete turn off to an impatient young man. Indeed, your intended suitor will probably choose to cop off with a girl who is flat-chested and doesn't need to wear a stupid brassiere... this contradicts the previous theory that these such Teen boys selected androgynous looking girls because they were gay. Budding breasts can be flattened by bandaging them flat, or sprinkling with anti-baking powder as this has an anti-raising effect, or taping two large heavy saucepans to the offending area).

How to Perform Different Sexual Positions Using The Minimum Of Effort
Most of the time it won't matter what position you force your unfit body into because the act of rumpy pumpy will be over almost as fast as you can say "a". It's just such a terrible irony that the famous missionary position is the easiest position to bother with because it requires you to face each other. That's why eyelids were invented. Sometimes, your parents' will selfishly refuse to go out and leave you to It on their bed - perhaps because there's a hurricane outside, or they've broken their neck tripping over your carelessly thrown shoes, or, they know you've programmed a locksmith's number into your mobile phone; so, you'll need to have a few alternative tricks up your skirt or trouser leg...

The Airing Cupboard Position

If you can master this difficult position it's definitely worth using in *all* other locations as being able to do It *standing* means that when you are caught by parents/teachers/coppers/their proper boy or girlfriend it's much easier to run away because you're already on your feet. Doing It in the airing cupboard has several advantages:

- It's lovely and toastie and warm so the Teen boy's manhood looks less shrivelled and pathetic compared to normal.
- There are lots of towels handy for mopping up afterwards.
- These towels can also be used for a fun, towel-flicking attack - it's a good idea to play this game *before* you've used them to clean up.
- It's dark. Occasionally, you can forget to keep your eyes shut throughout the *entire* sweaty session - being in the gloomy cupboard helps reduce visibility should this tragedy of sight occur.
- As the airing cupboard is warm you may overheat and thereby sweat off unwanted extra pounds, or indeed mili-ounces.

Behind the Bike Sheds Position

This is why free periods, break-times and bunking off are included in the timetable by your headmaster - your *absence* in the horribly overcrowded class makes teaching a little less dreadful for your teacher. You can learn all about reproduction and faking it *the hard way* (tee hee)...

because the corrugated wall will leave an agonising, permanent and attractive pattern imprinted on your back. Why not take it in turns leaning against the rigid surface so that neither of you misses out on this latest kind of "tattoo". This position is also great for providing easily available (and much needed) lubrication - bike chain oil. Squeak squeak.

The Cross Country Position
This is an ideal position for beginners and lazy Teens because not only do the little cute gym skirts provide easy access, but they also guarantee that the male will experience instant arousal (which is a bonus because, guys, it'll be *freezing* out there). More importantly, this position means you can also *avoid* doing any stupid running (tip: it's worth shagging *anyone* to achieve this). However, you will inevitably be mauled by nettles and bracken as you hide/do It in the undergrowth, so please ensure that you become covered in lots of neck love bites to act as a decoy to the P.E. teacher: he/she will be distracted by their jealousy. The real genius of this cross-country position is that, as non-running skivers, you're also traditionally obliged to smoke a fag… before, during and after sex.

The School Disco Position
In the olden days ten years ago, Teens lived in absolute fear of having no-one to do the last dance with. (Incidentally, girls back then believed that the bigger your hair was the bigger your boobs became, so many had perms to try and make their

chests more alluring to the boys. In reality, boys would get their fingers stuck in the curly barnets and many had to be cut free - literally - by firemen. That's why perms don't exist anymore. And why many of this male generation don't have all their fingers). Anyhows, girls and boys would line up on opposite sides of the school hall and when Chris de Burg's "Lady in Red" started they would hurl themselves at each other, not caring who they actually ended up smoochie-ing with - even if it was the science teacher. Nowadays, the pressure is on *how many* people you can cop off with even before the last dance. The last dance is **now** the time you're supposed to see who can pull off doing It on the dance-floor without the teachers realising.

Swotty, creepy types have, ironically, the best chance of pulling this public sexy position off as the teachers simply won't believe it possible that anyone vaguely fancies the brain-aches enough to actually do It. Of course, if the squares *are* doing It on the dance-floor it's because they've promised to do their fondle-friend's homework for them. If you're, hopefully, not one of these squaros you can increase your dance-floor prospects by:

     a) If you're a girl, threatening your chosen victim with jam-stained tampons.

     b) If you're a boy, threatening your intended target with spiders abducted from the changing room showers.

The Detention Position

This position is formerly known as an illicit relationship between a pupil and a teacher (the most likely teacher candidate for such an affair is the R.E. teacher, just so you know). This position will result in heartbreak, stalking, arrest and imprisonment, but hey, at least your parents will approve.

The Assembly Position

In 2007, assembly will become humanitarianly recognised by the UN as an abuse of a young person's personal rights.

- It encourages others to leeringly check out your bootie whilst you're wearing the most *unflattering* of clothes, your school uniform.
- It permits your jeering peers to humiliatingly count your spit ends to help them pass the time. They should at least be given scissors - *not* to stab you - but to trim off the frizzy blighters.
- You are no longer capable of standing for more than seventeen seconds - and this excessive amount of time on your feet was only under extreme duress whilst waiting in a burger queue.

Assembly will therefore, be turned into a GCSE module in "Speed Mating"; after all, all those lines and lines of faceless individuals is an ideal opportunity to practise flirting/sex with strangers. One housepoint will be awarded for every unromantic liaison. Go to the top of the class. For once, you couldn't try harder.

Now you've mastered the positions, you *may* want to avoid ruining the rest of your life by **not** getting pregnant. Then again, you'll never be able to afford getting on the property ladder so having a baby is the only guaranteed method for getting your first home… off the council. **Warning**: having a baby as a Teenager will *seriously* affect your already average looks: with dark shadows under your eyes from sleep deprivation; crows' feet from making faces and pretending to smile and make faces at the needy infant; and permanent lines around your mouth from screaming at it.

How To Obtain Contraception Without Embarrassment

There is no way on earth you're going to go in to a chemist and buy yourself contraception, even with your parents' stolen money - the cashier could quibble over the size you've selected. You're never going to go the Doctors, even though it's almost legitimate time off school/college - the Doctor might want to use the opportunity to give you an evil potentially life-saving injection for some deadly disease. And you've certainly never ever going to ask your Parents to provide you with the sperm-busters - you don't want *them* to start asking *you* for sex guidance (although you could have a right laugh giving them rubbish advice, for example, "not eating green vegetables is an aphrodisiac"). So, you're going to need to be able to make your own contraception. Should be easy enough, you've watched "Art Attack"...

How to Build Your Own Personalised Condom
The beauty of making your own condoms - obviously aside from being able to make it XXXXXXXXXX-Large - is that you can colour the condoms in. Guys should decorate their jonnies with pictures of canons, anacondas and Pamela Anderson. But in the more likely event that it's the promiscuous girl who's making the condoms for her lazy boyfriend, they should draw cutesy pictures of puppies, rainbows and maggots.

If you're a bit thick (i.e., most of you) then follow option A. But if you're middle-class and destined to go to university and a life of unappreciated privilege, you should use obnoxious smarty-pants option B.

Option A
Take one sausage balloon. Er, that's it.

However, if you reckon you're a "genius" because you've been predicted a Grade D at GCSE, you could try making your balloon condoms into amusing shapes like a doggie, elephant or the Blackpool Tower. But be careful about the colour of balloon you select... choosing pink if male will only arouse suspicion, whilst selecting black - unless genuinely black yourself - will only illicit charges of "Liar liar, tangas on fire").

Option B

Firstly, you need a rubber (tee hee) houseplant - fortunately, every proper bourgeois mother has one because she uses it to spy on the cleaner to see if she's dusting *everything*. Make an incision on the stem using the diamond-plated vegetable knife, then attach a gold receptacle like the milk bottle to collect the natural latex milk. Now add stabilisers (try stealing a friend's kid sister's bike, what larks), chuck in some preservatives (use your Mama's very expensive face cream) and vulcanising agents (that means fake big ears) in the private home laboratory Daddy built you to help you get to medical school.

Now, pour the latex mix into a temperature controlled tank (your private swimming pool will suffice) and take a line of glass penis-shaped moulds (try your local corner shop, Harvey Nichs, or if it's shut, a bunch of fairish-trade bananas) and dip them in the latex pool. The 'condoms' must then be dried using filtered air to prevent contamination... why not pop by your celebrity hairdresser and borrow all their hairdryers - those A-list clients can wait. If it's raining and you can't risk hair frizz, breathe heavily on the drying condoms; although, if you're a podgy "asthmatic" you'd better have the ambulance on speed dial.

Then - this is the hardest bit - try lifting your idle finger to gently roll the edge of condom over to form the rim. The condoms should then be baked in an oven to vulcanise the latex (you won't know where or what this "oven" is, so give them to your nanny to cook. So what if it's not in her job description, tell her you'll tell your Mum what she's really been up to). Finally, remove condoms from the moulds using high pressure jets of water - utilise your parents secret champagne stash. Tra la. And for the ultimate condom experience, try flavouring them with jam, peanut butter, space dust or caviar.

But that about other forms of contraception? It's nigh on impossible to make your own version of **The Pill** unless you have a stash of 3"x2" foil sheets with thirty-one tiny pockets in them that you can seal over on a factory production line specialising in pharmaceutical packaging. However, if by chance, you do, then simply fill the cute little holes with little mints. Easy peasy. As for **The Cap**, don't really know what that is, so moving on... And then there's **The Diaphragm**. Uh? Whatever.

WARNING: besides, guys should take the full responsibility for the contraception because girls can't be trusted to take The Pill as they are famously reluctant to swallow anything with calories. Condoms are the *__only__* 90-something% reliable form of birth control. Oh, or doing It standing up.

How to Handle Post-Coital Embarrassment
As a fully half-developed Teenager, you're physically mature enough to rumpy around (though

not with any skill), but what of the emotional, turbulent aftermath? How should you cope with those long uncomfortable silences as you both pick sex bits out of your mouths? And, most importantly, how can you get rid of them quickly…

1. Ask them their name.
2. Shout your mum for two cups of coffee (you don't need to worry about bad breath now).
3. If you're a guy, put on her bra and panties… this will guarantee that you'll never have to see her again. *Warning*: you may like it.
4. If female, put on your everyday, greying underwear and *not* the sexy bra and panties you stole from your adulterating Mum/teacher/slutty neighbour's washing line to impress him… this will absolutely guarantee that you'll never have to see him again.
5. Ask them if they'll accept you homework late. It's their fault for seducing you, after all, so you haven't had time to finish it.
6. Tell them how old you really are. They'll vanish.
7. Roll over and go to sleep (this manoeuvre will serve you well for decades to come).
8. Say "Was that it?"
9. Light up… your farts (this is particularly beneficial if you're having sex outside and it's cold, but be careful about burning yourself).
10. Start faking convulsions.
11. Pretend you are dead.

-o-

How to Lose your Virginity Successfully

WARNING: IT IS ILLEGAL TO HAVE RUMPY PUMPY BEFORE THE AGE OF SEXY 16*. THIS IS BECAUSE YOUR PARENTS GENERATION - WHO MADE THIS LAW - WERE MUCH UGLIER THAN YOU AT THIS AGE DUE TO THE LACK OF LIP GLOSSES, HAIR GELS AND COOL CLOTHES, AND *COULDN'T* ACTUALLY PERSUADE ANYONE TO HAVE SEX WITH THEM. THEREFORE, THEY CREATED THIS LAW TO SPOIL YOUR FUN AND BECAUSE THEY'RE JEALOUS OF YOUR SOCIAL AND SEXUAL SUCCESS.

Still, you don't really want to get sent down for being a sexy criminal because:
- You're in your prime right now - typically, it's only ugly people who go to prison so you're hardly going to want to cop off with anyone once you're there.
- The prison's are massively overcrowded, supposing you ended up sharing a cell with a bean-eating vegetarian.
- You can't go shopping - unless you go the same cushy prison that Jeffrey Archer went to.

However, if you don't lose your virginity before the legal age of sixteen, you will be the laughing stock of your peer group. And that's worse than doing time.

How Hard is Losing It (tee hee hee hee hee hee hee hee hee hee hee hee hee hee hee hee heee heee heeee heeeelp pass the ventilin inhaler)

Firstly, to be able to lose your virginity you actually need *someone else* to help you. If you're too ugly to get a girl or boyfriend, all is not lost as there are always blind people, irresponsible teachers and very realistic prosthetic face masks from film companies such as Dreamworks.

Now, is it a good idea to let your chosen accomplice know that you're a virgin and that they are your first? NO. Not only will this cause them to snigger (they will, *even* if they are a virgin too), they may well turn you down on the (correct) grounds that the intercourse will be both rubbish and over too quickly. (Of course, *once* you've successfully lost your virginity you should tell every *subsequent* partner that you're *still* a virgin as they will be so impressed that, as a novice, you're actually rather good at It. Why not continue this scam into your thirties... after this age, it's highly unlikely that you'll have sex ever again).

How to Romantically Set the Mood for Dumping Your Virginity

No special efforts necessary.

How to Get Rid of Your Affliction ASAP
In order to lose your virginity *effectively*, you should wait for your parent(s)* to go out - not only does this add much-needed excitement due to the thrill of them possibly catching you at It, but doing It at home is vaguely more comfortable than your school locker. However, your oldies should ideally be *further away* than just the back garden (where they go to escape you)... Your ageing parents now suffer from incontinence and will make frequent trips back inside to empty their colostomy bags... remember, colostomy bags make deadly missiles. (Indeed, Bush could have won the Iraq war by now if he'd pelted the baddies with poop - they don't *even eat* with their bum-wipey hand). Therefore, your decrepit parents need to be away from the house for a *maximum* of fifteen seconds.

Now, which room to do It in? The kitchen? Too advanced for a beginner - too many implements to get impaled on. The Living Room? Too many family photos. The Bathroom? No, if you get the tap end it's really annoying. Besides, it's filthy. Your bedroom? No, it's too much like being unfaithful to your hand. That only leaves your parents' double bed. Perfect. Stain-free sheets. Ish.

How to Prepare the Scene of the Crime
Don't bother doing this *before* your virginity-thief arrives as it'll look like you're trying to impress them, or that you care. About anything. Instead, make them

stand like a muppet whilst they time you with a stopwatch to see how fast you can do all this - then, on subsequent sexy occasions you can try and beat your personal best. What larks.

1. Barricade the door with your least favourite toys... *least* favourite because they'll get broken when your siblings, pals or police burst in with the camera.
2. Romantically drape 284 old sheets and towels over the sacrificial divan altar for the ensuing bloodbath (have bleach, bucket and rubber gloves handy in case of excessive wall splatter).
3. Coyly draw the curtains - not to conceal your embarrassment, but to hide your oddly-shaped body parts.
4. And light scented candles - obviously, not for the romance factor but to disguise the noxious stench of nervous fartings.

What is Foreplay and How to Pretend You Know What You're Doing.

"Foreplay is the act of fiddling with each others bits for a few seconds before you get bored and stick the saveloy in the roll", *Reference Source:* Boy's Toilet cubicle, Wood Green School, Witney, Oxfordshire.   This procedure can last from anywhere between one and five seconds. It doesn't really matter what you *actually* do so long as you make some "Mmmm" noises (N.B. *not* the "Mmmmm" noises you make when you eat a burger, that's a special noise to be saved for your eating pleasure only) as this will intimidate your participant into thinking that because *you sound* like you are enjoying yourself, therefore, you must be good at It; they will then *copy* your groaning to give the impression that they are also moaning because they are good at It too.

But, firstly, you must take your cool clothes off[1]. However, you **shouldn't** let the other person remove your clothes because:

a) They probably have lovely dirty, burger-greasy hands (not worth the embarrassing stain risk.)

b) They might try and see what clothes size you *really* are - if you're a girl you've already lied and told them you were a size 8; or if you're a boy, you've told a huge porky (tee hee) and said you are extra large.

c) They might fold your clothes and put them carefully on a chair… that's a *huge* turn-off.

Therefore, you should stand facing each other - if you can stomach looking at them - and play the "Who can Get their Kit Off the Fastest" game. Whoever wins gets to give the loser a wedgie… If your competition appears to lose suspiciously easily and they're male, you should be aware that they're definitely gay.

Right, now you're ready to stare lovingly-ish or repulsedly into each others genitals. If you want to distract them from looking/laughing at your bits and pieces, whisper sweet nothings into their waxy ears - these "nothings" can literally be any old nonsense as simply whispering in the ears is ticklishy horrible and they won't be able to concentrate on anything else, least of all your pre-gastric bypass body.

Then, once your mutual nudey embarrassment reaches a crescendo of mickey-taking you're finally ready... for a pillow fight. Well, it'd be a waste of your parents' big bed not to have a feathery fisticuffs. Show no mercy as the winner is entitled to the loser's pocket money. In fact, why not offer the stupid ugly loser the chance to play double or quits by seeing who can trampoline the highest... clearly, you will have previously fixed the results by removing all the springs from their side of the bed. Warning: try to avoid getting your head stuck in the ceiling as the fire brigade will wet themselves laughing when they come to rescue you - in 2006, 368 Teenagers told their Fireman rescuers that they were trying to XXX. So, even a Teenager, *the most accomplished liar on the planet*, can't fib their way out of this one.

Once you've run out of games to play you might as well get on with the boring task of doing It.

How to Commit Intercourse Quickly, Effectively and Selfishly

The male takes his sticky out rubbery thing and sticks it in the slimy female pee-pee pot. Wiggle it about. In. Out. In. Out. Shake it all about. And writhe about comically like you've seen in the movies. Finally, spasm away like you've just been shot by a 44 magnum and, then, run over by a hit and run police car.

How to Handle that Embarrassing Silence Afterwards

Who cares? You've finally done it. Just sit or lie there - preferably with *your back turned* as you should now begin the process of trying to forget who was the idiot you lost your virginity to - and wait for the parents to return. Then, you can *at least* enjoy the notorious mad scrabble back to the living room; you can totally live life on the edge and really add to the excitement by having a bash at making the parental bed... remember not to leave any tell-tale cuddly toys behind!

* Ha ha ha, if you're *still* a virgin *over* the age of consent, *and* still living at home with your parents, you're most likely to get rid of your virginity on Ebay.

[1] If you're a fatso it will be in your interests to keep your clothes **on**, therefore, you should only attempt to lose your virginity in the *winter* when you can use the cold as a pathetic excuse for remaining fully dressed. If your accomplice is stroppy about this, remove a sock, then, they'll be only too delighted for you to stay fully clad.

How to be a Born-Again Virgin

For the rest of your sexual life (until your thirties) you should pretend to be a virgin. Firstly, because your subsequent sex partners will think you're amazing in bed for a crappy beginner; secondly, because when you're famous this will provide a good marketing angle (re: Britney Spears), and thirdly and most importantly of all, the other person will spend 10% more time and effort trying to impress you and not being completely rubbish either. This is because once you've "Lost It" you're morally obliged to go round bragging about it and they don't want everyone hearing that they were a second-rate virginity thief.

Besides, being a "virgin" will get you free coffee and cakes if you hang out at your local church/ place-of-worship-run youth group. Homemade cakes, no less, you won't have had these delicacies before... they're very bulimia-friendly when made by religious people - they probably even use actual butter. In fact, pretending to be a virgin amongst these extremists has numerous benefits.

Reasons for Faking Virginity and Hanging Out with Religious Nutters

1. You can sneakily swipe the best clothes and bric-a-brac before the jumble sales - not for personal use, obviously, but for resale on ebay.

2. Your parents will be chuffed you're going on a "camping retreat" with your new-found, wholesome friends... here you come, Brighton.

3. You will look way cool by comparison to these sensible squares.

4. They'll be able to do your R.E. homework.

5. If Jesus *does* return to earth for the Second Coming, as one of his gang, he'll be able to perform a miracle on you - a nose job, liposuction and botox without surgery.

How to Pull Off Pretending to be a Virgin
If you're female all you have to do is just lie there, a bit corpse-like, and say "ouch" every 4.5 seconds. If you're male, simply giggle throughout the funny business. Easy.

-o-

How to Find the Erogenous Zones*,
A.K.A. How To Borrow The Things Your Pulling Partner Said They'd Never Lend You

Sometimes, a quick grope and giggle round the back of the bike-sheds or sofa when your parents are watching "Corrie" won't fully satisfy you. You may be left feeling cheated, used and annoyingly short-changed - in other words, your canoodle comrade *still* won't permanently lend you their I-pod. Outrageous. This is the time to take your foreplay to *the next level...* it's time to graduate from merely *turning up* for a fondle to actually searching for those mysterious-sounding erogenous zones. Huh?

But don't risk ear nibbling (wax potatoes), toe sucking (stringy cheese) or finger sucking (as a Teenager yourself, you'll know where they've been)... the edible results of these amateur foreplay fumbles only takes up valuable burger-space in your tummy. Besides, they *don't* work - they just annoy the hell out of both of you, as it involves spending even more time together. In fact, the G-spot is an urban myth created by chicks to make the guy feel inadequate as they search for it. The *real* erogenous zones are actually really easy to find and arouse…

The Teen Male

(Annotated visual of Teen Yob in novelty underwear)

Brain – stimulated by closeness of remote control
Eyes – easily excited by the sight of a football
Mouth – aroused immediately by availability of kebab
Ears – turned on by the presence of a belching challenger to their throne
Nose – responds favourably to the aroma of curry and fart
Neck – immediately aroused by passing souped-up Novas
Arm – turned on by mere mention of games console
Stomach – aroused by anything covered in fat or ketchup
Bottom – turned on by chance to sit for hours/days in front of TV
Leg – thrilled by falling over and being able to pick the resulting scab
Hand – titilated by challenge of holding 5th consecutive burger
Elbow – excited by prospect of giving it to current needy girlfriend

Finger – stirred by the opportunity to pick and flick bogies

Feet – alas, too easily aroused by rap music

The Teen Female

(Annotated visual of Teen girl in cute bedwear)

Brain – aroused by even the vaguest prospect of gossiping

Eyes – turned on by seeing someone to gossip about

Mouth – stimulated by chance to gossip for 13 hours non-stop

Ears – titillated by the discovery of fresh gossip

Nose – instantly stirred by the smell of a sale in the air

Hair - roused by joy of singeing it to oblivion with straighteners

Neck – easily turned by the presence of any male with more muscles than current boyfriend

Arm – stimulated by opportunity to carry numerous shopping bags, but only when Mum's paying

Ring Finger – naively aroused by hormonal delusions that current fella is "The One"

Other Finger – easily titillated by opportunity to pick G-string out of derriere

Stomach – overcome with passion at wearing a crop top, regardless of muffin-ness

Bottom – turned on by having a huge dump in the hope that she is now pounds lighter

Leg – quickly aroused by news of clothing sale
Hand – can only be turned on by buying new shoes/handbag (the only time she'll part with her own money)
Ankle – aroused by 6" heels and twisting ankle on them (= day off school)
Foot – a tantric zone capable of sustaining shopping for days on end

-o-

How To Make Sure Puberty Is A Living Hell For Everyone Around You

According to the Universal Dictionary of Parents, Puberty is a time "when their already unpleasant, spoilt, whining child turns into a rabid creature more malevolent, evil and toxic than that spinning head girl in "The Exorcist". Cool. That Regan chick is your idol. Forget Charlotte Church - what a wussy amateur. In fact, that bile spewing, greasy-haired girl wasn't *actually* possessed by the naughty Devil, but simply experiencing - and enjoying - an overload of teenage hormones and hilarious body changes. She was *only* spinning her head so that she could see if her arse had gotten as big as her pubescent boobies.

S o ,   p u b e -rteeheeheeheeheeheeheeheeheeheeheeheehee is a turbulent and stressful time of physical and emotional change and pain - for you, your "friends" and, hopefully, your family. Hurrah. It's *so* worth it.

The Physical Changes of Puberty (snigger snigger)

- If you're a girl, you'll get sexy boobies - even if they're tiny beestings, you'll still be much more attractive to boys... bra-strap snapping is such a hoot.

- If you're a fat boy, you'll *also* get boobies - lucky you, you don't need to bother getting a girlfriend.

- You'll develop pubic hair that is excellent for creating static to stick balloons to walls (ginger people are advised against trying this lark as their pubic hair is a weirdo texture and can result in spontaneous combustion. Then again, you might as well try it, no-one's ever going to fancy you).

- You can demand repossession-costing presents from your parents in the feeble hope that buying you off will keep your hideous hormonal self out of their way. Tcha.
- If you're a boy, your voice will break and you'll finally stop getting bullied at school. Incidentally, whilst your voice is in the process of breaking, the high and low tones are ideal for guy/girl role-play while masturbating. But if you're voice *doesn't* show any signs of breaking, it's worth

swallowing a conker to create the illusion of an Adam's apple; also, when the doctors perform a tracheotomy to save your life the resulting soreness will fortunately temporarily make your voice sound much lower. Alas, this effect will eventually wear off so you will have to perform the conker swallow procedure ad infinitum.

- Boys will swear that their willy has finally becoming much, much bigger. This is a blatant porker (phnar) that they genuinely believe. Until the day they die. The ironic thing is that girls don't care about the size of the manhood, providing a) it's not bent; b) it doesn't smell like you haven't washed for a week (air freshener, guys, air freshener); and c) so long as you have a car, private jet, or better still, a skateboard.

- Girls will start the embarrassing, painful, traumatic business of menstruation. They are *so* lucky... as this is the ultimate green light to behaving like a psychotic snarling maniac. If you're a male, it's definitely worth pretending that you want a sex change so that your Doctor gives you the female hormone, oestrogen, a.k.a. "Bitch". Why should girls have all the fun? Plus, then you'll grow your own set of cherry buns.

- You'll develop a much more expensive taste in clothes. Tell your Mum that you saw it on David Attenborough's show and this is simply part of the homo sapien mating ritual; she won't really believe that you watched this quality TV but she's *so* desperate to be a granny because she knows it'll be *so much better* than being *your* Mum.

But these are all the obvious physical developments that you've already learnt about from "The Tweenies," what about the more subtle, confusing changes you may experience... In the olden days you would have been able to go and ask your cool P.E. teacher, nowadays they're all a bit dodgy...

The Male Puberty High-lights
Eyes will turn into magnets and become hypnotically attracted to boobs - irrespective of size, age, hairiness or quality.

Head hair will either start to fuzz and resemble pubes, or require grooming for several hours until it looks like you just got out of bed, or starts thinning at an alarming rate and shaving it all off makes your head look like a willy.

Ears will develop bionic powers so you can overhear your parents finally going to sleep after row-whispering for hours in their room, enabling you to sneak out to stand on street corners. Coo-oool.

Chin will develop an impressive 3.37 O'clock shadow. And regardless of your actual hair colour, your "beard" will mysteriously contain ginger hairs.

Chest will grow a few piddly hairs that will appetisingly smell of chicken. Or you will turn into a yeti, which is fine if you live in the Andes or East Kilbride because it's freezing there, but not fine if you want to have a non-lesbian girlfriend. You'd better shave it off with your Dad's new razor approximately every three hours. What laughs you can have as he nurses his major shaving rash.

Neck will develop a taste for cheap jewellery that you will pretend is real. Even when your neck turns green. You're fooling no-one. Who cares.

Arm will require a badly-done tattoo and your Mum will ground you for a month. When that (obviously) fails, she'll show your baby photos to new girlfriends for the **rest** of your life. In revenge, you'll show them her secret "sexy" polaroids.

Hand will grow mysterious calluses. Strange that.

Stomach will demand to be shown shirtless as soon as the sun starts shining (even in the winter months) because you confuse malnutrition for a six-pack. Even fatsos will want to flaunt their six-rolls-pack.   Girls only ever fancy these boys because the flab rolls make ideal storage pockets for make-up etc.

Fingers will become your chief method of communication thanks to texting, leaving your mouth free to eat burger 23/7 (save one hour for swearing). Your fingers will consequently develop impressive muscles which you can also pretend is down to your prowess as a champion masturbator/ games console king/nose-picker (take your pick, HAHA).

Legs will not develop in any way whatsoever as you will entirely concentrate on building tiny muscles in your arms using dumbbells and carrying fat girlfriends, leaving your ignored legs to resemble sprawny sparrow legs. That's why you will never remove your long shorts in the summer.

Feet will develop a stench worse than death, or worser, soap. They will also start stomping and skulking all on their own. When your parents scream at you for doing this, calmly utter the phrase, "I'm rehearsing my rhythm percussion. The world famous stick banger Evelyn Glynnie is a millionaire - and she's deaf." Suddenly, they'll hear a till ringing.

The Female Puberty Highlights

Hair will develop badly broken ends, common-as-muck root re-growth and be burnt to a frazzle from straighteners… unless you live in the NE or Liverpool, where it will be permed curlier than a pube on a poodle.

Ears will develop an uncanny ability to hear only what they want to.

Nose will develop a sense of smell capable of sniffing out a bargain at 100 metres. You won't actually buy the item, but smear your foundation and powder all over it – especially if item is white.

Your lips will develop the appearance of a permanent snarl or sneer, depending on the light. This only changes when you want something when it momentarily turns into a fake smile.

(shoulders) For a while you will develop the posture of a hunchback because you're embarrassed by your swelling boobies.

Your chin will develop an orangey line from badly-applied foundation that you think looks like you've got a suntan. You're fooling no-one.

Your nipples will sprout thick coarse hairs that you will attempt to pluck out with your fingers. You'll never admit to these, even when they get caught in someone's teeth.

Your boobs will grow and be pert for approximately one week, then they will begin their lifelong journey to your knees.

(belly) You will develop rolls and rolls of flab that you alone are blind to, you'll think you have a tum to rival Britney's and therefore only wear cropped tops. Even in winter.

(left hand) You will develop hideously expensive acrylic names which you'll make your parents pay for, only to pick at them until they ping off.

(right hand) Your hand will develop extreme reluctance to pay for anything when a parent or male is nearby. Your hard-whined pocket money is for essential, self-esteem items like lip gloss.

(middle finger) Middle finger will be used to communicate with parent/teacher/boyfriend when you can't get your own way.

(fanny) Mercifully your hideous vagina will grow a slightly less hideous carpet of fuzz reminiscent of living in a squat. You'll spend the rest of your life shaving it with your fella's razor. But if you're posh and smart, you'll have it waxed and sell the strips to pervs on Ebay to fund your drug habit.

Your knees will develop mysterious bruises. Yet you haven't fallen over. Curious.

Your legs will become more hairy than a Yeti. You will secretly like stroking them – it's like having a doggie. Attempts to remove it with razor will result in loss of 19 pints of blood over the course of just one week.

Feet will develop never-healing blisters from ill-fitting, cheap but cool-looking shoes (you think). It will result in witch-hag feet no man will ever caress. Unless under the influence of (bogus) promise of sex.

How to Outsmart Your Parents Who Think They've Been There, Done That However, your parents will have experienced puberty themselves and will already be well-versed in the usual Teen "Blame it on Puberty" routine, but they'll also have a survival strategy prepared for your atrocious behaviour. So, if you seriously want to be able to get away with blue murder, not only **must** you be able to back up your appalling behaviour with the latest (bogus) medical facts about the blame-free hormonal challenges of puberty…

-o-

How To Enjoy The Birds And The Bees Chat With Your Parents

It's undeniably true that Kids today grow up much more quickly. Thank heavens for the escalation in crime rates forcing you spoilt Teens to toughen up. Indeed, your parents have been preparing themselves for the cringe-worthy Birds and the Bees Talk since your very first birthday. So don't allow their lengthy rehearsal period give them the upper hand during this mortifying Chat about the facts of life; prepare *now* how you'll mis-behave during this embarrassing Talk to make sure that they'll wish you'd never been born...

Of course, the only reason parents talk to their Teens about sex and its serious ramifications *isn't* because they're worried that if you had a baby then you'd ruin the rest of your life... they know that it's *their* life the baby would ruin, as they'd be the ones who'd end up stuck looking after It.

How to Spot "The Chat" is Brewing
If you're a guy:
- A toilet roll will mysteriously appear on your bedside table.
- You'll find spy-busting strands of hair attached to your Dad's unemployed condom batch.
- Your Dad will start heartily slapping you on your back - not in an attempt at Father-Son bonding - but to see if you've got any agonising nail scratches on your back.

If you're a girl:
- These strange woolly cigars with tails will inexplicably appear in your make-up bag.
- You'll wake up covered in hair removal cream - your Mum's hoping that without your werewolf coverage you might actually get a boyfriend and stay out of her way more.
- Your Mum will start shrinking and dyeing all your best lingerie in the wash, thinking skuzzy underwear will put boys off. As if.

How to Spot the Signs that "The Chat" is Just Hilariously Moments Away

Neither parent wants to be the one to have to give The Birds and Bees Chat with you - partly because they're not sure if they've got their facts right, and partly because you're such vile company. Good for you. In fact, the chance are that if you hear them arguing for hours and hours on end it's because they're playing "Scissors, Paper, Stone" to see who's going to be the unlucky Chat giver, and *not* because they're divorcing. *That'll* happen next year. You can tell that The Chat is just *seconds* away, when:

1. You see one parent coming directly at you, and this time - unusually, without shouting or throwing something at you.
2. You spy the other parent pretending to hide so that they can earwig, and trying not to pee themselves laughing - quite a difficult task for the incontinent oldie. (Better spray the air with *their* duty free to avoid foreign urine inhalation).
3. The worried, embarrassed parent is sweating, groaning, bleating on about pins and needles (what a moaner - pins and needles are well funny), and clutching their chest... they'd rather try and have a heart attack than talk to you about sex.
4. They're drunk.

Warning: your natural instinct for self-preservation will be to run a mile. Well, not exactly run, more like, slouch and stomp. And not a mile either - more like fifteen metres to your room. Still. Fight this urge. Because permitting your parent to talk to you about sex will prove to be the funniest seven minutes of your life.

How to Survive The Birds and The Bees Chat
You can employ many tactics to amplify your parent's huge embarrassment, shame and discomfort:

1. Say absolutely nothing throughout this creepy experience, keeping a deadpan face (try imagining you're having sex, or dead, or at school).
2. Alternatively, say "Why" to *everything* - if you're a girl this will soon lead your parent to give you a large sum of money to go buy a book on reproduction (which, of course, you'll blow on pick or mix); or, if you're a boy, you're supposed to spend the cash on a prossie (which, of course, you will).
3. Put your hands on your ears and sing "La la la, la la la" really loudly. You'll either be discovered by a passing talent scout or your parent will cry in front of you. Either way… result.
4. Repeatedly put your hand under your armpit to make farty noises and ask if this sounds like a fanny fart. If it's your Dad giving you the Chat, he'll probably find this really funny and slip you secret money for the chippie. If it's your Mum, she'll show you that if you

wet your hand first, you'll achieve a more realistic sound. NOT.

5. Whenever your parent utters the words "penis" or "vagina" try repeating the words like you've never heard them before, for example, "pee-nus?, "pi-ness?", "pen-nes?" Your parent will then be obliged to teach you how to pronounce them in the hope that this'll stop you being bullied in the playground... hilarpenis.

6. At the end of The Chat give them a round of (sarcastic) applause - they'll thickly think you're congratulating them on the quality of their presentation, which will lure them into revealing hysterical juicy tit bits from when they were your age. One word - blackmail.

7. Shake your head in patronising disagreement whenever they provide factual information - they'll seriously panic that perhaps they *really are* rubbish at sex, and bribe *you* for advice. This money can be used to purchase whoopee cushions.

8. Finally, when you're sufficiently bored, occasionally flicking your tongue like a lizard will bring The Chat to an abrupt conclusion.

Questions To Ask Your Worn-Down Parent About Human Reproduction

There will come a blissful point during this Birds and Bees fiasco when your Parent won't be able to stand another second with you - you'll be able to spot this moment by the enthusiastic way they'll reach for the noose/shotgun/pills. This is most selfish of them, as you'll have additional, knowledge-hungry and thoughtful questions with which to terrorise them. Plus, you don't want to get spit/blood splatter/vomit on your expensive trainers. So, why not ask them unanswerable sex questions that will keep them alive whilst they try to come up with an answer (and keep you free of bodily fluid stainage):

- Are redheads destined to stay virgins until they die?
- Is it morally bankrupt to use used condoms as a cheap, plentiful alternative to water bombs? Isn't this recycling?
- If you have rumpy in the bath, will It create a vacuum causing the thingy to get stuck? Is this pleasurable (the getting stuck, *not* the ensuing fire brigade rescue)?
- If you're male and enjoy the sensation of a big, ripping poo does this actually mean you're gay?
- Does a female prefer to go on the bottom so that the male can't see her flob?
- Does the male prefer to go on top because it's easier (and more preferable) to look at the headboard from this angle?
- Ask if they've ever tried the Nagabandha postion, page 1736 of the Karma Sutra?
- Do you still fancy your life partner?
- Do you still do It?

Your other remaining parent will be feeling really smug that they escaped giving you this terminally embarrassing facts of life chat. They'll think that they've got off scott-free. Don't they know you *at all* by now? Treat them to a few special manoeuvres so that they don't feel left out...

1. When you see this parent for the first time after this Chat, either laugh, wink, or grimace at them - as if you know something *truly* horrendous about them (even more horrendous than the contents of their secret diary).

2. Do this for the rest of their life.

3. Throw your water-bomb used condoms at them.

4. Whenever you're out in public with this parent, randomly slip a novelty condom on your head and announce that the other parent said you can't be too careful about STDs - they weren't.

5. Pretend that due to mis-information you've actually caught a STD by sticking rice crispies to your face.

The ultimate conclusion to this cringey rites of passage experience is to announce to your parents that this Birds and the Bees Chat was all well and good, but that you really need the Birds and the Birds Chat (if female); or if you're male, the Bees and the Bees.

-o-

How to Make Sex Actually Fun by Playing Cool Games

It doesn't matter how nifty at sex you are, or how frequently/infrequently that you do It, it will always become incredibly tedious about half way through, after approximately five seconds. So in order to see the session through to its tedious "climax", spice up proceedings by playing these much more entertaining games. The winner gets to give the loser a dead arm. Leg. Stomach. Knee. Elbow. Little toe. Eyelid...

Shadows

Only 0.1% of couples actually have rumpy pumpy *with the lights on* (they're egotistical, perfect-bodied gits, or blind); the other 99.9% only dare use a bedside lamp shoved far, far under the bed to provide just enough light coverage to help minimise toe stubbings, accidental head-buttings and laughter. Fortunately, this shadowy glow can *also* be used to make amusing or impressive wall images using your flobby bodies. Compete against each other, or when you soon realise you're much more crap than they are at creating pictures, suggest making shadows together. Don't try to make a pantomime horse.

Examples of Positions for Beginners
    a) Try "The Pencil" - just stand there.
    b) Or "The Carrot" - just stand there.

c) Or "The Eiffel Tower" - just stand there…
with a beret on your head.

Now you've realised just how hard pulling off the above positions actually are, you'll probably want to do shadows together…

For the Inter-mediates
a) Try "The Short Fence" - both just stand there, adjacent arms touching each others shoulders.
b) Try "Two chips" - both just stand there, one at a jaunty angle because the base of "the chip" hasn't been cut flat.
c) The "Humpback Bridge" - lie on top of one another, the one with the fattest arse goes on top.

But should you discover that you're a natural at this shadow melarky (you square freakoid), you should go solo. And call the Arkinsaw State Freak Show on 03000 35 873072.

For the Advanced Show-Off
a) "The Taj Mahal" - put your right arm at 45 degrees to the horizontal access, your left arm at 17.6 degrees to the Equator in British summer time, GMT; raise your clavicle to face the North star on the 23rd of the month; followed by pointing your left middle toe to Mecca. Then, bend your right elbow 180 degrees to create the

Chameli Farsh, and twist your torso 360 degrees to replicate the Chhaka plinth. Now separate every strand of hair on your head and spit down the middle, hair must be plaited and coiled into a perfect circle, cut, then stuck to the thirteen vertebrae in your back - the remaining half should be electrically charged using a dodgy plug socket to create the illusion of the rising sun over the river Yamuna. Finally, you should sever your torso in two and position them - before dying - side by side to ironically create the Cenotaphs of the Mausoleum. If you want to *really* go for platinum gold, get a Barbie doll and seat it in front of your Taj Mahal to represent Princess Di.

b) "The Pompeii" - for this, you'll need some kind of exploding liquid (phnar).

c) "The Great Wall of China" - this can only be performed at orgies, just get all tangled together.

The Counting Shoes Game

This is a version of the counting-sheep-to-bore-yourself-to-sleep game. It's had to be adapted because it's possible that you may find the woolly animals seriously much more attractive than your actual partner so counting shoes, for example, is a safe alternative. Or, women players could also count handbags, make-up, chocolate bars or women you know who could use cosmetic surgery; whilst the guys could count lager, curries, footballs and women you know you think could use cosmetic surgery. This game can also be enjoyed at many other boring occasions like job interviews (count the items you intend to pinch from your future employers stationary cupboard), whilst performing life-saving surgery if a doctor (count medical instruments left inside patient), or at weddings (count the weeks you think it'll last) and funerals (count your inheritance).

Join the Spots

This is great for doggie-style positions, simply take a permanent marker or tattoo kit and connect the zits on their back to reveal the hidden picture. Have even more fun by not telling your partner what you're up to. If, whilst joining their back zit-dots, you discover an effigy of Jesus Christ, you are morally obliged to contact the Pope or, better still, the tabloids - you could make a lot of moolah. If the selfish zitty person doesn't agree because they're embarrassed about their poxy acne, just menacingly whisper to them, "The Silence of the Lambs".

Memorise the Stains Game

This is for advanced players only as you'll need a good memory and 97% of Teens don't eat fish - the other 3% think they're pelicans. Study the stains on the bed-sheets, then, the next time they're washed* see if you can remember where the old stains were (*this can be anywhere between one week for an uptight Teen girl to three years for a Teen boy). If your Mum is having a me-me-me nervous breakdown, she may foolishly forget to wash your Teen sheets at 90°, and do a 40° wash - the stains will still be there, thus spoiling your nifty game. To make the lazy loser do the wash at the correct temperature (ideally, this is 1469°), send her to the centre of the earth where the very boiling water will remove even the most persistent of Teen stains. Pst, keep your eyes out for the Turin shroud stain - this could keep you in Pick and Mix for the rest of your life.

The Ready, Steady, Cook Game

Having rumpy pumpy can make you very hungry... after all, the average couple burns a whopping three calories per hour in the missionary position! So, gather all the crumbs in the bed and see what kind of tasty snacks you can improvise from the "ingredients". For the first time in their lives, fat Teenagers have the advantage over their skinny peers as there will simply be *more* crumbs in *their* beds; this is actually why some skinny people actually choose to cop off with fatties, as they're too weak from their eating disorder to make it downstairs to the kitchen for a life-saving snack.

The Knit the Nose Hair Game

This is a great pastime for the winter months when it's a bit chilly in your room for secret sauciness because your parents are sadistic cheapskates and won't let you have the heating on full for 30 hours a day; so, using your partner's nasal hair you could knit scarves, hats, gloves, fur coats. When you become a knitting pro, don't stop with nasal hair...

girls actually go out with repulsively hairy boys because the guys own enough "body wool" to make a Barbie horse and stables; whilst boys only go out with hairy girls in order to be able to knit themselves a Ferrari. Oh, and to see if the girl's a lesbian. And if she is, to cure her.

Ventriloquism
The mouth can become particularly bored during sex as most couples don't bother with kissing after the first couple of minutes, or seconds. Normally, the mouth is then used to issue annoying sexual instructions, or discussing how to redo the bedroom décor... you'll never agree on this because guys pretend to hate pink in case it awakens gay tendencies, whilst girls - for some peculiar reason - aren't fond of ceiling mirrors. Therefore, use your mouths to practise ventriloquism and play tricks on each other by throwing your voices. For example:

a) "This is the police – you're surrounded."
b) "(Insert their name), cooey, it's your Mum."
c) "Wooo-ooooooh, clank clank."
d) "This is God speaking."
e) "We come in Peace."

If you find that you are losing more games than you are winning, then this is the time to dump your partner, but not before you've raided their piggy bank. Put itching powder in their hoodie (nits! Hahahaha). And stick bogies on their naffo shoes.

-o-

3 FRIENDSHIP

How To Make Friends With People (Who Are Much Cooler/Naffer/Sexier/Nicer/Nastier/Better-Looking/Uglier/ Smarter/Thicker/Funnier/Unfunnier Than You)

Social success in life is entirely dependent on *how many* "friends" you pretend you have, and *not* the quality of friendship. God forbid (or Kaballah/Buddha/Cruise/Allah forgive - better not leave those sensitive Muslims out - don't want a fatwah) you should be mugged for your mobile phone only to be mercilessly mocked by your attackers when they discover that you have less than two hundred and forty seven thousand numbers stored in your address book. That would be worse than getting repeatedly stabbed by your assailants, or being given the deadly Front Wedgie.

But here's the irony (ask a boffin who's appeared on "Mastermind" or, better still, "Bullseye")... it is *incredibly easy* to establish friendships with other

Teens because they're all *equally desperate* to have as many phone(y) numbers as possible (this fortunately also massively increases the number of people they can get off with, or give vicious dead arms to). ***However***, this will mean that any old scum can potentially call themselves the Teen's friend. Tricky one... what about quality control?

How To Pick "Friends" Who'll Make You Look Better Than You Actually Are?

- Shouldn't your clique be ***better-looking*** than you? This will finally force you to make much more effort to improve your dodgy appearance using cosmetic surgery, drastic dieting and volunteering to become the first full face transplant patient. If those stingy surgeons unreasonably turn you down, get your face bitten off by a rabid poodle.
- Shouldn't they be ***better-dressed*** than you? Then you can borrow/steal their coolest outfits, regardless of whether you can actually squeeze your pimply dimply arse in? In fact, it's a bonus if the clothes *do* rip because it's much more likely that your irate friend won't want them back; you can always have them fixed by your mum or send them to a sweatshop in China who'll do a bit of a better job, minus the nagging.
- ***Cleverer*** than you? If you're still in education you'll be able to pinch and copy their homework - you won't get caught because, fortunately, you're too stupid and lazy to copy it 100% accurately and will

thereby avoid detection by the beady-eyed teacher. And, if you're no longer in education, having a cleverer friend totally works in your favour when it comes to copping off with people, as everyone hates a smartarse - you'll always, automatically, be picked for a kiss and a grope over your brainy pal.

- Shouldn't they be *car-owners?* After all, legs are only for kicking, stomping and cronking. But this doesn't have to mean doing your parents out of their job - they can now give you piggy backs up the stairs to make up for no longer being their 23/7 taxi service (the "24th" hour being reserved exclusively for eating, sleeping, preening, gossiping and farting).

How to Pick Friends Who'll Make You Look Less Crap Than You Actually Are

So, does it sound great just hanging out in a gang of gorgeous, sexy, sophisticated cool dudes like on "The O.C", "Hollyoaks" or "Biker Grove"? **NOOOOOO**. Remember, remember, it's ***only*** the *number* of numbers in your mobile that counts, people, NUMBERS. Who cares if 97% of your phone numbers belong to losers - you're only being friends with them to boost your phone list kudos and stop the muggers laughing at you when they nick your mobile. In fact, it's positively Stephen Hawkinesque to have at least 2,476 "friends" who are fatter, or uglier, or thicker, or smellier, or more boring than yourself... otherwise how else are you ever going to pull? You need the skanks to make yourself look good.

How To Pretend You Like These Mutt-face Muppets

Luckily, it's not as if any of these "friendships" will last longer than two weeks, so you should be able to stick it out - you live with your parasitic parents, after all. A fortnight is the recommended amount of time necessary it takes to go through their entire possessions and select your items for theft; *and* also make your way through their friends to get off with. So, during this torturous fortnight, you can pretend to like your "friend" by:

- Walking/skulking in their proximity - even in daylight.
- Sitting on the same bench (though draw a line at swigging from the same Tennents Extra can - you know where their mouth's been).
- Copying everything they say, wear, and do. (But secretly, do it better).
- If the "friend" is visually repellent, you can wear sunglasses all the time and stick images of your fave celebrity lusts on the *insides* of the shades. Then, if they ever do speak/swear at you, you can retaliate whilst actually looking in their direction.
- Give them a loan of your current getting off girl/boyfriend (obviously, not telling them first that this person leaves more slime behind than a giant slug.)

How To Make Even More "Friends" - And With No Effort Whatsoever

In the olden days, you needed a really good hair flick to be popular, preferably held in place with superglue or jism. Nowadays, though, you don't even need to be funny, cool, or going to go to stage school to be a soap star/one-hit wonder to win "friends" over. You simply need:

1. A credit card - preferably your own; however, your parents or pensioner granny will do.
2. Unrestricted internet access: if your oppressor parents have put a web block on your computer, a crack can be found at www.crackwhores.com
3. Spare i-pod earphones: it doesn't even matter if they're waxier than Madame Tussauds.
4. More than one mobile phone number - the more you have, the more popular you'll be. Therefore, repeatedly pretend to your parents that you keep getting mugged for your mobile; they'll keep replacing them because they'll be vaguely relieved that you weren't stabbed, as this would mean visiting you in hospital and probably catching M.R.S.A.
5. Just be the mobile mugger. Everyone will want to be your friend.

How To Fall Out Like Chernobyl

Clearly, once you've spent the compulsory disgusting two weeks together as fake friends, they are then allowed to fall out in any of 45,937 ways… the clincher is usually to hold a "Who's Got

The Best-Looking Little Toe Competition", (make sure you win by amputating a toe from a foot model in Soho). Of course, you're then morally permitted to leave their stupid ugly stinkface number stored in your mobile.

However, if they are *really* clever (e.g. B-Tec) they'll start sending you intimidating and abusive texts, i.e. they are spelt correctly and in full, *and* with impeccable grammar, to try and scare you into deleting their number. How stupid of them - you're too stupid to actually know if something is spelt correctly or properly punctuated. But get your Dad on to them any way. Or Gripper Stebson (you infants won't get that joke - you *could* ask your parents but that would mean speaking to them).

Why Some Teenage Friendships Last Longer Than The Fortnight
But why do some Teens appear to genuinely like each other and stay friends beyond the compulsory two weeks??? If certain Teenagers appear to be real friends it's only because there's something **hideously** wrong with the pair of them...

1. They have something terrible on each other that forces them to stay loyal, e.g. they may have killed someone together and need to keep schtum to stay out of prison, or worse, they both peed their pants laughing at the old lady who fell down in the street.

2. They are hideously ugly... possibly deformed or have naturally curly hair. They <u>have</u> to stick together.
3. They both still like it when their Mums try to kiss them goodnight/at the school gates/ dropping them off in the car. Normal Teens *only* ever let their weepy parents kiss them at family funerals because allowing this physical contact makes vulnerable parents more susceptible to your material demands.
4. Their parents' are tie-dye wearing hippies, police, traffic wardens or royalty - these weirdo sects have to stick together in society in order to survive.
5. They are conjoined twins.
6. Or they became "horribly" stuck together following a hilarious tragic accident at a glue and plastics factory.

How To Cope If *You're* The Uglier, Fatter, Thicker, Smellier, Boringer, Naffer Friend

You don't know how lucky you are, you festering squat-faced mank. This is pole position on the friendship circuit. *EVERYONE* will want to be your better-everything friend. Your peers may be the sirloin steak, but you're the chips. And greasy chip shop chips, at that. Who cares if you know and they know that you're way out of their league. In fact, it's defo worth getting uglier, fatter, thicker, smellier, boringer and naffer because you'll become the most popular Teen on the planet. Consequently, you'll have the most mobile numbers ever to impress the phone mugger... Uh-oh. Problem.

Trouble is muggers don't mug manky losers like you in case they catch naffitis off you. Still, you *could* pay them to assault you with all that extra pocket money your parents give you for being the runt of the litter.

How To Pretend You've Even More "Friends" Than You "Really" Do
It's quite likely that your parents will go through your private mobile address book - not to try and find out where you are and if you're still alive, but to find out if you're more popular than they were at the same age. Parents *detest* having offspring who are cooler and more hip than they ever were, as it reminds them of how big a failure they are. Therefore, rub salt, burning alcohol and poison ivy into their wound by adding hundreds of bogus numbers into your mobile. For example: Wayne Rooney 03739 736694, Madonna 071 466 393, Paris Hilton 08000 836 872 cell extension 42, Jesus 0845 666666, Lena Lovitch 01 1111111, Nena 099 999999, Postman Pat 077 382765, Homer Simpsoh 0880 8008135.

But, hahahahahahahahahahahahaha, if you really abhor your parents, you can really mess with them by memorising all your "friends" phone numbers in your head... leaving you're mobile address book stark empty (to memorise these 30,000 something numbers, simply pretend they're your favourite e-numbers. Your parents will conclude (perhaps rightly) that you have no friends because you're a sociopath who'll probably, one day, turn into a serial killer. They'll be horrified - not because of the potential future grief you'll inflict on the families of your victims' families, but because they'll probably have to move house after being hounded by the press - and their house may not yet have peaked in value. If your "psychotic address book" is empty, your parents will attempt to keep you from your killing spree with very nice food from M&S and the latest high-tech camera phone - they'll think it encourage others to be friends with you as you're clearly loaded... of course, you'll use it to take snaps of potential victims...

-o-

How To Break Friends, Shake Friends, Never Ever Re-make Friends

This is truly the most rewarding aspect of forging "friendships" - getting well and truly shot of the minging, cling-on loser. So, clearly this is an ideal opportunity for you to perfect your prowess as a callous and spiteful Teenager. Hopefully, it's quite likely that your "friend" will *also* be trying to dump *you* as a "mate", which will result in a marvellous duel of malice - the victor being the one who's level of devilishness most impresses and terrifies their peer group. Or, even better, the winner is the one who succeeds in making the other cry first in public (of course, cheating by pulling nostril or pubic hair doesn't count. But do it anyway.)

Why Teenage Friendships So Easily Break Down In Today's Culture

In the prehistoric twentieth century, friendships had to be founded on the basis of living *near each other* - this was due to parents' cars being seriously naff so no self-respecting Teen would be seen dead being ferried around by their Mum or Dad. Friends **had** to live near enough for the Teen to be able to walk there - typically no more than 100m. Consequently, friends were literally lumbered with each other for ever. In fact, *if* these olden day friendships *did* break down it was due to trivial problems like:

- one of the Teens moved to the other side of the world, like Devon;

- or, one of them had a disgusting, embarrassing affair with one of the other's parents (nowadays, this is just plain funny and cool);
- or, one of them was divvy enough to die in a road traffic accident. (Incidentally, most Teenagers - then *and* now - aren't smart enough to leave a will, so when the RTA victim snuffs it without legally leaving their 7" picture discs to their "best mate", this is a legitimate reason for the still-alive Teen to terminate the friendship with the corpse).

Nowadays, however, mid-life crisis Dads have much sexier cars and are veritably enthusiastic to act as your very own personal chauffeur (so they can drive around looking for girls to beep after you're dropped off), so your "friends" can live on the other side of town, country or world. This makes it dead easy for you to have *hundreds* of fake mates and feel like a real celebrity. But blimey, just remembering your pretend friends' names is bad enough... Never mind whose embarrassing secret is whose for you to cruelly let slip (there's nothing more irksome than inaccurate gossip - not even gulags)... Or keeping track of who's not getting off with who (so you can get in there)... No wonder these "friendships" can so easily turn nasty. Yippee. Inevitably, then, 21st century Teens have many more difficult, emotional and traumatic problems to luckily destroy their fake friendships...

The Top Ten Friendship-Busters

1. One of the "friends" selfishly becomes anorexic, and therefore much more attractive (right up until the point when they look like a corpse, then they don't look quite so hot)... this leaves the other lardy Teen feeling resentful, bitter and in dire need of finding a fatter friend to make them look good.

2. One of the friends has your skanky braces removed, which immediately puts them back on the tongue baguette market. Previously, the brace-free friend could always secretly rely on no-one wanting to snog their Metal Mickey pal *over them* at parties or in the park bushes. (If you're the *non* brace-face, you *can* maintain your snog-superiority by inviting your newly brace-free "pal" for a spinach-sandwich tea, then, whilst they're eating, pin them down and superglue 8" nails randomly to their teeth - permanently trapping unsexy food in these new homemade "braces" will buy you a bit more tongue time.)

3. One of them unexpectedly achieves an impressive Grade D - the proud parents will relentlessly brag about this to the thicker thicko's parents, rendering the thicker thicko's life more unbearable than usual.

4. The outrageously unreasonable "friend" won't permanently lend you their lipsalve, i-pod, life savings, homework, quarter pounder, best underwear, or the ultimate friendship-breaker - their girl/boyfriend.

5. One of them takes an egg sarnie on a school/college/bunking off/music festival trip.
6. One of the pair (probably the one who has just eaten the egg sarnie) deliberately lets the other walk through their fart cloud.
7. One of them becomes seriously ill, leading them to suddenly - and unjustifiably - becoming the centre of everyone's attention and therefore really popular. But ha, this is only because:

a) everyone is really nosey about what someone looks like when they are *properly* ill (so they can learn how to apply more believable make-up when they are faking a sickie);

b) the "sympathetic" "friends" know that this can mean blagging time off school, college, or work for visiting the sickoid in hospital;

c) they're just so relieved *it's not them* as now the probability of them contracting a serious condition is *massively* reduced. This secret glee at other people's health misfortunes will continue through adulthood.

8. Only one of the Teens is asked for a dance/snog/grope by the person they both fancy... normally Teens share snog-partners - this time they hog the tonsil-tickler.
9. The uglier friend during the above scenario promptly informs their so-called friend's tonsil-tickler that their "mate" has a STD. It's irrelevant if this is actually true or not, claiming this really naffs off the "diseased" friend as they won't know what this condition actually is, making them look

really thick. Tip: the most baffling STD to pick is the tongue-twister Chlamydia (pronounced: *clam-mid-eeh-aaahh*).

10. The bogey flicking from one Teen "accidentally" lands on the other - ideally when that person is yawning as this demonstrates great aim and skill.

11. One of the Teens informs the other that they have a terminal disease - the "Healthy" Teen will run a mile in fear of being morally obliged to give the canceroid all their cool possessions whilst the ailing friend is still alive. The friend won't want to have to go back to the "dead friend's" house in case they see an adult crying.

How To Destroy A "Friendship" With The Minimum Effort and Maximum Pain

Sometimes, even your bestest efforts to mutilate a friendship go unrewarded - your "friend" seems masochistically willing to put up with your unadulterated evil. However, be warned, this isn't because you're the sexiest, cooliest cat in town, but because they are *using you* to make themselves look good... their parents think you are the Devil incarnate, so by comparison, they believe their Teen to be not so monstrous after all. Cunning. You're almost impressed. NOW is the time to finally take them daaaooooowwwwn.

How to Break the Unwritten Rules (you're illiterate) of Teen "Friendships"

1. Suck up big-time to your soon-to-be-ex-friend's parents: laugh at their crap jokes; eat their shit food; even offer to clean their naff car. They will LOVE you. Your friend will consequently want to dismember you, but will settle for letting you telling everyone *you* dumped *them* - even this peer humiliation is preferable to their parents banging on to them about how great you are. Of course, you don't want any of your perfect Teen behaviour getting back to your own parents, so tell your new surrogate parents that your parents are heading for a vicious divorce - your "adoptive" parents will then give yours an embarrassed, wide berth. (Also, their Mum will give you extra ice-cream).
2. Execute *The Front Wedgie** on them - this tactic works a treat on either sex, with the added bonus that you can also give them your infamous Evil Eye whilst knackering their genitals.
3. Permanently borrow their hair - it can't be worse than your fuzz-mop.   Invite the gullible idiot over for a sleepover*, then when they're sleeping in an e-number fuelled, sherbert stupor hack off their crowning glory using pinking sheers. The downside of scalping them, though, is that people may mistake their baldness for serious illness and then pretend to be really nice to them. *In the olden days, Teenagers had sleepovers to watch over 18 scary

movies and, more importantly, to get secretly drunk from the drinks cabinet and be really annoying to the host parents; today's Teens know that they can cause a *lot more misery* if they stuff themselves with sweets and fizzy drinks and pretend that they have Attention Deficit Disorder.

4. Chuck a stink bomb, or if you *really* hate them, a Brussels sprout in their mouth whilst they're pretending to be Mariah Carey, Kanye West or Westlife.

5. Stop pretending to be someone you're not - just be yourself. That'll do it.

How Friendships Change As You Grow Older and Less Wiser

There are currently 13,973,836⅔ Teenagers living in the UK today, so you'll never run out of "friends" to make and break up with whilst your still in your Teens - you'll actually run out of new friend options when your turn twenty-one. From this old age onwards, you'll spend your life desperately and pathetically trying to hang on to your social circle, which will then consist of a maximum of four people. In fact, the only thing keeping these fickle "friendships" alive is that you'll all need someone to be your best man or bridesmaids at your eventual wedding... as *soon* as you get hitched you can dump these dullsville acquaintances as fast as you dump your new spouse. Phew.

Then, when you turn thirty-three and start having vile children of your own because you've got nothing better to do, you'll suddenly realise that - with no friends whatsoever - you're depressingly and terrifyingly LONELY. Not only do you have no social life (your spouse soon put a stop to that), having kids has seriously ruined the chances of you ever going out to have fun ever again. Most importantly of all, with no friends around, who the hell is going to baby-sit for you as you go down to the pub alone to drown your sorrows!!?! Consequently, you'll then spend the rest of your life trying to track down your old Teen "friends" from school. They'll only agree to reconnect in the hope that they are earning much more money than you, have a better-looking spouse, and that you have kids with special needs. Did you know that in seven years time, "Friends Reunited" will be re-branded "Friends Reunited - But Not For Long When They Discover That You're Still A Git".

How To Behave Towards Your Ex-Best "Friends"

It's simple. Treat them like a pussing leper who's holding an egg sarnie whilst wearing a baseball cap back to front and singing "I'd Like To Teach The World To Sing".

***Warning**: performing *The Front Wedgie* can have very *serious* medical repercussions... your victim may come after you with a wet bogie, freshly-picked scab, or worse, a used tampon.

-o-

How To Be The Worst Best Friend In the World

Traditionally, Teenage friends *expected* their pals to be back-stabbers, sarcastic, spiteful, hateful, physically abusive and experts in bogey bombing. Nowadays, that's a parents' role. So, the 21st century Teenager has to be far more creative, evil and ruthless in their quest to become *The Worst Best Friend in the World*. In fact, there's even an underground movement for Teens to compete for this very title at www.worstbestfriendintheworld.com. Teenagers are invited to submit their most impressive dastardly acts of evil inflicted upon a friend online *now*, the closing date is 31st December 2007. The winner will receive a crown of blue "Smarties", their own reality TV show called "(Stinks Like) Teen Spirit," and a year's supply of saliva to use as you see fit (it's been kindly provided by residents of Guantanamo Bay after being tortured with a dvd of Gary Rhodes' "A Cookery Year"). Naturally, standards are expected to be very high so you'll need to practise, practise, practise at becoming someone truly nasty enough to deserve to win - who says you can't apply yourself?

How To Impress The Judges Of "The Best Worst Teenage In the World"

The judging panel consists of ex-Teens who've already wowed the World with their malice: Amy Fisher (shot her adult lover Joey Buttafuco's wife in the head), Shannon Doherty, Charlotte Church, Wee Willie Winkie... so simply convincing your friend that they're fat (if thin) or fat (if fat), or even executing the perfect front wedgie just won't cut it. You need to think smarter, harder and more originally than is actually possible for you. So cheat using some of these ideas found written in code at the back of the diary of a clearly bored Anne Frank:

1. *Be on time* - few things are more annoying to a Teenager than a friend who turns up punctually at their house to witness their futile attempts to style their barnet individual hair by hair, find a clean spot on the mirror to squeeze their zit on, or catching them giving their manic depressive Mum a potentially life-saving hug as they put on their shoes (making damn sure the laces are still there).

2. *Agree with everything your friend says* - this is life-threatening to any Teenager because arguing is even more important for staying alive than hamburgers and CO_2. Now, agreeing with someone will be completely alien territory to you so here are a few examples to get you in the swing of it:

a) They say: "That Nicole Richie isn't anorexic - she's got really fat eyelids", you say, "You're so right".

b) They say: "Does my arse look big in this?" you say, "It looks big in everything."

c) They say: "Can I borrow your boy/ girlfriend?", you say "Of course."

However, agreeing with everything they say will actually prove quite difficult so it's worth cutting your tongue out for a bit as they'll have less reason to expect you to argue back (you can try re-attaching it later using the brilliant invention of blue tack - trouble is, though, it'll leave an annoying sticky, blue mark afterwards). But if your gobshite friend starts demanding that you use nodding or shaking your head to have an argument with them then try self-decapitation (you'll find a guillotine in the local library).

3. ***Return their borrowed/stolen possessions in perfect condition.*** For clothes that means washing (especially with lovely fragrant fabric softener), and ironing them (make your Mum to do all of this - she'll jump at the chance; she won't realise that they're *not* your clothes and she'll suddenly be hoping that you're turning gay and will become the spawn of her dreams). Your friend'll be disgusted at this barbaric act of hygiene inflicted upon them as now all your peers will think *they're* turning gay. Items such as music players, trainers and skateboards should be returned as *if new...* <u>unscuffed</u> possessions are the ultimate sign

of geekdom. To achieve this "brand new" look simply replace the item with an actual new item that you've either shoplifted or suckered out of your own parents by pretending that you think you might be gay/ lesbian (your dad'll hope that buying you off will keep you on the straight and narrow). Or use Tipp-Ex. That's what shops do to re-sell returned goods.

4. ***Compliment your friend*** - a "compliment" is when you say something nice to someone, this is *not* to be confused with "condiment" as your friend will be most confused if you say "You look salad cream today". If you flatter your friend, they'll instantly detest you, not because they think you've started batting for the other side, but because - despite their deepest darkest desire to be a tortured, hateful, nasty piece of Teen work - they desperately *want* to *believe* you when you say that they look pretty/handsome or are really cool or kind or clever or charming or aromatic.

5. ***Being positively delightful to their parents*** - to help you pull off this barbaric act of pleasantness, just imagine that their parents are really loaded and will leave you all the dosh when they top themselves because they can no longer stand being the parents of such a foul Teenager (actually you *will* inherit). Recommended enchanting behaviour includes:

a) *not* slamming the door in the parent's face as they innocently leave the room after you;

b) *refraining* from gagging when they accidentally come near enough for you to smell their rancid breath;

c) and actually having a whole conversation with them when they ask you a probing question, e.g. instead of unintelligible grunting, mutter a "Yes" or "No" (pst, *of course* it doesn't have to be the truth).

Warning: your friend will be horrified at the prospect of being disinherited, and may secretly retaliate by smarming it up to your parents. Ha. Let them. Your parents are skint - you've made sure of that.

How Far Teens Around The World Have Gone To Try And Win

Instead of scouring internet chat rooms for dodgy grown-ups, go and check out your competition at www.worstbestfriendintheworld.com - you'll be stunned at the lengths many Teens around the planet have gone to, to try and secure victory:

- Chad Willis in Minnesota, USA told his morbidly obese pal, Brad that he could perform a cheap gastric by-pass using a long balloon, a pair of pinking shears and a picture of Nicole Richie stapled to Brad's oesophagus wall to stop it wanting lovely burgers. Astonishingly, the DIY operation accidentally worked, so Chad was instead forced to spread the rumour that his now-thin pal was a Republican.

- Amongu Nafusta from Nigeria superglued her pal's water collector to her head - not only did this result in her pal's suffering from near-death dehydration, but the removal of the water jug severely bodged her corn braids.
- Amelie Camus of France filled her best friend, Nathalie, cigarettes with addictive cheap British chocolate - over the course of three weeks, not only did the ever-vain Frenchie put on 2 whole pounds but she also got a spot.
- Dieter Koch of Germany orchestrated a complicated lederhosen accident for his friend, Klaus... having sewn up the legs of the ledenhosen, Klaus fell into the nearby "convenient" hole and broke his meta dorsal clavicle - a very rare fracture that requires the arm to be set in plaster in a kind of Nazi salute position.

How To Bribe The Judges To Make Sure You Win

Consequently, you may realise that you only stand a chance of winning if you bribe or blackmail the judges...

Amy Fisher - if you type her name in Wikipedia you'll read that on May 14th 2007, The New York Post reported that she had left her husband and had had a meeting with Joey Buttafuoco in Central Park to either reconcile or pitch an idea where both of them would live together for a money-making reality series. Pretend you are a producer from NBC and will give her the lucrative show if you bung her the title. Sorted.

Shannon Doherty - according to Wikipedia, she is allergic to wool, chocolate and guinea pigs. So send her a jumper wearing (grannies can be useful after all) choccie-smeared pig in the post... with a note saying that if you don't win, next time it'll be a <u>guinea</u> pig.

Charlotte Church - you don't even need to bother Wik-ing her. Now she's up the duff to try and hold on to Gav, just waft a glass of wine or alcopop under her nose. In her sobre-ish attempts to get rid of you and your lovely liquid, you'll be the competition victor faster than you can say "Barf".

Wee Willie Winkie - again, you'll need to refer to Wikipedia as you won't have the foggiest idea who he is. He's a well-known ASBO Teen delinquent who's troughed one too many Blue smarties and runs around doolally at night in Liverpool trying to wake everyone up. Slip him a cup of Horlicks under the pretence that it's an e-number kiddies cocktail. Once he's had a good sleep he'll wake up feeling horribly normal and well-adjusted, and will be "Play Doh" in your hands.

Hey, who knew that Wikipedia would become the Teenager's Best Friend for Celebrity Stalking!?

How To Behave When You Win "The Best Worst Friend In The World"

Fortunately when you're crowned the winner as "The Worst Best Friend In The World", you won't be expected to cry and make a nauseating speech. Of course not. The audience'll be hoping for, and expecting a veritable symphony of hand gestures and expletives. Secretly rehearse on your parents or granny first - your goal is to become the world's fastest talker/swearer as this'll make it a f!*?!*g nightmare for the bleeping sound engineer.

Warning: next year you'll be supposed to hand over your title to the "The Worst Best Friend In The World 2008" champion. Balderdash. They'll have to fight you for it. To increase your chances of victory, as you grapple:

- Croon Chris de Berg's "Lady In Red" softly in their potatoey ear - they'll probably die of pain;
- Stump their in-growing big toe (every manky Teen has one) 2,983 times on a handy brick that you carry everywhere with you;
- If male, fill in the shaved "scar" on their eyebrow with crayon - they'll do a runner faster than Lee Harvey Oswald (he shot JR).
- If female, cause them to spontaneously combust by rubbing their shaving stubble re-growth with a piece of kindling you handily carry everywhere with you; after all, you

never know when you might need to start a fire. Incidentally, if you ever get spot searched by the cops, simply tell them it's for the second ice age - as are the harpoon, stolen pick and mix and, whoopee cushion.

- Pretend you're a hypnotist by growing a goatee and losing your hair on top, then go cross-eyed at them and tell them that they are a Duke of Edinburgh gold medal winner. They'll disappear faster than a bulimic at a buffet.

-o-

4 EDUCATION

How To Pretend You're Getting An Education

The single most important qualification for being a success in life is being good-looking. Ridiculously and ignorantly, your parents' still believe it to be e d u c a t i o n ! ! ? ? ! W h a t , j u s t l o o k a t them?!!!?!!??????????!!!!!!!!!. Therefore, you'll need to know how to con your oldies that you're getting terrific schooling whilst you *actually* bunk off to scour the pavements looking for loose change to save up for that much-needed plastic surgery. (Tip: try outside old people's homes - Alzheimer's makes the oldies' life savings shake out of their pockets; luckily, the Grim Reaper-ites no longer leave their money under the mattress as dodgy care assistants will pinch it).

How To Mis-Educate Your Illiterate Parents
Fortunately, deceiving your parents about your education is easier than forging your CV because we live in a shallow, fake cool media-age... presentation is *way* more powerful than content -

it's not *what* you argue, but how *obnoxiously* and *loudly* you scream it. Besides, your parents are obviously even thicker than you (they married each other, after all), so once you start rattling off the following educational chicken nuggets of wisdom, they'll think you're a flipping genius. Consequently, they'll even eagerly agree to you taking a fake sickie whenever you get so much as a pimple because they'll start living in fear that you'll get bullied/stabbed at school because you're so brainy. (To obtain several successive days off, try leaving pretend puncture wounds using ketchup or blood from a menstruating friend).

WARNING: If your parents are actually quite brainy (0.8% of them, i.e. those with beards - this applies to Dads *and* Mums), and question your "facts", look patronisingly at them (a cinch) and remind them that in the olden days they didn't have computers at school so they haven't had the same amazing educational access as you. Plus, before legging it out of the door, scream that they're both having secret affairs.

How To Bluff Your "Education"

ART
   1. The "Mona Lisa" is, in actual fact, a Polaroid taken by de Vinci to save time. He simply coloured over the face using Crayola, being extra careful not to go over the lines. In fact, if you scratch the canvas in the Louvre, you'll actually reveal Mona's giggling face

underneath. You see, Mona was sitting on a leather chair and every time she moved it made a farty noise causing her to giggle like a girl on alcopops; after 25 hours of Mona's squawking, a naffed off de Vinci coloured her face in miserable as revenge.

2. Van Gogh's "Sunflowers" was a complete cock-up. He *was* going to paint a lovely cheap and cheerful bunch of wilting carnations from the garage, but VG forgot it was "Stranger Neighbour's Day" and all the flowers were gone. VG had to pop across to the really trendy, rip-off florist - those sunflowers cost him 75 quid! Being a poor artist, he had to cut off and sell his ear on "Ebay" to a cauliflowered rugby player who needed a transplant.

3. Picasso's cubist "Crying Lady" is, in fact, the world's first Etchasketch. That's why it's rubbish.

English

1. Full stops were originally invented to stop adjoining "K's" from adjoining sentences from kicking each other, which throws the surrounding letters into disarray and turns both sentences into jibberish. E.g. *No onea cared that thke ship hd sun evin criKd for yeears.*

2. Apostrophes on plurals have been known – on the third Wednesday of every fifth month and a full moon – to move from the right places' to the wrong place's. Or is it the other

way round? Where's that Lynne bird when you need her.

3. Big Will Shakespeare was the UK's first commercially successful rap artist - unfortunately the *musical* score to his texts no longer exists as during The Great Plague, people needed excessive amounts of paper to wipe their poo poo bottoms. Shakespeare's play *texts* were *only* saved from being wiped out – literally – because all the poo-bummed plebs fortunately died.

Maths

1. Algebra was created by the ancient Greeks as a form of torture: at the Battle of Waterloo the Greeks double dared the Vikings to solve a strange looking sum. Had the Vikings actually succeeded in cracking the puzzle it would have revealed the solution to being able to remove the female bra in less than five minutes. To this day, Man is still trying to figure out "alge-*bra*".

2. If you're thicker than an old lady's ankles at maths it won't ever, *ever* matter. Kerry Catona doesn't have a G.C.S.E. in maths and look at her.

3. 1 + 1 is not actually 2. In the time it takes to process this seemingly simple sum, the real value of "1", in the E.U., has increased to 1.0036. Therefore, the actual answer is, er, more. (Your parents' will be clueless about the European thingy and just agree with you

to avoid admitting their embarrassing ignorance).

History

1. The Great Fire of London in 1963 didn't start in Penny Lane by a gormless YTS lad in a bakery. Well, not exactly. It *was* him, but the fire wasn't caused by oven sparks and thatched roofs... he was trying to impress the new Saturday girl by lighting his farts; trouble was, he'd had a dodgy vindaloo the night before. Wooo-oosh

2. King Harold did *not* die at the Battle of Hastings in 1066 from a cool arrow through the eye. What *really* happened was he was trotting through the slaughter of his foot soldiers, singing "Agadoo" when a *fly* hit him in the eye. In a blind panic, King Hazza fell off his horse and landed in a huge horseshit and - hee hee - promptly suffocated to death. (Don't worry, the horsey-worsey was OK).

3. Queen Victoria is not actually dead. She merely faked her own death in order to pursue her lifelong dream of being a stand-up comedian. To this day, she earns a decent living working the working class men's clubs of the North East circuit, and is renowned for her much-loved catchphrase, "I am *not* amused!"

Geography

1. If you eat enough limestone (approximately 23 tonnes) you'll have enough calcium carbonate inside you to be able to use your finger as a stick of chalk, which can be very handy if the teacher runs out... in return, not only will you receive extra milk at break and house-points galore, but your classmates' ears will amusingly bleed profusely whenever you touch the blackboard.

2. Volcanoes are, in fact, hormonal spots on the earth's skin which occur when it hasn't washed itself properly using the sea. They only erupt when the earth laughs hysterically at India's favourite joke: "What are those things at the end of your arms?"... "Me Andes". Luckily, volcanoes can be stopped from killing innocent-ish humans by being told any joke by Joe Pascali.

3. Stalagtites were first discovered by a gout-ridden woman called, ironically, Pretty Polly who used the hanging rock formation as moulds for her self-serving invention - American Tan tights for thick, knobbly old lady legs.

Science

1. If you sit under an apple tree and throw an apple upwards, there is a global, temporary *loss* of gravity. For example, you know when you go over a hump-back bridge and you get that funny tummy, it isn't due to the bridge but someone, somewhere chucking a

Braeburn skywards in an attempt to execute a pigeon (this is because killing the flying vermin with a machete is illegal in Faggy Bottom, Dorset).

2. The biggest threat to the planet's survival is _not_ the depletion of the ozone but the accumulative impact of methane and sulphur gases from homo sapiens fartings. If the 21st century's love affair with curry does not abate, there'll be a fatal nuclear explosion on 27th May 2008. (Wicked, a day off school).

3. If you hide the physics teacher's bifocal glasses, the time spent

shouting at his pupils is directly equal to the time spent looking   for his specs (funniest place to hide them is on his comb-over).

$$\text{Glasses} = \underline{a\sqrt{b}+d-\approx}$$
$$\text{Anger} \geq (\text{worth it}) = \text{detention}$$

Of course, succeeding in conning your parents that you're more intelligent than you really are will eventually backfire, as they'll believe that you will, one day, get a really well-paid job and be able to put them in a non-abusing care home. As if. Let them be deluded.

-o-

How To Survive Exam Stress

The stress of pretending to revise for once-a-year exams is a doddle compared to the extreme stresses you have to cope with *every single second of every single minute.*

Real-life stresses of Today's Teenagers:
- Surviving having naff so-last-week trainers - it's not just social suicide, it's peer group euthanasia.
- Owning hair that's been badly straightened with cheap ceramic irons. You might as well stick pubes to your head.
- Living with V.P.L. (Visible Penis Line - this is only cool for 1% of males).
- Losing an acrylic nail (call the National Nail Nightmare line 0870 8008135 for support and financial help to advertise for the safe return of your much-loved nail extension; or for finger transplants from Africa - ironically, despite their shitty lives, these third world people *don't* bite their nails. They should, it's valuable nutrition).
- Having ugly parents or worse, having better-looking brothers or sisters.
- Getting your wet dream sheets in the wash without raising suspicion.
- Eating your bogies only to discover that they're annoyingly dry.
- If male, having to wax or pluck your werewolf eyebrow and running the risk that you'll overdo it and end up looking gay.

- Walking through a teenage vegetarian's fart cloud - this is almost worth turning vegetarian for (you can still get (veggie) burgers).
- Wearing mum-bought jeans that humiliatingly *won't* fall down to reveal your greying Calvin's or fraying g-string.
- *Not* getting mugged for your mobile because it's crap.
- If female, being told you have a camel's toe (because you're wearing the compulsory size-too-small trousers).
- Losing your virginity to someone you don't know.
- Losing your virginity to someone you know.
- Being caught using the green cross code when you're crossing the road/motorway/ railway by your mocking (but soon to be squashed dead) friends.
- Getting the words wrong in public to the song of any black rapper.
- Getting the words *right* to any tunes by 'Coldplay'.
- Receiving a million paper cuts when you rabidly scour the latest celeb gossip magazine for unflattering pictures - it makes you feel heaps better about your own mobile phone picture album.
- Your evil mum washes Mr. Snuggles.
- Dropping one of your 267 chips on the ground and it landing on a dog poo - anything else, and you'd have still eaten it. Dog poo is hard to wash off.

- Waking up after your 17 hour kip to find you've got a sheet wrinkle imprint on your face that looks like a disfiguring scar - and annoyingly it hasn't 'cut' through your eyebrow.
- Not having your full 17 hour kip.
- Passing your driving test first time - what are you, square!? You're supposed to *at least* knock down an elderly cyclist carrying their only grand-child in a toddler seat.
- Finding papers confirming your "parents" really are your birth parents.
- You get run over and annoyingly, that morning, you'd put on your crap underwear.
- Being approached by a parent for the "sex talk" and having to pretend you know it all anyway;
- Forming a band and the only people who come to your first gig are all your parents' (and they clearly pretend that you're good).
- Fancying someone who isn't cool.
- Fancying someone who is cool - you're way out of their league.
- Being caught laughing.

So, compared to these very real stresses, failing your stupid exams is easier than falling off a park bench, blottoed. However, claiming to be revising in your room is still a great excuse for not only spending time depressingly alone and isolated from your family, but also an *ideal* opportunity to cash in some extra sleeping, texting, and practising kissing on your pillow.

How To Beat Your Sadistic Parents At Their Own Game

Your parents will secretly relish the sight of you suffering hideously from exam stress because they foolishly believe this is giving you a taste of the real world. Er, no-oo: that'd be film premieres and a threesome with Vic and Dave. So you should milk it by appearing totally stressed out by your looming exams:

- To create even blacker circles under your eyes, simply let your cheap eyeliner run (nowadays this applies to both girls *and* boys).
- Bite your already gnarled nails right down to your knuckles - by the way, the bloodied stumps are also excellent for using for graffiti.
- Mess your hair up… Fortunately, to your peers it'll just look even more cool. Or go for the jugular and actually brush your hair neatly - you parents'll think you're going off the rails.
- Ask your parents to buy you some rope. If they actually *do* provide you with rope, you should consider doing *really well* in your exams so that you *can* get a good enough job to enable you to leave this abusive home. Now, you're natural instinct will be to stay put and make their lives even more of a misery, but the cunning of your plan is the sheer horror of your return in your twenties when your house is repossessed because you clearly can't manage

your finances. Hopefully, they'll have kept the rope.

How To Pass Exams Without Any Revision or Effort Whatsoever

Everybody knows that every year exams are becoming as easy to pass as wind at Glastonbury (all that larger, bean-burgers and all those potential victims helplessly stuck in the mud). This is because:

- Exam marking is now farmed out to third world workers in Indian telecentres. They are *actually* better educated than the average UK teacher exam marker, but they daren't mark correctly in case they get fired for showing off and are thrown back in the gutter.
- There's a chronic famine of red biros on the planet due to a psychotic teenage crush of one Sarah Walker, aged 15, Berkhamsted, Herts who's writing the longest love letter to David Beckham to get in the Guinness Book of Records. Consequently, all exams are being marked correct with the only available blue biros.
- It's not well known, but the exam setters for multiple choice papers all suffer from O.C.D. As regimed pattern-lovers, all answers follow a simple criss-cross formation. That's a zig-zag, you thickie you.
- If writing an essay, simply end your piece with "In conclusion and therefore..." it's dead clever. In fact, the exam marker will be

completely won over if you just write this phrase over and over.
- The government is deeply and rightly concerned that the regularly declining yearly crappy exam results will lose them the next election; they therefore bribe the exam markers with hollow promises of lovely apples to pass you for simply writing your name at the top of the paper. You can actually buy a stamp with your name on it from an art shop to help you with this difficult task.

Anyhow, next year, all exams will be taken via text. So you're bound to pass, whatever. And it'll take half the time. Don't forget to include a smiley - your exam marker will worry that you're a druggie raver (an olden day phenomenon they just about remember) and be afraid that if they don't pass you, you'll come and get them with your neon stick.

In conclusion and therefore, it doesn't even matter if you don't get *any* qualifications. The only people who need letters after their name are rock stars, eg. Kurt Cobain R.I.P. It's clearly obvious that all employers (except those working in the sciences, politics and TV chefs) now hire purely on the basis of physical sexiness. No boss* wants to have to stare at a minger all day. They have their wives at home for that. So you'll be well alright then.

*This brazen statement implies that all bosses are male. Yes, that's correct. If the boss looks 'female', they don't know it yet, but they're a pre-op transsexual.

-o-

What to do if you're the Victim of Bullying*

In the olden days (say, the Eighties and Nineties) being bullied by your peers was seen as a rite of passage... character-forming... a necessary evil for toughening you up for the real world. In this bygone era, you could have been persecuted for having the wrong kind of hair-sprayed flick (i.e. not smelly enough), uneven creases in your nylon trousers or, worse, for not wearing enough caked-on blue eyeliner.

How Bullying Has Changed

Back then, the bullying often took the form of amusing *name-calling*: "You Howard Jones-wannabe", "You foil-wrapped-sandwich freak" (cling film was new and trendy); or, "You non-bleeding heel whore" (if you weren't wearing stilettos you may as well have been dead). Or you could have even have suffered mirthful *physical attack*: a wedgie, a Chinese burn, a dead arm or, worse still, a nipple twist. Today, innocent bullying has taken a turn for the worse... name-calling is much meaner and much less creative: "You're dead meat, you geek" or "You're gonna die, you Teenager". And physical attack has escalated into, for example, uninvited leap-frogging, and unsolicited raspberry tummy blowing (very embarrassing - not because of your muffin top, but because you actually secretly wash and smell nice and clean). So, in this politically correct, killjoy climate, bullying is now seen as wrong... as socially unacceptable...as child abuse; and sometimes, in its worst manifestation, as just plain naughty.

How To Beat The Bullies (To A Pulp, Ideally)

If you are the victim of bullying, the current advice is to confide in your parents - but they'll actually be privately mortified at: a) having a child that's naff enough to be bullied, and b) having to actively do something to help you... that's because it's marginally less effort than arranging your funeral. Your parents will then deliberately embarrass you and contact the school; or worse still - keen to prove to themselves that they could win a fisticuffs now because they never could when they were your age - confront the bully or their psycho parents, and consequently make the whole situation terrifyingly worse.

Wise up. Don't, *whatever you do*, tell your parents. In fact, you have to wonder that perhaps they subconsciously hope that they do make the bullying situation worse for you. You need to take matters into your own chewed-to-the-quick hands. You can *easily* get rid of your bully on to some poor other victim by:
1. Moving abroad under a new identity.
2. Winning a reality TV show so the bully will want to be your bestest friend.

3. Doing their homework/domestic chores/ eating veggies/sleeping for them.
4. Taking up disco dancing - the bully'll be too afraid to come anywhere near you in case it's contagious. (Actually, it is).
5. Catching your face in the sandwich maker so you can have extensive reconstructive plastic surgery (trouble with this method is it may put you off your cheese toasties for life).

How to be a Better Bully**

The bittersweet irony about being a bully is that picking on your victims is the *only* thing you're good at - seeing as you're ugly, thick and hated by your chavvy parents. And always will be. You're clearly destined for life as a doley, convict, or regular 'X-Factor' auditionee. Bullying is the only thing you'll ever excel at, which consequently gives you much-needed self-esteem, self worth and reason for carrying on living. Therefore, does society have any actual right to deny you your only chance to be happy? Should you *really* be condemned for mercilessly tormenting some clever geek who will, one day, automatically be a great success in life anyway?! *Of course* society should pick on you! A gang versus one lone individual is human nature.

You're not even a genuinely talented bully, because if you were, you'd pick victims who were much bigger and better than you - like prime ministers, evil dictators and invading aliens. Paradoxically (thank goodness for computer thesaruseseses), if you simply channelled your bullying talents (particularly stink bombs, paper spit darts and bra-snapping) away from your peers and directed it against adult meanies like Hitler or Simon Cowell, you'd be seen by society as a modern-day hero like Vin Diesel or Paris Hilton.

* The author wishes to assert that 1% of her conscience is worried that her parents and in-laws will think any jocular writing about bullying is irresponsible, immature and downright impish. Therefore, the author is morally obliged to state that if you are the victim of bullying you *should* inform your parents, the school or police, or call Childline on 0800 something something. Plus, you should get a better haircut and clothes.
** If you are a bully, this is no laughing matter so stop it you effing ugly, chivvy, thicko.

-o-

How To Do Your Pointless Homework
(Without Ever *Actually* Doing it)

GOSSIP-FLASH: Homework has absolutely *nothing* to do with making you smarter, teaching you discipline, giving you a sense of pride in yourself or keeping you out of your parents' equally thinning hair whilst they fight about their divorce settlement or have bitter rumpy-pumpy. Homework was actually **invented** by teachers to provide them with **marking** which helps fill the lonely, empty, tedious hours between home-time and 7pm when their partners reluctantly come home from *their* soul-destroying work.

Furthermore, if a particular teacher gives you *loads* of futile homework it's simply because they're hideously ugly and clearly single, so there's nobody at home to spend their evenings bickering with, or murdering, before bedtime. It is, therefore, an act of humanitarian kindness to single out these Quasimodo, desperate teachers for *even more* harassment in lessons than other tutors - it'll help fill their sad free time with paranoid worry.

Consequently, your teachers *couldn't care less* about what they're covering in red ink, they're paying *no attention* whatsoever to what they're marking… they're too busy looking out of the window and day-dreaming about how to seduce Head-boy/girl. Grading has **always** depended on the following qualities:

- How neat your handwriting is (ironically, left-handers have an automatic advantage as your writing is illegible and the teacher will be afraid you're autistic and bash them if they grade you badly).
- Whether or not you bring the teacher an apple a day (or drugs if you live in an inner city ghetto, like Kensington).
- If female, how short your skirt is - obviously, you should wear *full*-length skirts (that's just above the knees) to female teacher classes to receive good grades, and change to a bum-mini for your male teachers to receive straight As.
- If male, wink at the female teacher to receive excellent grades and wink at a male teacher to receive straight As.
- How scary your parents are (give them 'Halloween' masks on Parents evenings; or, if you know you've really screwed up, 'George Bush' masks.)

However, all the above tactics require you to actually attend school and that's just not practical, so, instead, just cut out these pieces of homework and stick in your exercise book using your secret glue stash or bogies (fresh ones are best). Then, threaten your dog with a brown sack and the river, or worse, Battersea Dogs Home to force him into taking your exercise books to school for you. Wouldn't it be blissfully ironic if your starving dog *really did* eat your homework on the way in!? Try

Marmite. Or cat juice. Here you come Cambridge, Oxford or Bognor.

Warning: just remember to NEVER hand any homework in **late** as this gives the teacher far too much time to sit and ponder the meaningless of their life and increases the likelihood that they'll give you duff grades in an attempt to try and drag you down with them.

English

> *The language of Shakespeare in this play is not only rich in visual metaphors and smilies, but is an intricate tapestry of sub-textual mirkin meaning which reveals the hidden boobies feelings of his characters: the contradiction betwixt arse words and fart action; the painful dichotomy between love and hate; the energising battle regarding penis power and booby subservience; the moral peepee constraints of religion and the social willy disorder created by class. Indeed, Shakespeare's subtext is not only a pubies barometer of Elizabethan times, it illustrates how little smeggy humanity has changed. Centuries change. Gimpy Man, apparently, does not. Therefore, this is why Shakespeare's work is as relevant knickers today as it always was. In conclusion, will the same be said in centuries to come of Alan Bennet or Eminem? Amen.*

Maths

The following gibberish can also be used for physics and chemistry homework because all these ugly teachers wear glasses which they remove as soon as they return home to avoid seeing just how foul they are in the mirror or, indeed, *any* reflective surface, e.g. their uglier partner's greasy, shiny forehead. Consequently, they can't even *see* what they're marking. Incidentally, hiding these teachers' spectacles in lessons is an incredible act of generosity as not only does it mean they don't have to look at your repulsive face, but it forces the teachers' eyes to strengthen themselves, thus by-passing costly lens surgery that they'll never be able to afford on a teaching salary. Plus, they may comically head-butt the blackboard or accidentally fall on a Bunsen burner.

History

In World War One and a Half, the Germans used the Schlieffen Plan to enable them to invade their neighbouring countries one at a time. They initially invaded Belgium but soon left because it was sooo boring, and entered France instead – largely due to the availability of croissants and wine. The Germans quickly walloped the Frenchies using their dangerous saveloys - the silly Frenchies foolishly used fresh baguettes to duel with the Germans (had they used stale, hard baguettes like the ones from Aldi, the end of the war would have come much, much sooner).

However, then the Germans guffed up by forgetting to surround gay Paris because they were too busy arguing about whether or not the Eiffel Tower was a phallic symbol (74% thought so, the remaining 94% thought it was a willy). This gave the French and British troops time to get their own act together (they were busy squabbling about whether or not hairy female armpits were sexy), and there was a huge pillow fight at the Battle of Marne. Then, the two sides had a giant trench digging competition north of the River Aisne, but when it was declared a draw by boring-never-take-sides Switzerland, the competition turned into whom could stay in the trench the longest. It lasted four years! Britain won - because they love waiting in queues.

Geography

Alas, glacial moraine the recent romantic comedy blockbuster, "The Day After Tomorrow" will indeed one day become a tragic reality (but luckily not in my lifetime). Calcium, er, carbonara. In fact, conspiracy theorists believe water table that the film is actually a reality TV show charting the devastation caused by stalactites and the Western World's excessive plundering of fossil fuels without adequate alternative investment in renewable energy development.

If only, market gardening, the West invested heavily in developing green sources of energy - such as wind power - in areas of high Vindaloo consumption like inner city Birmingham.Or, plate tectnotonics, why not harness the water power from male urinals at the weekend to power the hospitals that these same men will visit when they've become so intoxicated they get run over or get in a fight?

Furthermore, solar panels could be legally required on all new builds (excluding, obviously, sunorexic Scotland)… this sun power could then be hanging valley utilised to power the rise in use of sun-beds (which, ironically, are a necessary consequence of the global warming that has resulted in dodgy weather). Whilst deforestation of the rain forests could be challenged much more effectively than Sting's tonedeaf efforts, for example, why do the bad men have to shout "Timber" *so* loudly? What about all the sleeping birdies?

But most importantly of limestone all, people should use their legs as transport — unless, of course, travelling further than 100 metres, then it's fair enough to use the car.

In conclusion, we're all going to dieeeeeeeeeeeeeeeeeeee. Photosynthesis?!

Art

"The Last Supper through the Eyes of An Innocent Child" - a stick figures of The Last Supper

"The Meaning of Life" - a big messy swirl of different colours, called "Adolescence", with words written like pain, confusion, nag, fear, zits

"Still Life" - a collage of a dead person, chalk outline and fruit bowl on head as murder weapon

"My Art Teacher" - a picture of a halo

N.B. Your art teacher wanted to be a proper artist but wasn't actually talented enough so has to pretend to find teaching young people rewarding. These bitter and twisted teachers are very useful for buying you booze from the off-license, having a cool student-teacher affair with, or getting a backie home on their moped.

Biology, Home Economics, French, R.E...

- You do not need to hand in any homework whatsoever for any of the above classes because these teachers picked these thicko lessons because they weren't clever enough to teach proper subjects. These "teachers" will be eternally grateful to you for sparing them the trouble of marking your work as they can barely read themselves. In fact, milk it. They should:

- Tye your tie in a cool knot... after all, you've never used two hands simultaneously to do anything before.

- Adjust your socks to the legally correct slumped level.

- If you're a boy, they can follow you around and make sure you don't unconsciously pull your trousers up to your waist.

- If you're a girl, they can follow you around and reapply your cheap lipgloss every time it wears off, e.g. every 4 seconds.

- If you have a long trendy fringe, they can tap out any obstacles in front of you with a white cane.

- If you get into trouble and are sent to the Head, they can act as your body double. Er, no they can't. You're far too gorgeous. Mind you, you could temporarily scalp your face off and stick it on them, then, when it has to be reattached by a top surgeon, you could ask them to bung in a facelift whilst they're working.

Just DON'T ask these thicko teachers to do your other homework for you. You'll end up in the Special Needs department.

-o-

How To Get A Masters Degree in Bad Language

Now, we're not talking naughty F*!XX*?! words - you should be at least Grade 8 at swearing by now, having begun learning vulgarology in the playground at primary school. We're talking about *really bad words* that you *shouldn't even know*, never mind have the hairy genitalia to utter in front of your parents. *But you should…* because it'll result in you getting sent to your room without any dinner. Hoorah, because this'll leave you free to tuck into your secret stash of decent food like fat and sugar. Furthermore, you can *totally* naff off your fuming, ignorant parents *even more* by *explaining* what these foul words actually mean…

"Proportional representation"
Meaning: representation of all parties in a legislature in proportion to their popular vote. (Don't bother trying to actually understand this – just simply learn it as if it were the lyrics to a pop song).
How and when to use irritatingly: whenever your parents moan about politics, using this baffling phrase to rub in that the thickos are politically ignorant, and probably don't even vote.

Alternatively, why not say the expression willy nilly… it's simply hilariously annoying, whenever. (But don't bother using this phrase if your Dad is clever Gordon Brown; you can if it's David Cameron).

"Oedipus complex"

Meaning: in psychoanalysis, a subconscious sexual desire in a child, especially a male child, towards the parent of the opposite sex, usually accompanied by hostility to the parent of the same sex.

How and when to use irritatingly: when you're wittering folks next fuss that you outstayed your curfew by just 14 hours, inform them that this Oedipus thingy is why you don't get on, and why you must get out a lot. You'll truly creep them out, and they'll leave you well alone to practise your conscientious snogging the bedroom mirror practise.

"Onomatopoeia"

Meaning: the formation or use of words such as *buzz* or *bang* that imitate the sounds associated with the objects or actions to which they refer.

How and when to use irritatingly: become a one-person percussion band using household items. Whenever you make a deafening racket, say "onomatopoeia" repeatedly. They'll start to wonder if you're actually a genius or have autism - either way you'll get sent to a special school. Bonus. With any luck you'll go deaf from ruptured ear drums too.

"Scatological"

Meaning: "obscene language or literature, especially that dealing humorously with excrement and excretory functions."

How and when to use irritatingly: whenever you're being childish (i.e. awake) and making poo poo jokes, instruct your parents that what you're doing has a posh name, so you're *actually* being an intellectual making jokes about shit-wee-love-juice.

"Revisionism"

Meaning: the revision of an accepted, usually long-standing view, theory, or doctrine, especially a revision of historical events and movements. Huh?!?!?!?! Again, learn as if trying to memorise a f r i e n d ' s p i n n u m b e r. *How and when to use irritatingly*: parents often perform revisionism *unintentionally*, in order to try and manipulate you into doing what they want. E.g. your Mum may argue that if *she'd* got a better education she wouldn't be a stay-at-home-Mum. Er, yes, she would, it's cushy. So, tell her she's a revisionist. She'll be confused, wonder what exam you're talking about, and go and do the vacuuming whilst cooking dinner and doing the ironing.

"Egalitarian"

Meaning: the affirming, promoting, or belief in equal political, economic, social, and civil rights for all people - think Martin Luther King, Bono or Chantelle being allowed to be on "Celebrity Big Brother". *How and when to use irritatingly*: if your unreasonable folks won't let you paint your room black, scream this word at them - in the time it takes them to find the dictionary, you'll be able to redecorate. The entire house.

"Algebra"

Meaning: a stupid maths system.
How and when to use irritatingly: the only word in the whole world that can instantly get your parents off your back.

"Abstemious"

Meaning: careful (a.k.a. frigid) in the consumption of alcohol.
How and when to use irritatingly: at cool, booze-fuelled occasions like weddings, Xmas and Monday evening, and *particularly* if your folks start displaying nauseating affection for each other instead of other people, then hiss should this word at them. Their irritate confusion will start a hilarious drunken row.

"Hyperbole"

Meaning: a figure of speech which is an exaggeration.
How and when to use irritatingly: if your Mum ever whispers "If you masturbate you'll go blind" offer to prove her wrong. When she backs down (hopefully she will), you should then tell her she was guilty of hyperbolising, as the very most you may suffer will be a sore hand. (Hopefully you won't go blind for genuine medical reasons as this will spoil your argument somewhat).

"NSPCC"

Meaning: the ability by a Teenage to blackmail their parents into doing whatever they like by uttering this acronym.

How and when to use irritatingly: whenever they come near you… Of course, they may retaliate with their own threat, "Dr. Barndados". Stalemate.

Not really. Spike their drinks cabinet with water.

-o-

How to Pull an Oscar-Winning Sickie

The trouble with today's Teenager's attempts at skiving off school/PE/Saturday job/family do/life in general is the fact that they forget that their parents were once Teens too (but clearly not cool like you). Your folks have pulled their own fair share of sickies too, so simply moaning, groaning and making the droopy-eyed, slack face just doesn't cut it any more. In fact, your parents won't even be able to tell the difference from your usual appearance. You're going to have to take your performance to the *next level*…

Furthermore, TV hospital dramas like 'E.R.' and the outstanding 'Casualty' have unfortunately raised everyday plebs' expectations of medical special effects. Ketchup blood and sausage string intestines just don't cut it any more. So, to see real gore for yourself, why not take a trip to A&E… you could try standing in the middle of the road until you get knocked down but there's no guarantee that you won't get a bit of gravel indentation on your face; the easiest way is to ingest a poisonous substance like a sprout - the resulting digestional agony will be mistaken for appendicitis. Luckily, with the NHS being as rubbish as it is, you'll probably be stuck in a hospital corridor, lying down, for days. Bliss.

How To Make Authentic-Looking Sick

In the halcyon eighties*, you could happily get away with just opening a can of chicken soup for imitation vomit before emptying it into the toilet, bucket, shoe or floor (that's if you had the willpower to resist eating it, mmmm). Nowadays, a far easier and cheaper way to produce convincing puke is to take a huge swig from every bottle in your parents' drinks cabinet, jump up and down like a pogo stick - this will hopefully result in you *actually* vomiting.

If you can't resist drinking too much from each bottle, you can avoid arousing suspicions over liquid levels by refilling with tea or pee. It's also shrewd to freeze portions of your puke for future pulling-a-sickies: it's best to hide your pouches behind the frozen ice-pops (your parents don't tend to touch them... then again... what a laugh if they should 'accidentally' find your gourmet convenience meal). Alternatively, if your parents are freaks and tea-totallers, simply remember your first kiss, that should be gross enough to induce a chuck.

How To Create A Worrying Looking Rash

Meningitis is every parents worst nightmare - because if you were to catch it and lose your arms and legs it'd cost them a fortune in having their house adapted for your disability. Consequently, you can reap the rewards of their paranoia by making a simple permanent rash on your body, that won't disappear when a glass is pressed on it. Take exactly 1000 rice crispies and colour them in red using your best felt tip (if you run out, a Sarah Walker of Berkhamsted has a reservoir supply of red pens), then simply glue them to your body using very small bogies.

How To Fake A Fit

This is tricky because it may look like you're just having a normal strop - for example, you already know how to roll your eyes to the heavens. So, to help differentiate between a fit and your everyday tantrum, you'll need some froth at the mouth… this can be obtained from a local rabid dog (local as in take a lovely trip to France and offer the frothing dog some decent sauages). A fit is also most convincing performed whilst lying down - which is just as well because having an authentic looking fit is well knackering.

How To Behave Poorly For An Unidentified Illness

You'll need to vary your "illnesses" for pulling sickies to stop your parents from becoming suspicious - unless of course, you're going for a biggie like T.B which'll result in you getting sent to the cool seaside for several delirious months to convalesce. T.B. is *highly* contagious so your shit-scared parents won't waste any time in shipping you off. To fake T.B. "cough" ketchup blood in a *hankie* - that's a piece of cloth or material used by adults for nose wiping.

So to perform the symptoms of a mystery condition, it's wise to remember that in war, it is the *quietest casualty* who is the *most near death* (they're probably just faking it too, because they know if they don't whinge like all the other wounded drips then they'll get treatment the quickest). Therefore, instead of the usual clichéd writhing, moaning and groaning, opt for complete stillness and silence. For added plausibility in front of suspicious but slightly worried parents, flinch spasmodically but *look like* you're trying to hide your 'pain'. This'll truly freak your parents out, making them worry that you may actually be dying (again, funerals are expensive). Crying silently in front of them will also seriously disturb your parents, particularly if performed in front of laughing siblings because you'd normally lynch them for this. Literally.

How To Behave If You Suspect You're About To Be Rumbled
Sometimes, your parents will be annoyingly suspicious about the sincerity of your symptoms... especially if you feebly ask your folks to be your witnesses as you draw up your will - this is overkill and will give your cunning game away. However,

you can always clinch it by faintly whispering this hideous phrase: "I… love… you…" They'll think you're about to snuff it and are (rightly) worried that they'll finally have to clean your room. They'll be on that phone for the ambulance faster than you can say "burger" which is blinking brilliant because this'll result in several days off in hospital as the doctors try to diagnose your mystery illness, being waited on hand and foot… which is infinitely better than at home because nurses aren't allowed to nag you.

How To Look Whilst "Recovering"

If female, simply abandon your normal truckloads of make-up and you'll instantly look like death warmed down. You could also give yourself a neat hairdo with side-parting to look even more dodgy. If male, actually *apply* make-up and you'll look like you've contracted a highly infectious tropical disease. Or, better still - and longer-lasting - your parents'll think that you've gone embarrassingly gay and will want to keep you in your room indefinitely.

*The constant nauseating referrals to the perfect Eighties clearly indicates that the author was a Teenager during this heavenly decade. The author wishes to assert, however, that she was, in no way shape of form, an obnoxious Teen, and was in fact a perfect A-Grade youth. *Now*, she's obnoxious.

-o-

How To Forge Illegal Sick Notes

If you break into your head teacher's office and look up that big secret file that says "Etiquette of Truanting" you'll be delighted to discover that you're actually *legally* entitled to 22 days off sick per annum before you are investigated for bunking off by the local council's social work team. Therefore, take 21 days off using these fool-proof sick notes.

(visuals: coffee stains, chewing gum, I ♥ AP, phone number, bogey, on backof envelope, on naff notepaper/kiddy notepaper, sticker)

Between the 2 pieces that are torn from same sheet

TIP: To avoid arousing suspicion, do not give these two sick letters to the same teacher as they may put them together in their crime lab and see they're torn from each other.

How To Excel At Truanting
In fact, truanting is an important and vital aspect of a Teenager's emotional, physical and sociological development, because bunking off gives Teens a valuable sense of what it's going to be like when they become an adult, with no job, no money and no hope.
The Emotional Value Of Truanting

As the Teen wanders aimlessly round the shopping centre or park, they'll learn what it's like to be bitterly lonely, even if surrounded by bunker-off accomplices. Fortunately, they'll also then discover how to cope with the endless hours of boredom by realising time can be frittered pleasingly away with the amazing array of bodily functions.

The Physical Skills

The truanting Teen quickly learns (now there's a first) that skipping school can be very bad for their health. Firstly, there's all that endless pounding of the pavements which can result in blisters, red cheeks and unsightly muscles in the calves. Secondly, external weather conditions can be extremely detrimental to their hairstyling. Consequently, these hazards lead the Teenager to a Darwinian revelation - that they should take a taxi (a *real* one, not your parent) to the nearest major shopping centre, or back home. Ideally, the shopping centre should be at least 200 miles away - not because you'll be afraid of being recognised by one of your teachers who's also faking a sickie to get a much-needed day off, but because you already memorised every item of clothing in every shop in your nearest mall. If you choose to return home, you don't worry about your housewife mum being there to rumble you… she's out having an affair with several of your neighbours.

Truanting Teens will also suddenly and miraculously discover the use of their legs and actually realise that they can, in fact, *run* if they should see a police officer. This invaluable physical revelation teaches a Teen that they can easily outrun the cops - who are, by professional necessity, fat - it's now their only insurance against stabbings and bullets.

The Sociological Development
By bunking off the illiterate Teenager is wisely preparing for the School of Hard Knocks. With limited financial resources and intelligence at their disposal, the almost astute Teen is forced to use all their cunning and evil to get what they want with the minimum of cash and effort:

- Free burgers can be blackmailed out of your local chippie by claiming that you've found a dead rat in your chips. You can easily find a dead rat by looking under your squalid bed. If you're lucky, you won't even need to go to this bother because you may actually legitimately find a deep fried rat in your packet of greasy love.

- Extra loot for Pick and Mix supplies can be readily obtained by begging - don't busk as this is totally degrading. You'll be thrown loads more dosh if you tuck your leg up like a stump… best do this sitting down on the dirty (bonus) pavement because if you attempt this manoeuvre whilst standing, you're guaranteed to fall over instantly as you've never attended a single P.E. class in your life.

- Massive reductions off already sweatshop-cheap clothes can be gained by soiling the desired items with: a) lipstick; b) vomit (look at a piccie of Nicole Richie running on the beach - fit cow); c) dog poo; d) bogies (preferably the runny smeary variety): e) unidentified white stuff.

- Free taxi rides home can be obtained by lying in the road and waiting for an ambulance to pick you up: they'll be so annoyed at you for time-wasting that they'll ferry you back home for a parental scolding. Ha. You know they're not in. She's out having an affair. And your Dad's at work… having an affair.

It is currently rumoured that Gordon Brown is to revise the government's existing policy on Truanting and actually *include* it on the academic timetable. Pupils will be required to skive off school for a double period every week, with extra house-points to be awarded to those pupils who manage to get even fatter on free burgers *and* acquire a whole new (but dirty) wardrobe (which the fatties will then need). Pupils who fail to play truant will be duly punished with having to comb the creepy physics teacher's beard.

-o-

How To Run The Greatest Sponsorship Form Swindle Ever

Sponsored activities are an excellent and easy way to make extra cash for salon hair products, Ibiza week-ends away and pick and mix. You see, your sponsees don't actually care what's your chosen activity, or whether or not you actually do it, *all anyone cares about is who has sponsored the most money so they can beat it.* Hey, you're an entrepreneur. A veritable Robin Hood, robbing the rich to give to the rich, you.

Sponsorship Form for
Belching-the-Alphabet

Name Address   £ per letter

```
Ivor Biggun     2 Gay St, Here, H3!8*$
                £21
```

Cough up now or else!

Sponsorship Form for Chinese Burn-athon

Name	Address	£ per victim (double for a policeman/royalty/ serial killer)
Ted Bundy	*Cascade Mountains, Washington*	£6.66

How To Speak In Foreign When You Go on School Exchanges
(or Naughty Week-Ends Away If You're A Drop-Out)

Should you be lucky and middle-class enough to go away on a school exchange you may be nervous about being in a strange land, a different culture, alien customs. Nah, what you're bothered about is not being able to make yourself effing understood. Forget "Where is the library", "How much is that?" and "Where is the British Embassy?" all you *really* need to know to get by is right here...

Phrase 1
"I wouldn't snog you if you were the last person on Earth."

French – Je ne ferais pas snog vous si vous étiez la dernière personne sur la terre.
Spanish – Yo no me besuquearía usted si usted era la última persona en la tierra.
German – Ich werde snog Sie nicht, wenn Sie die letzte Person auf Erden waren.
Italian – Farei non lo snog lei se lei erano l'ultima persona sulla terra.

Phrase 2
*"Get out of my !?**!?! face NOW!"*

French – Sort de mon ?!**? ! Faire face à maintenant !
Spanish – ¡Salga de mi ?!**?! ¡Encare ahora!
German – Steigen Sie von meinem ?!**?! aus! Stehen Sie jetzt gegenüber!
Italian – Uscire dal mio ?!**?! Affrontare adesso!

Phrase 3
"I'll get my parents on to you."

French – Je vous obtiendrai mes parents dessus.
Spanish – Diré a mis padres en usted.
German – Ich gelange meine Eltern an an Sie.
Italian – Otterrò i miei genitori sopra voi.

.

Phrase 4
"Your food sucks, where's McDonalds?"

French – Votre nourriture suce, d'où est McDonalds ?

Spanish – ¿su alimento aspira, de dónde es McDonalds?
German – Ihre Nahrung saugt, woher ist McDonalds?
Italian – Il vostro alimento succhia, dove è McDonalds?

Phrase 5
"You stink of garlic/cheese/B.O./salami".

French – Vous la puanteur d'ail/le fromage/B.O./le salami.
Spanish – Usted hedor de ajo/queso/B.O./salami.
German – Sie Gestank von knoblauch/käse/B.O./ salami.
Italian – Voi puzzo di aglio/il formaggio/B.O./ salami.

Phrase 6
"Your European clothes are hideous".

French – Vos vêtements européens sont affreux.
Spanish – Sus ropas europeas son horribles.
German – Ihre europäische Kleidung ist schrecklich.
Italian – I vostri vestiti europei sono spaventosi.

Phrase 7
"Let's sneak out after midnight".

French – Laissons le mouchard hors après le minuit.
Spanish – Permitanos a chivato fuera después de la medianoche.
German – Lassen Sie uns schleichen aus nach Mitternacht.
Italian – Insinuiamo fuori dopo la mezzanotte.

Of course, there *are* seven more countries in the entire world - but you don't want to go to any of these places - their TV is really crud. The TV programmes are duff in France, Spain and Italy too, but at least the folk on telly are quite good-looking;

whilst in Germany, the TV people are quite hairy and good for mocking.

-o-

5 HEALTH

How To Eat Like A Typical Lardy Teenager (And Decrease Your Life Expectancy... Well, Life's S!?t Anyway And The Earth's Going To Explode In 2028, So What's The Point In Healthy Eating, Jamieeee?!)

Today, in the UK, one in every six Teenagers is obese. Well done you! (that's the only cheesy exclamation mark you'll find in this entire literary tomb*). That shows real strength of character in being able to resist media, cultural and survival-instinct pressures to be slim, alive and, most important of all, attractive. That's *real* Teen Spirit. In fact, you should be awarded an OBEse because it takes considerable, heart-felt effort to be a lardy, muffin-topped fatso...

Why It Takes Real Guts To Be Morbidly Plumpy
1. You have to moan *for hours** at your selfish parents until one of them cracks and

chauffeurs you into town fully believing that you're going to buy a schoolbook (idiots), when you're actually going for your bi-daily burger fix. This is, in fact, a piece of cake - well several - but it *is* a waste of time that could be better spent scoffing cholesterol.

2. Being revoltingly porkoid requires you to go *all the way* to the kitchen *yourself*; and if that wasn't tiring enough, to *streeetch* up to that darn biscuit tin - Mums' put the tin high up to try and discourage 'you' and Dad (i.e. herself) from downing them. Consequently, you should gorge on *quadruple* the number of biscuits you'd normally scoff to replace this lost energy (approx. 2745 kc).

3. Munching packet after packet of crisps is actually *quite hazardous* as crispy bits are jaggy and can cause *serious abrasions* to the roof of the mouth. Therefore, it's recommended that you eat only salt and vinegar crisps for maximum stinginess which is dead funny and means that you're well hard.

4. Eating bulimic quantities of chocolate leaves suspicious-looking brown scum under your nails which may lead others to believe that you've just wiped your botty with your hand. Teach them to not be so judgemental by sucking merrily away on your sausage trotters. (P.S. If you've run out of chocolate, who's to say that poo doesn't taste nice - flies like it. So do people in Wales.)

5. Going to the sweetshop can cause (amusing) rifts between you and your 'friends' as the "Only 2 at a time" policy forces you to reveal which 'friends' you don't really like. Hang on, you only have one other 'friend'… problem solved.

6. You have to *attend* tedious family functions like funerals and weddings to gorge on your fave kind of food - high fat buffet fayre. Frequenting such torturous get-togethers requires you to endure *slobbery dog granny kisses*, so thank Allah for cheese and pineapple on sticks and unidentifiable balls of, er, 'meat'.

7. You *actually* have to *queue* in the chippie!!!!!!!! If this was any other shop, you'd storm out of if there was so much as a blind, wheelchair-bound, recently widowed old git in front of you.

How To Survive If Your Probably Even Fatter Parents Try To Force You To Eat Healthily

Your parents may attempt to sabotage your noble efforts at rebelling against the "Body Beautiful" culture by trying to make you eat healthily. *Not* because they care about your future health - they'll be rotting, maggoty corpses long before your heart disease kicks in, but because they're jealous that they can't enjoy your full-fat approach to life. If they *were* to join your gorging, your dimply parents would put reeeeaallly gross amounts of weight on in annoying site-specific places like under their chin, or eyelids - they are hilariously bitter about how your fat is spread *evenly* over your *entire* wobbly body. Besides, it's in their interests to stop you not being morbidly obese because your disgusting appearance puts them off tucking into their own greasy trough-loads.

Sadly, though, the days when they could smack you for not eating your lovingly heated, 'low-fat' convenience dinners are long gone - now they face life imprisonment if they so much as give a Chinese burn. Indeed, they can no longer even blackmail you into eating your veggies by threatening that Santa won't come - because you know he always comes no matter how vile you've been that year. However, the fear that they'll get an ASBO for letting you die young, or worse, that they'll get struck off your neighbours' Christmas cards list for child abuse (Christmas is the only time of the year your Mum and Dad feel like they've got any 'friends') will result in many lazy parents pretending to go through the motions of providing you with some healthier food options.

How Parents Try To Evilly Save Your Heart Diseased Life
They will attempt to serve you:
- Food that's not fried.
- Fruit that's not fried (banana fritters are the closest you've ever come to fresh fruit).
- Liquid that's not fried.

Just throwing this 'food' back at them can quickly become boring... largely because your aim is rubbish (so why not try and improve it by imagining you're throwing a brick through the window of your school/workplace). However, your parents will actually be quite good at ducking because they've had loads of practise during their heated rows. So instead, you can utilise that untapped creativity you never intended to use...

How To Hide Your Pigswill Health Muck
1. On the rare occasion that you eat at the table (e.g. your sofa and armchairs have been knicked by burglars), remember that under the table isn't *just* for wiping bogies. Try plastering on the lumpy mash and soggy broccoli... plus, if you're a bit of a thicko you'll also discover if you're going to make a good plasterer or brickie (actually, it won't matter if you're any good or not). When there's no room left under the table, use the underbelly of the family pet(s). Or wrinkly granny.
2. Your body also contains many spacious orifices to fill with unwanted healthy slop: your ears (there's nothing between them), your nostrils (pre-stretched by fingers), or your belly button (try removing existing fluff to create extra room - you can use that fluff later on for a pillow on a plane).
3. Tell your Mum it was delicious, but alas, due to the secret gastric by-pass surgery you've

just had on the NHS you're already full. Fortunately, though, your school's collecting food for the greedy third world and produce a collection box made from her wedding hat. This scam can last for *weeks* because the hat is massive - incidentally, wedding hats are so big in a vain attempt to distract wedding goers from the size of the hat wearer's massive arse.

4. Learn magic for several years. Then, wave your wand and, hey presto, the muck will have miraculously disappeared. In the likely event that the food remains stuck firmly on the plate, chuck it on the ceiling - this is another well-used magician's technique.

5. Even if you're caught at the following sting, your parents will be most impressed that you've watched a film that doesn't star Vin Diesel or Lindsay Lohan (of course, you haven't). The scam's based on an old, old film called "The Great Escape" (durr, give the ending away, why don't you) - simply shove the green food down your jean legs and then leave little deposits wherever you go, e.g. just your room or in front of the telly.

6. The easiest tactic for healthy food disposal is to make a sibling eat it by threatening them with a bogey wiping, killing Mr Snuggles, or giving them a kiss. (If you're a sad, only child, you can victimise your Dad instead... by threatening him with revelations to your Mum of hidden porn/alcohol/female underwear).

How Low Will Parents Stoop To Save You?
Your parents will probably hate you enough to try the cruellest, cleverest act of chid abuse known to mankind. They may attempt to smuggle this healthy pigswill into your body by feeding it to you at the only time you can't fling it back at them - *in your gaping snoring mouth when you're asleep.* To make this impossible for them you can:

- Place a spider in your cavernous cakehole as this will deter any tip-toeing Mums from coming near you… ever again. To stop the spider stupidly going in to your stomach (after all, it's not fried), block off your windpipe with a brick.
- Put some froth at the corners of your mouth (use any of the numerous cappuccino takeaway cups you've left moulding in your room). Your parent will think you've had a fit and possibly snuffed it; they'll then - so as to avoid any potential blame - leg it back to their room to wait for the other parent to 'discover' you in the morning.
- Just stay out all night. Every night.

How Society Tries To Scare Teenagers Into Feeling Bad About Being Fat, Happy and Bad-Assed Sexy

When the oldies were growing up they got their teenage kicks by being scared of cruddy episodes of "Doctor Who". You aren't div enough to be frightened by such nonsense because, luckily, you've been exposed to on-screen violence from babyhood. So, the grim reaperettes have had to resort to creating *lies* about you dying young from your unhealthy lifestyle to give you the same sense of excitement and fear that they enjoyed from Tom Baker's long stripey scarf. (Praise the Lard that they don't *really* know what scares today's typical teenager:

1. Never getting off with an ex-soap star.
2. Vomiting in your own hair (in the olden days, this only applied to girls, now pouffy-haired boys fear the same social shame).
3. Not being famous for doing naff all (ugh, what stupid idiot wants to be mega successful for actually achieving something socially valuable).
4. Getting a white-head on your lip... the greatest torture on the planet, and currently employed by dirty fingered interrogators at Guantanamo Bay).

The Horrifying *Real* Reason Behind The "You'll Die Young" Medical Conspiracy
Anyhow, all this scientificy hoo-ha about Today's Teenager having the lowest life expectancy since

the Medieval Ages is _really_ a grown-ups scam to stop fat Teens showing off their celebratory, nihilistic muffin-tops, bottoms and sides. _Jealous adults are just trying to kill your admirable self-confidence and considerable self-esteem with their big fat lies...._

Big Fat Lie 1: _"You need a balanced diet to grow."_
You can easily disprove current medical opinion about The Youth of Today needing to eat a balanced diet to develop properly because in the olden days, people didn't eat _any crap_ and they were _midgets_ - Queen Elizabeth the First was in actual fact the height of a meercat. Junk food _clearly_ makes Teenagers taller... as you're obviously tall enough to read the small menus above the fast food counter; plus, all those burgers must also be good for your eyesight. Now **that's** evolution.

Big Fat Lie 2: _"Salt is a condiment of the Devil."_
This is pure hogwash about lovely salt - fast food's conjoined twin. You actually **need** loads of extra salt in your diet because, as a fatso, you sweat a lot, _lot_ more, so you need extra salt for that. The "recommended" six grams of salt a day only gives you about enough saline to sweat off going up the stairs. To get enough salt in your diet you should make bi-weekly visits to the Dead Sea which is swimming in salt - plus, you'll also get to find out what it's like to be a corpse floating in the sea. Cool. (Coincidentally, you'll also - effortlessly -

look like a corpse that's being floating in the sea *for ages…* bloated.)

Big Fat Lie 3: *"Five a day keeps the doctor away."* This is a downright nasty porky, after all, the average Teen *does* eat five portions of fruit and veg a day: chips, chips, chips, chips and chips. And all *this* has done for the average Teen is to give them zits. Then you *will* need to see a Harley Street 'doctor' for your chemical peels and laser resurfacing. Mind you, you can actually *avoid* permanent acne scarring if you only pick each zit for a minimum of 42 times… after that, you'll get moon-sized craters, although these holes are very handy for storing your chewing gum. And hip flask.

Big Fat Lie 4: *"If you don't eat your crusts your hair won't go curly."*
If some balding crony throws this codswallop at you, just innocently ask, "So, if I start eating crusts will my pubic hair go straight"? Talk about tumbleweeds.

Big Fat Lie 5: *"Your body is 90% water so you must drink two litres of water a day."*
That's bloody obviously not correct - your body is clearly 90% lard. What you do need to drink is large amounts of fizzy pop because it's been scientically proven in Hollywood that the bubbles in pop internally massage the fat globules and therefore help reduce the appearance of cellulite. Also, when you can't be arsed to flush the loo

(pretend you're deliberately conserving the planet's water), the 'water'll' be a pretty/gross colour for the next person - who says you're not thoughtful. Anyway, drinking too much water is bad for you… it's called drowning*.

Bigger Fat Lie 6: *"Eat your spinach or you won't be strong like Popeye."*
That's pure poopoganda. Popeye was defo on steroids. Anyway, who wants to be like Popeye - he was well ugly, and sounds like Beckham sucking helium. You can buy steroids from any reputable high street stereo retailer.

Ironically, there is **one** piece of health propaganda that *is* true, and that's the saying "You are what you eat". Correct. Burgers are gorgeous and popular.

How Old People Will Go To Any Lengths To Stop You Being Sexy
These old fogies are just one incontinent wee away from having a waltz with the Grim Reaper so they'll do <u>anything</u> to stop younger generations from looking good and having dangerous, illicit fun. They'll make up any old nonsense to golden rain on your parade…

Big Fat Lie 7: *"Sun tan booths give you skin cancer."*
Piffle. They give you a lovely, healthy orange glow. Not to mention that all important body confidence: having a tan makes you feel and look slimmer… this, in turn, massively boosts your self-esteem and

encourages muffin-topped girls to wear hipster jeans and cropped tops; or going shirtless if you're a booby boy. Sun tan booths should, in actual fact, be legally protected by the UN for Human Rights as they enable lardy lonely teens to finally feel good about themselves.

Big Fat Lie 8: *"Nits actually prefer clean hair."*
The blatant stupidity of this is enough to make you want to tear your hair out. This is a pathetic adult's attempt at 'the double bluff'… the adult naively believes that you'll think that they're lying and that nits like dirty hair so you'll promptly go and wash your festering barnet. It's a well-known gossip that nits prefer chemically treated hair because then can get mega high off all those peroxides and styling agents. You don't care anyway… so long as your hair doesn't move once you've styled it. In fact, having million of nits in your crowning glory will probably help thicken your hair and keep it in place.

Big Fat Lie 9: *"There are more germs under your mauled nails than in a public toilet."*
And the point is…

Big Fat Lie 10: *"Your Great Aunt Gertrude Died Suddenly Aged 35 From Heart Disease - It Runs In The Family."*
Good. Anything to escape your parents' nagging.

How To Live To Well Over A Hundred

Actually, you can be as fat, unhealthy and inactive *as you bloody well like* because you'll **automatically** live to well over a hundred due to the huge advances in medical science. In fact, it could easily be argued that your elders and worsers are evilly *manipulating* you into being fat, unfit and dying because hospitals can now so easy-peasy fix whatever terminal condition you've given yourself; indeed, the *more* you try to kill yourself with your unhealthy lifestyle, the *longer* you'll live. Plus, ridiculously, on the NHS, it's **free**... now that's blatantly going to downright encourage you to squander all your hard-earned, 'borrowed' or stolen dosh to squander on even more crap food, booze and fags... nirvanaaaah.

Why Being In Hospital Getting Weeping Bed Sores Is Better Than Being At Home

Of course, there are the inevitable niggles:

* You may well have to endure a bout of MRSA (although you'll probably get a fat stash of secret dosh from the government to shut you up... mind you, talking with your nerve-damage, disfigured face'll be too hard to bother talking and selling your story anyway)
* You'll need to stay awake 24/7 to avoid getting snuffed out by Nurse Euthanasia (a fun game is to pretend that you're asleep and then shout "Boo" just as she's about to slip

in the needle. Don't mis-time this one as you'll miss the next episode of "X Factor").
* The food is shit - but marginally better than your Mum's.

But, on the other anti-bacterial liquid soaped hand, your hospital stay has much to offer:

1. The absence of parents - they'll be obliged to visit you on the first day for appearances sake, but then they'll accidentally forget that you exist. You'll then only receive visits from your friends (who are using you to bunk off work/school) and the chaplain (who'll be very nice and want to cuddle you all the time).
2. You can piss in the bed as often as you like and, by law, the nurses have to change your sheets.
3. Everyone brings you presents. Then hopefully, you'll contract some MRSA and be forced to stay in hospital indefinitely which'll force your visitors to bring you much better gifts than the first wave of grapes, mags and sweeties. Bring on the games consoles and i-pods.
4. Bed baths: you may find these hugely embarrassing but it's a far better option than having to wash your own goolies.
5. If you're young and lucky enough to be on a children's ward you'll receive regular visits from a 'hilarious' clown. So, your moral duty is to:

- Give them the Evil Eye.
- Trip their big feet up.
- And throw your own version of a custard pie at them - your bedpan.

Those of you old enough to be put on an adults ward must try to avoid these wards at all costs - you do NOT want to be on a ward with senile, dribbling and mad adults; therefore, you must pretend to be mentally retarded and need to be treated like a child. So, just act normal then.

6. The shiny floors are excellent for skid practise.

How To Get A Life-Saving Transplant

If your appalling unhealthy lifestyle results in you needing an organ transplant you can relax knowing it's come from someone far, far healthier than you... probably from someone really, really, really poor who lives in Eastern Europe or India where they don't eat crap. Not only will having a transplant entitle you an amazing, unquestioned amount of *paid leave* off work/homework-free time off school, you'll also get a wicked scar which you can pretend was from getting stabbed whilst trying to defend your wicked mobile. Don't get a hand transplant from any of these donors, though, because you'll find that it'll keep spontaneously sticking itself out in a begging motion.

The key organs you may wish to consider replacing are:

- *The Heart*: simply continue eating your regular cholesterol-friendly diet.
- *The Lungs*: carry on smoking like an industrial chimney. Clever Teens will learn how to breathe through their ears.
- *The Kidneys*: alcopop it to your heart's content - your gross kidneys will then be a pretty colour for the surgeon to admire.
- *The Brain*: don't worry about this one, it's been *naturally* rotting since the day you were born.
- *The Skin*: if you're Caucasian, you intrinsically suffer from a pasty white demeanour, thus, 100% burns will qualify you for skin grafts... you should screaming well demand for the epidermis to be from a Latin-type donor, because then your new skin will be a dead sexy tanned colour. No-one will dare argue with you because they can barely bring themselves to look at you. Plus, you'll stink. You can acquire sufficient burns to qualify for this skin grafting by lighting your farts after a kebab with extra hot chilli sauce.

How To Start Preparing For Your Death Now
Smart, lazy Teens will also be cunningly aware that when they finally retire at age 83, their state pension will be so pathetic (current estimates suggest approximately three pence per week) that they are **duty bound** to start make themselves terminally ill *now* with poor lifestyle-related diseases in order to get their money's worth out of

paying taxes all their life. When you're an old, decrepit (but, of course, still sexy) pensioner these long stays in hospital will provide you with slightly better standards of hygiene and care than at home from your own, despising family.

Alternatively, if you currently aspire to be a welfare benefit scrounger all your life, you'll be relieved to know that you'll *still* be entitled to these free stays in hotelospitals… and they'll provide a welcome change of scenery from chronic OAP loneliness in front of the telly or net curtain. Paradoxically (author doesn't know what it means either - it just looks good), though, once you're stuck in hospital being saved from your self-inflicted fast food death, the actual NHS food will definitely kill you. But you can always pay some illegal immigrant auxiliary worker to sneak out and get you a kebab or falafel - they're born smugglers.

How To Have An Eating Disorder And Annoy Your Fat Friends

Some weird Teens choose to eat healthily because they have an eating disorder like anorexia or bulimia. This is a terrible, serious problem for society as a whole because it's not easy knowing how to *pronounce* them *correctly…* mispronunciation can make you look like a right spanner:

Anorexia is pronounced "An-oh-woe-is-me-rex-ee-ahhhhhhhhhh"

Bulimia is pronounced "boo-lee-me-me-me-aghhh"

Giving yourself either of these illnesses is <u>very</u> anti-Teenager because it suggests that you reject suffering traditional Adolescent Angst like everyone else such as acne and street stabbingobia, because you believe yourself to be worthy of potentially much more serious, life-threatening, lifelong problems. Wake up and smell the chocolate milkshake. Being thin does *not* make you happy - everyone's miserable - you'll just look better than everyone else.

How To Find The Right Eating Disorder For You
Basically, which deadly disease you choose depends on whether you enjoy eating or not... and this largely depends on if your Mum can cook. If your Mum's a veritable Nigella in the kitchen, you're better off opting for bulimia; but if you're not middle class, anorexia will be best for you. However, if you're too weak from not eating to think clearly (even more so than a make a traditional Teenager), here's a medical summary to help you pick your mental disorder:

The Pros Of Anorexia
1. You don't have to look down a toilet.

2. The downy fur you'll grow all over your skin will keep you nice and toastie in the winter.

3. You'll have excellent cheekbones which'll photograph like a supermodel... you'll look dead wicked on your facebook.

4. You can automatically be a supermodel. Even if you're a munter.

5. If you're good enough at anorexia, you'll be sent away to a rehab or hospital. Either way, you're away from family and school. Result (the downside is you'll be surrounded by skinny cows).

6. Your hair will thin - what better excuse can you have for getting celebrity style hair extensions.

7. You'll stop having periods (only if you're female) - this alone is worth getting the self-hating, terminal condition; although you'll still be exceptionally moody. Result.

8. Male anorexics will experience a loss of sex drive. Good. Who wants such self-obsessed, burger-hating blokes to reproduce.

The Cons Of Anorexia
1. Death.

2. Worse still, because you're supposed to hate your body, society expects you to cover up and wear baggy clothes. What!?! And not let others admire your sculptured physique!?!!!!!!!!!!!

The Cons Of Bulimia
1. You have to look down a toilet. Although, most eating disorder devotees are middle class (therefore, too self-absorbed to care about real suffering around the world) and will therefore be

clever, so you're probably bright enough to vary where you hurl: green Wellingtons, cut crystal vases, horse boxes.

2. Your teeth will rot... mind you, your embarrassed parents will be more likely to cough up for expensive dental whitening.

3. Your fingers may become calloused from sticking them down your throat, which makes putting on your cheap bling more tricky.

5. Constipation - as with anorexia, you're unlikely to be very fertile so at least you'll know what it's like to *look* pregnant.

6. You'll perfect the art of secrecy - eating alone, puking privately... which is good training for when you become a celebrity and want to avoid the paparazzi after you've had your plastic surgery.

Bulimia pros

1. Puke in the hair is actually an advantage as you will stink and all mere mortals will avoid you.

2. You can eat everything you ever wanted without so much as stretching your perfect size eight clothes.

3. When you're a grown up, your bulimic history will be a free pass to show business, which is just as well as you missed passing your exams because your were too busy hurling up your chewed off nails.

3. You can have fun timing yourself with a stopwatch as you gorge on the contents of the entire kitchen. Teens with eating disorders are extremely competitive - there should be a toilet bowlympics.

How To Be A Stupid Vegetarian

There are three and a half reasons for a Teenager becoming a Vegetarian:

1. Some nobly turn to vegetarianism in their Terrible Teens because they love cuddly wuddly animals and fishy wishies. However, these fakers are well-documented by Sky One as being secret sleepwalkers who scour the motorways for scavenging for bleeding, rotting road kill in their starving sleep.

2. Some choose to become a Veggie as a protest against the capitalist, barbaric practise of factory farming... how commendable (though, deeply unlikely - nowadays, Teenagers don't even know what a farm is).

3. Whilst some forgo the flesh because they have a massive eating disorder and believe that not eating meat will help them stop getting fat(ter). Hell-loooo - cheese is 70% cellulite.

1/2. But the absolute majority of Teens become Vegetarian purely to   really get on their parents nerves.

Therefore, these deliciously spiteful and crafty Teens must find *secret ways* to gorge on lovely, fleshy, juicy meat without being caught by their irritated parents.

How To Scoff Meat On The Quiet

A) Genetic Cloning And Mutation

Become a human guinea pig by checking your local post office window for adverts (- there are always weirdos/scientists looking for 'volunteers'), and have your DNA crossed with a Gecko lizard. Then, at Sunday dinner, you can use your faster-than-the-speed-of-light, flicking tongue to snatch chunks of the roast without any of your family noticing. Plus, ooh ooh, your webbed feet will be really handy in school swimming competions.

B) Join The Vampire Club

Try the next best thing to fresh meat. Blood. Look in the Yellow Pages for your nearest vampire group. Your mum will happily tolerate the black clothes, cloak and fangs just because you appear to be joining in with others. Fortunately, the inevitable puncture marks in your own neck will be mistaken for well impressive love bites by your peers, and the resulting deathly white complexion can later be improved by 3,862 visits to the sun-bed shop. (Tip: to get extra, free sessions, try inserting chocolate coins in the machine, it probably won't work but it'll make the choccie all lovely and gooey).

C) Vehicular Windscreens

Windscreens provide a much under-rated source of nutritious protein, and it's easily available. Plus, the meat's already gutted. If you're really in need of a meat frenzy, visit a truck stop - here you'll find much bigger windows... well, that's if the hillbilly truckers haven't got there first.

D) Roadkill

This is a very convenient form of fast food flesh. Not only will you find a choice of cuts, but you'll also revel in a variety of expensive, exotics meats: bunnies, Bambi, protected species badgers, squirrels, foxes, rats, pet dogs. Yum yum. Avoid the carcases with flies.

E) Cannibalism

Make "play" fighting more rewarding by taking a swift chomp of your siblings or friends irritating limbs as you apply a distracting Chinese burn. Siblings are very much like worms, and if you scoff a hand a new one will eventually grown back. Who cares about your 'friends'.

F) Self Cannibalism

For the ultimate in convenience foods, just tuck in... to yourself - at least you know where you've been. For example, scoffing that fun bit of skin around your nails is almost as good as picking a scab. If your stumping fingers become too red raw, down a few bogies instead until your trotters heal.

How To Spot A Real Vegetarian (And Avoid Them At All Costs)

Under no circumstances, do you want a genuine, bona fida vegetarian in your circle of friends:

* They tend to be uglier than average, and although this may temporarily have the effect of making you appear more attractive, ultimately this'll reflect badly on your ability to attract sexy pals.
* They often wear foul clothes made of natural materials like cotton and wool because they pretend to be against all things man-made. Stripey rainbow fluffy jumpers are a sin against synthetics.
* They usually wear braces on their teeth and this'll make them spit gob over you when they speak; and you *do not* want to get accidentally pregnant with them.
* They look malnourished and have terrible skin because their bodies are sorely lacking in bloody iron.
* They make stinking shits.

Why One Type Of Vegetarian Makes The Perfect Friend

Veggies can usually be found living clustered in the South East and attending public schools. These veggies ironically make great friends:

1. They're desperate to be friends with someone common and therefore rough as muck (i.e. you) as they believe (wrongly) that you'll help them stop being bullied in their private

school. Cool... someone new and easy to pick on.

2. They'll have a limitless credit card (their parents hope their embarrassing geeky, eco-child will use it to disappear and travel the world), and they'll be eager to buy your friendship with whatever you so desire. Burgers, burgers, and burgers, it is then.

3. Their loaded parents will have an overseas property that you'll get invited to on their family holidays (their parents believe your yob-like appearance will deter any local burglars - ha, *you're* the burglar).

How To Show Up A Bogus Vegetarian

Some Teenage Vegetarians are - inevitably - incredibly thick or just plain liars and think that they can pretend to be a full-blown veggie **but still eat fish**!!!!!!!!!!!!!!!!!????????????? Mind you, their brains are wasting away because they're not getting any meaty gristle. You can spot these porky-telling veggies easily by either:

- Their rancid fish breath.
- The fact that they're *always* really bragging really loudly wherever they are that "I'm a Vegetarian... but occasionally I'll eat sustainable fish for protein."

If you encounter one of these gobby charlatans, it's your honour-bound duty to truth and justice to proclaim even more loudly; and therefore make them look a right prat:

"The Vegetarian Society's definition of a vegetarian is: the   practice of a diet that excludes all <u>animal</u> flesh, including poultry, game, fish, shellfish or crustacea, and slaughter by- products. So there."

Then you should pelt them with animal entrails - just pop down your local burger takeaway.

There also exists a mysterious sub-strata of Vegetarians called the Vegans, don't worry about them, you'll never meet any because - due to lack of anything they're allowed to eat - they're all dead. Actually, it may well be in your interest to encourage some of your fad-loving friends to turn to Vegetarianism as this will help evolution, and the survival of the meatiest. Due to malnutrition, they're bound to snuff it earlier than you due which'll leave you with a bigger share of the overall welfare benefits (it can take *years* for BSE to show up).

Amazingly, 99% of Teens grow out of pointless Vegetarianism... normally around the time that they leave home and have to start cooking for themselves. In the meantime though, if you're one of the hardcore few who insist on being an annoying Veggie (i.e. you really want to bug your folks) then you might as well *be the most obnoxious Veggie you can with irritating facts...*

How To Eff Off Anyone Who Eats Glorious Meat

A) Pigs: approximately 80 per cent of UK breeding sows are housed permanently indoors and repeatedly made pregnant and their babies taken from them. The sows are put into 'farrowing crates' - these are barren, metal and concrete cages designed to restrict the sow's movements so that she cannot accidentally crush her young. She can't even turn around and she's stuck here for 6 weeks. Then, although the natural weaning process takes two to three months, piglets are usually taken away at three to four weeks so that their mothers can be impregnated again. The growing piglets are raised in concrete pens. Piglets are subjected to mutilations such as tail-docking and teeth-clipping to prevent them wounding each other in their bored anger. Bred to grow much faster than nature intended, piglets are often unable to support their own weight. Heart and respiratory problems are endemic. A lifetime spent on hard concrete floors causes breeding sows to suffer a high incidence of lameness.

Infections run rife on pig farms due to the filth, the heat and the overcrowded conditions. Their feed is laced with antibiotics, simply to keep them alive. Then you eat them.

At the slaughterhouse, pigs are first given a powerful electric shock to their head - an attempt to render them 'insensible to pain' - before their throats are stabbed with a knife (known as 'sticking').

A three-year study of 29 slaughterhouses in the UK revealed that stunning is often ineffective. In one study, 35 per cent of the pigs were found to have been stunned in the wrong position, and an average of 30 seconds elapsed between stunning and sticking - enough time for the animal to regain consciousness.

Enough already. This ex-Teenage Vegetarian can't take it any more…

((List of animal welfare organizations))

The Vegetarian Society

Animal Aid

Animal Liberation Front (for *genuinely* obnoxious Teenagers only)

-o-

How to Smoke Stylishly and Kill Yourself Coolly

In 2007, 1 in 4 Teenagers are regular smokers. The other pathetic 3 in 4 Teenagers are nerdy gimp wimps. So, of course the moral dilemma is how to smoke *really individually and stylishly* and not at all like your lemming, unoriginal peers. Oh, and how to stop your parents finding out. Not because they care about your health and future welfare but because your 'secret' smoking will stink their house out and devalue the price of the property; the *only* thing keeping your parents' will to live alive is the prospect of selling the family home for a huge profit and permanently disappearing whilst you're at the park bench or police station.

Besides, if your folks discover you're a puffer, they'll only try to steal your secret stash as their own form of stress relief… for being your parents. Although, the advantage of allowing this crime to be committed is that *they* may well die early from lung cancer and you'll inherit the house. Wee-hey. So why not hold lit cigarettes in your parents' mouths as they sleep, knocked out by the Valium.

Is Smoking Actually Bad For You?

It is currently fashionable to believe that smoking is *really* bad for you - this is a toxic truth perpetuated by grumpy people suffering from personality -testing lung cancer. Their aim is to sue tobacco manufacturers by claiming that the cute little white sticks gives 1 in 4 smokers a painful, drawn-out death… but it's not as if they'll ever get to spend that large sum of money anyway?! Plus, shouldn't they be focusing on enjoying their last days at the hospice? Talk about *negative*. And adults have the nerve to criticise the youth of today for being pessimistic, narcissistic moody gits! Why not look at the bright side of terminal lung disease?!?

How To Enjoy The Health Benefits of Smoking

On the upside, you *won't* have to die from: testicular cancer; breast cancer; anal cancer; bladder cancer; oesophageal cancer; pancreatic cancer; stomach cancer; bone cancer; cervical cancer; chronic myelogenous leukaemia; boredom; laryngeal cancer; myeloma; retinoblastoma, eyelash cancer; ovarian cancer; bowel cancer; liver cancer; an inoperable brain tumour; cardio-vascular disease; split ends; rhabdomyosarcoma; carcinoma; HIV; auto-asphyxiation; bovine spongiform encephalopathy*; achonodroplasia; uterine cancer, mesothelioma or sprout anaphalaytic shock.

After all, many of the above terminal conditions are annoyingly *random*. They strike willy nilly (tee hee). Surely, it's infinitely better to know *how* you're going to die, and to know that you're *100% to blame*. Indeed, *y*our parents are always moaning at you to accept responsibility for your actions, so please them by taking up smoking with the full knowledge it's smoky suicide.

How To Outlive The Uptight Health Nuts, Ha Ha Ha Ha Ha Ha Ha

In fact, it's highly likely that if you start smoking at the *earliest possible age* you'll be guaranteed to live, well probably, forever... having abused your body so massively with other substances and lifestyle choices, your stem cells won't know which cancer to focus on and will, therefore, not bother with any of them (cancers are actually quite lazy too). This will hilariously annoy those pious, preachy healthy non-smoking green-munchers who'll probably get multiple cancers as their internal organs are so bored and want some action. It's called Sodd'em Law. However, there are some **very** hazardous, lethal side effects to smoking the sexy stick...

How To Handle The *Real* Dangers Of Smoking

Much more devastating than emphysema and ending your days retching your rotting lungs up (great phlegm for gobbing from high buildings, though), cigarettes will:

1. Make your hard-whinged-for clothes reek... mind you it's a nicer smell than your Mum's hideous girly fabric softener. And the stale ashtray pong'll cover the smell of your B.O.

2. Cause your hair to stink to high heaven - fortunately you're barnet is p e r m a n e n t l y slathered in stinking hair products. *Warning*: in 2007, 3872038 Teens were admitted to A&E with 3rd degree scalp burns from lighting up on windy street corners. Never mind. That's why God invented cheap and nasty hair extensions (incidentally, the real reason w h y Posh periodically dons hair extensions is because she's a prolific fart lighterer).

3. Turn your already dubious breath rancid. Therefore, you should eat even *more* kebabs to cover up your halitosis.

4. Burn a hole in your hard-sponged pocket money (that's why it's crucial to either steal loose change from sofas in furniture stores or pretend to go out with someone with a paper round... they're always the geekiest of the geeks and will gladly pinch fags from their newsagent.)

In conclusion, you'll end up stinking like a tramp but at least this'll guarantee that you'll always get a spare seat next to you on the bus… which you may one day have to take if your mum or dad are selfish enough to die on you. However, if your odour issues become sufficiently bad enough to make even yourself gag, just hang out with Europeans - they have the worst B.O. in the world. Plus, they're quite immoral.

How To Defend The Lifestyle Benefits of Smoking Like A Loser

Your parents, teachers, care-workers and hospice staff may nag you incessantly about giving up the fags. Again, not because they care about you but because they receive free money from the state to "look after you"… if you snuffed it they wouldn't get this free bootie and they'd have to go on the game. Or, worse, work in a supermarket. So, you need to be able to persuasively and angrily argue why your continuing smoking is healthy *for everyone* involved…

1. Your mouth will receive **plenty of exercise**: in turn, your gob'll be in better shape to pull a variety of Teenager Facial expressions, thereby turning you into a *more effective communicator*. Clearly, you should omit the fact that you'll simply only use your mouth to perfect the pout and the sneer. (Incidentally, using clever words like "thereby", "therefore", "wherein" etc. with your elders will help you to completely out-argue the thickos).
2. You'll **burn a whopping 7 calories a day** lifting your hand to your mouth. This is 7 more than the

grand total of a Teenager's average daily calorie expenditure… this will consequently entitle you to eat at least 3 bags of chips a day.

3. The **neon yellow fingers** you'll acquire from nicotine staining will prove most handy should you ever be buried underground in some annoying accident as they'll help your rescuers **locate you quickly**… so you can have another fag.

4. Stinking like an ash tray may actually **encourage you to wash occasionally** - something your non-smoking frigid Teenage counterparts won't be doing.

5. Smoking is a well-known **appetite suppressant** - if you *didn't* smoke you'd be clinically obese and be at risk of dying from thigh-friction spontaneous combustion. Ultimately, no parent wants to be repulsed/ embarrassed by having lardy offspring.

6. Smoking will stop you looking like a virgin… *even if you are* (although this is *most* unlikely as most Teenage smokers are also slags). <u>*Not*</u> looking like a virgin is vital in **preventing you from being bullied** by your peers, or passing strangers.

7. Passive smoking'll actually **help your adult carers to chill out** a bit, man. Besides, any ensuing cancer and death will be a blessed release from their pathetic existence… and a welcome escape from you.

8. Smoking is your **form of stress relief**. Teens today live in a terrifyingly pressurised culture, without the fags you'd be *even more* angry, vile and hateful. Yes, it is possible.

9. Your teeth will become **horrendously yellow** - everyone in your parent's ignorant generation

believes that yellow teeth are stronger than white. Furthermore, when your decaying nicotined teeth actually fall out (encourage this by eating only sugar), remember, you're entitled to FREE DENTAL TREATMENT ON THE NHS UNTIL YOU ARE 18. ROT ON!! (Mind you, it's dead cheap to get them unprofessionally whitened using Tipp-ex®).

How To Master The Art Of Smoking Stylishly

The majority of cancer time-bomb Teens are idly content to smoke simply by raising their hand to their mouth, shoving in the cigarette, and taking a drag. This is for unoriginal pansies. To set yourself apart as cool and a true individual, you should smoke with panache... or, failing that, with weirdness.

- Use a cigarette holder - these can be acquired from ageing drag queens (just ask your Dad), or simply take the magic wand you still have from your desperately sad childhood and chop a bit off. This is well chic and your peers will be mega jealous - even though they'll pretend they're not by shouting "gayo" at you. Then, you can also use the holder to spit chewed up paper bombs.
- Snort like a pig on cocaine when you inhale as this'll give the impression that you're really hard core and trying to get as much of a nicotine hit as humanly possible.
- Never, ever, ever be seen *without* a fag in your gob... even if you're receiving CPR

after suffering a really brilliantly executed body-severing wedgie.

- Smoke through your nostrils, as this leaves your mouth completely free to eat hydrogenated trans fats. Furthermore, this has the added advantage of singeing off unwanted nasal hair when the fag's nearly out.
- Employ an illegal immigrant to do all that heavy fag holding and fag-to-mouth manoeuvrings for you: the government's minimum wage for these gypos is 5 pence per day (naturally you'll underpay). They'll be well grateful for the work. Plus, this leaves your hands free to flick the air, or fat people's bottoms, at random.

How To Avoid The Kiss Of Death
Actually, smoking can sometimes be quite **fatal**. You may, at some point, have the terrible misfortune to **kiss a non-smoker**. You'll actually have been *conned* into this by the naff tobacco virgin who'll pretend to be a chain-smoker in order to get off with much more cool you. They'll have tricked you into believing they're a smoker by:

- Hanging out at family barbecues in order to get smoky smelly.
- Staining their pristine fingers with wee.
- Wheezing… they'll have stopped using their asthma inhaler.

However, once you start swopping saliva it will be bloody obvious that they've cheated on you because their breath *WILL TASTE ALL CLEAN*

AND MINTY!!!!!!!!!!!!!!!!!!!!!!!!!!!!!!!! This is a violation of your human rights and to get your own back you should chunder a chunk in their betraying gob.

How To Turn Your Deadly Habit Into A Life-Saving Act

Some monkish idiots on the planet believe in karma - in a nutshell, this means that if you do something really bad, if you then do something vaguely good it cancels the bad stuff out. Therefore, to make sure you don't get lung cancer before your twenties (when everything starts to go downhill) you should recycle your mountain of empty fag packets by turning them into mini hospital rooms for squashed slugs. To make the rooms as comfortable as possible for the slugs simply gob** in the packet as the slime'll make them feel most at home. This act of goodwill will probably get you an O.B.E., and result in you being featured in the back pages of "OK" magazine.

*Don't be so sure, burger face.
** How mature of the author to not write "jack off into".

-o-

How To Self-Harm Better Than Anyone Else

Self-harming is all the rage these days. Nowadays, no self-respecting self-loathing Teenager would be seen dead without loads of feeble little scars on their flabby, flaccid limbs. In fact, you can't even be a pop-star these days unless you try slashing yourself with a sharp instrument - er no, a triangle just won't cut it. Traditionally, self-harming involves microscopically mutilating yourself with a razor blade - **durr** - this is incredibly retarded because borrowing a parent's manky old shaver will result in the transference of their rubbish DNA back *into you.* WHY, OH WHY, DO THIS TO YOURSELF when you've worked so long and so hard to not only publicly deny that you are, in fact, related to your parents, but have also spent many conscientious nights trying to dilute your genetically contaminated blood with alcopops.

How To Be At The Cutting Edge of The Self-Harm Bandwagon

The problem with these conventional paper cut-effect "mutilating" scars is that they can be pretty darn unnoticeable... indeed, the disfigurements may just look like cat scratches or, when healed, like silvery slug trails. Under no circumstances do you want your slightly happier peers to *miss* the fact that you're terminally unhappy and full of hateful angst. Furthermore, there is no point whatsoever in scratching yourself repeatedly on *hidden* parts of your body: NO-ONE is ever going to look at your ugly arms and legs. If you want everyone to notice your self-obsessed, self-harming you *must* do it on your boobs or penis.

Therefore, your goal as a tormented Teenager is to create a new style of self-harming that is:
A) devilishly original;
B) and blinkingly obvious even to a blind man.
However, blowing your head off in the style of Kurt Cobain is a tad excessive - not only do you run the risk of there being no cerebral contents for the body removal team to clean up, but you'll *never* find out if Toadfish Rebekci loses any weight. Or that stupid goatee.

How To Self-Harm Like No Other Teenager In 21st Century History
1. Get a really bad hair-do...why not try a Eighties style hair flick. Immediately, your unparalleled, self-hate will be blatantly apparent, especially if you use noxious 'Silvrikin' hairspray. Cunningly, though, these massive waves of cemented hair also make great places for stashing your whoopee cushion and packets of 'Spacedust'.
2. Download the Greatest Hit of "Girls Aloud" on to your i-pod and play it so loud that your eardrums bleed. Hmmm. Actually, your ears'll bleed even when played very quietly.
3. Let your Mum use lovely fragrant fabric softener on your clothes. You clever masochist. No-one'll be able to stomach your poisonous clean fresh scent, whilst the

velvety touchiness of your clothes will make your peers suspect that you're turning gayo.

4. Don't pluck/wax your eyebrows: this applies to girls, boys and inbetweenees. Now, returned to your real natural werewolf state, you might as well have the bubonic plague. Your 'friends' will detest you almost as much as you do. (But not as much as your parents).

5. Get a tattoo that says "A-grade student" branded across your knuckles.

6. Carry a copy of Amnesty International's quarterly magazine wherever you go.

7. Be seen coming out of a charity shop - for maximum effect you should be holding one of their carrier bags. Don't be so naff as to buy anything though, just knick one.

8. Stick a currant or morsel of shit to your face. In the bygone Eighties this was called a beauty spot, when in actual fact, it is now known to be a contagious warthog. Your peers won't be able to stand looking at you, any more so than if you had one eye that looked slightly skewiff.

9. Wear a religious effigy around your neck. This clearly has bugger all to do with you getting Goddie to help you through your emotional turmoil, but purely because you know that your bible-bashing peers will rally round to support you… and they're well ugly, so you'll look well sexy by comparison. And if you get struck down by God for your naughtiness then, hey ho, time off school/ work, as a dead.

10. Wear *tasteful* jewellery, the more expensive and higher carat the better. It follows, then, that you should also wear clothes from BHS - you couldn't deform yourself any more badly (other than going to the same nose surgeon as Jodie Marsh).

11. Girls should wear <u>matt</u> lipstick (your frumpy mum will have a congealed one from her slutty past stashed in her bag - she no longer actually uses it on her thin puckered lips but keeps it in case she has to write a message on a mirror if she's ever kidnapped. Dream on.) Vile matt lippy is clearly an act of self-loathing.

12. Guys should wear "Hi Karate" aftershave (your Dad'll have some stashed in the glove compartment - he no longer wastes it on your mum but keeps just in case he's ever seduced. Dream on.)

Does Self-Harming Actually Work?

In a word, don't be so ridiculously stupid you gormless, naïve divvy twit. Self-harming is a lot of time and effort (say five minutes, slumped in your room) for even less reward... no-one could care less if you're miserable - they're far too busy trying to be *more* miserable to notice your useless attempts at disfiguring yourself. A far more successful strategy for letting everyone know that you're a tragic, angry, hormonal, moody but deeply creative arsehole is to **inflict unbearable harm upon others**:

* Wedgies.

- Chinese burns.
- Bogey bombs.
- Ear wax smears.
- Fart-in-face assaults.
- Bad breath burp attacks.
- Static hair balloon muggings.

-o-

How To Learn To Love Asparagus*And Beetroot

As disgusting, repulsive, evil, putrid and stewpid as these two vegetables clearly are, they're also invaluable to a disgusting, repulsive, evil and putrid teenager (note: you're *not* stewpid). In fact, they're your new best friends. Yes, even better friends than a cover-up stick. Firstly, asparagus makes your wee-wee smell absolutely ranking which is *really* handy when you've run out of stink bombs. So, to be able to stomach this phallic-looking nightmare, try imagining you're dead and it doesn't matter.

Secondly, then there's the beetroot... when eaten in large amounts, it'll turn your pee blood red. This is particularly useful when you want to skive an event like exams, or meeting up with someone dodgy from a chat room, or buying a present for anyone but yourself, because you can show the crimson-stained toilet water to your mum who'll have you in bed faster than a whitehead exploding on a mirror/ cake down the gobhole of a bulimic/piece of chicken down a recently-turned teenage 'vegetarian's' throat. To help you swallow this vegetable offal, try imaging that everyone else is dead... in the ensuing crazy celebratory state, you'll gladly eat these earthen sweetbreads.

6 FINANCES

How to Get More Pocket Money Out Of Your Tight-Fisted, Miserly, Stingy, Pound-Pinching Parents

Money really *does* make the world go round. And round. And round (hic) round (hic), tee hee... because money encourages you to buy alcopops and cheap cider. The trouble is, pocket money doesn't go far these days - designer accessories and 18 carat gold 'aint cheap. Furthermore, nowadays, the traditional Teen *top-up* of cash pilfered from your Mum's purse is suspiciously and worryingly low - she's busy siphoning off the child benefit and housekeeping dosh to do a bunk to Spain, Harley Street, or run off with your Dad's brother... or sister.

Then, of course, there are the unfair regional and class divides to contend with; amazingly, not every

Teen is born with a silver credit card in their mouth. Some have to steal them*.
*The Author wishes to assert that stealing credit cards is well dodgy - it's *hard enough* for you to do your *own* handwriting, never mind copy someone else's.

**20-29 year olds are now legally classified as "Teenagers, Plus" as they still live at home, or in the very least, still financially sponge off their debt-ridden folks *and* make their Mums do their stinking washing.

How To Get An Instant Pay Rise
Thankfully, your parents would rather have a debt bigger debt the Third World than appear un-wealthy or stingy *in public*. Therefore, adopt any (or all - much more fun) of the following tactics for embarrassing them into giving you excessive amounts of unmarked money for you to then squander on burgers, weird haircuts and new weekly mobile phones.
- Start mending* all the cool rips and tears in your clothing with dodgy patches: in the olden days ten years ago Mums fixed dishevelled clothes because they couldn't afford new ones. Now all your peers and neighbours will think that your parents must be going bankrupt. *Obviously, you're not going to do the sewing yourself... find out where sweatshop 'Top Shop' get their garments made and send them there. Don't

bother with a stamp, drawing one is effectively the same to the Post Office - they're going out of business so they're just glad for your custom.

- Make an illegal charity box out of an old peanut butter jar (use that brand new one you decimated at breakfast) and go collecting down the high street for the "NSPCC" - that's the "New Stuff for Pleasing this Cool Cat" charity. Remember to dress in black and white as passers-by will then be far easier to emotionally blackmail into donating their cash. Your humiliated parents will be bundling you into their car faster than a news reporter in the Gaza strip.

- Threaten your folks with the promise that you'll never leave home unless they provide you with a big enough income to start investing in I.S.A.'s (huh?!) which can eventually be invested in your first property, probably a mansion. Or squat. (I.S.A.'s actually stand for "I'll Spend it on Alcohol").

- Beg your parents to throw your landmark 16th or 18th birthday party (and 11th, 12th, 13th, 14th, 15th, 17th, 19th) *at home*. You see, it was previously believed that these major parties were traditionally thrown in lavish venues purely to avoid the home being trashed; this is incorrect - parents have, in the past, agreed to spending large sums on these dos purely to avoid their peers, and yours, seeing how crummy your home is. Your parents will shower you with pocket money, *and* you'll get a blinging party at the local golf club.

- Start hanging out with tramps and Eastern European immigrants, claiming to your parents that these poor people make you feel cosy and warm about how lucky you are to live in such relatively materialistic family. Ballsderdash - you know full well that your parents'll be terrified that your new "friends" will steal all their stuff, and will consequently shower you with loads of money and electrical items in the hope that it will 'buy you' some better-off friends.

How Trendy Leftie Parents Try To Abuse Their Teenagers

Unfortunately, some trendy middle-class parents may futilely attempt to resist your financial demands on the grounds that if you got yourself *a part-time job* you would gain self-worth, independence and pride. Er, no you wouldn't. You'd get dark circles from having to get up. And sore feet from possibly having to stand up!!!!! Your oldies are just jealous because when they were your age, if they wanted any money they had to go up the chimneys. Blimey, it's just as well you weren't a Teen a couple of decades ago, because you'd **never** get your fat arse up there. Mind you, imagine… all that soot on your body would look like one killer tan. *And* you'd smell like one amazing chain smoker. Huh, your parents don't know how lucky they were.

Of course, if your cruel hippie parents try this 'boost your self-esteem by getting a job' trick on you, just pretend that you can't possibly spend any of your free time working because you need every spare moment to study and therefore, get into a decent university. Incidentally, it *can* be a good idea to actually go to university - even a proper hard one - as there's plenty of sex, drugs, alcopops and lie-ins to be had; plus, it'll financially cripple your parents whilst you're there.

How To Stand On Your Own Two Idle Feet And Get A Part-Time Job*

There are pro and cons to getting a part-time job to supplement your high income.

The Pro
   1. Money.

The Cons
   2. Getting up.
   3. Staying up.
   4. Communicating with others.
   5. Naff uniforms.
   6. Loss of precious time that could have been spent terrorising your family.
   7. Loss of precious time that could have been spent terrorising your friends.

So, as you can clearly see, there's actually naff all in it for you to make working part-time worth it - unless, of course, the job's in a *busy* burger joint or clothes shop... if you catch the drift (pst. that's what rucksacks were invented for). Besides, today's namby-pamby, politically correct climate means there are probably lots of laws making child labour and exploitation far more challenging for the hard done by employer. So, if your parents try threatening to cut off your weekly bottomless-pocket money if you *don't* get a job, then inform them of these Europeany laws against illegal child labour (your thicko parents won't be any the wiser...).

The E.U. Legal-ish Guide to Child Slavery

A) Pre-16 year olds are now protected against *"The Newspaper Round Rip-Off"*. Quite frankly, you'd be financially and emotionally better off working as Henry 8th's food tester (at least you get to die when the food's sucks - not like your Mum's borderline poisoned muck, *and* it's far better way to go than the pussing bubonic plague). So, ignore your parents' shallow claims that it's a well-known fact all youngsters who are entrepreneurial enough to do a paper round end up successful and rich - that's rubbish, you'll end up cold and wet. Retaliate with two simple words… "child abduction". Long live the lie-in.

B) 13-16 year olds can no longer by exploited by *"The Odd-Jobs for Loose Change Scandle"*. This is the *most heinous* illegal form of child labour (even more so than sweatshops in China) as the pay is pure crud; and, **more** importantly loose change *weighs a lot* - so if you're male it makes your pockets sag unfashionably, or if you're female, the small change takes up valuable room in your handbag that should be saved for flavoured lip glosses and flavoured condoms (tip: flavour your own condoms using your lip glosses - not only will they taste *much* better, you'll also come back up with glistening lips). However, there is an upside to this Rip-Off because if you do the chore *really badly*, your parents will eventually pay you more **not to** do the odd job.

C) 16+ years can no longer be oppressed by "**The Saturday Job in A Shop Scam**". Ironically, though, this has nothing to do with the minimum wage effectively being slave labour; if you lived in Africa where everything is dirt cheap you'd happily slave away for £5.50 - you could live like Katie Price out there! No, the truth is that no-one on the planet wants to be served by a surly, rude, sneering Teenager, such as yourself. Besides, not having a Saturday Job actually keeps your Dad sane and in the marriage, because the more time he has to spend working to keep you in the lifestyle to which you demand to be accustomed, then the less time has to spend at home with you and your Mum.

The *Only* Time In Your Life When You'll Want To Get A Job
When you turn 18, you can offset the terrifying knowledge that your best-looking years are now *behind you* with the fact that you're now legally old enough to have *The Best Job In The World.* Clearly, though, these jobs are highly desired and only ever given to only the best-looking - mingers need not apply**. YOU ARE NOW LEGALLY OLD ENOUGH TO SERVE ALCOHOL. This entitles you to:

- Get drinks bought for you - even off dodgy arseholes, a free shot's free shot, right?
- Down spirits straight from the optics when your boss's back is turned. It's amazing

how there's physically no room in your body for vegetables, but your legs suddenly become hollow when there's booze to be necked.
- Take your pick of the most drunken customers to get off with.

In fact, who cares what the pay is? Offer to work for free. Pay them - thanks to your parents, you're already loaded.

*Ha ha, got you. Obviously, this Bible isn't going to advocate you getting a part-time job, it was a cheap verbal trick to give you a cool adrenalin rush.
** If you are a ming, you could easily still get a bar job in a holiday camp... because all the clientele are equally ugly.

How To Make Heaps Of Dosh Without <u>Ever</u> Getting A Job

Your parents are always banging on about how quickly you've grown up (though not fast enough for their liking - you're still sponging at home). Exactly. So, why should you get a part-time job in your Teens because this'll only give you a horrid taste of what it's going to be like as an adult and having to work in a job you hate, for shit money. *Not working is protecting your precious innocence.* You should aspire to put off working for a living until you're at least 27, when either the 'Jobstart'

Nazis start threatening to cut off your arms (let them - then you can claim loads of disability benefits) and your dole money, or you finally make it on to "Big Brother" and obviously win the prize money.

How To Acquire Money Without Technically Stealing
Besides, you're more than sly enough to make loads of cash from enterprising ventures that would have the 'Dragon's Den' team bending over forwards to invest in your genius.

1. *The Changing Room Change Con* - Whilst fat people are ripping off their clothes in a deluded hopeful frenzy to see if that (way too small) sale bargain fits, or in their flabby embarrassed race to leave the communal changing room asap, hundreds of pounds in loose change falls on the skin-debris covered carpet. Finders thievers. Remember to choose upmarket shops like the ones you take your mum to when *she's* paying (like Harrods), and not the cheapies you shop in when it's your money. You can then exchange this annoyingly huge amount of coinage at charity machines in supermarkets... to stop the machines from fleecing you for a percentage of your hard-fumbled cash, throw down some foreign coins to confuse it.

2. ***The Family Function Fiddle*** - Weddings, christenings, birthdays, funerals… at last, there *is* a valid reason to attend these mind-numbing functions. As the "grown-ups" get more and more legless, they'll start dancing like lunatics, then watch the money fly from their fake designer pockets - they always have lots of big notes to look flash in front of their distant family. Try using a discreet trawler fishing net to capture the bootie… and what fun if you pretend the notes are like organic salmon swimming gloriously upstream to get their heads bashed in before they lay their eggs. Your newly inherited small fortune will *just* about make up for the humiliation and grossness of seeing your parents' slow dance.

3. ***The Seasonal Events Scam*** - You're *never* too old to go carol singing, do penny for the Guy or trick or trick or treating (sweeties can be sold on for a large profit to the greedy fat kids who are starved of love and affection at home). All these clever forms of begging are **easy money** - people will pay you *to go away*. Furthermore, your divvy soft mum'll think you're trying to recapture your long-lost childhood, which gives you huge leeway to misbehave later. Indeed, to maximise profits:

   a) At Xmas sing so baaaaaaaaaaadly that Simon Cowell would want to give you a record deal.

b) At Trick or Treat threaten to set the Guy alight - or yourself (especially if it's cold) - if they don't give you any money.

c) At Halloween just look really scary on your neighbours doorsteps... so there's no need to dress up.

Plus, if you perform any of the above begs at the *wrong time* *of the year*, your victims'll think you're a bit simple and double the money.

4. **The Piggy Bank Racket** - Currently in the world, there remains enough small change in ungrateful children's piggy banks to get rid of the entire Third World Debt. So that should just about see you through the next couple of weeks, then. To locate these piggy banks all you have to do is offer your services as a babysitter - cheapskate adults will jump at the chance of not having to pay for an expensive agency sitter; and in addition to Robin Hooding the piggy banks, you'll get to raid their fridges and wardrobes too. Plus, one of the parents will probably make a pass at you when they take you home.

5. **The Benches Sting** - Possibly your easiest, most reliable and biggest source of income. As your mates get more and more drunk on cheap cider at the park bench, and start performing breath-taking stunts like

handstands or playing kiss chase, they'll lose <u>all</u> the money that's been pilfered from their parents from *their baggy pockets*. You could even just *put your hands in* those ridiculously baggy trousers (they won't feel a thing - and even if they do they'll be too busy enjoying it to stop you); or, raid their handbags whilst they're drunkenly snogging and busily concentrating on *not* puking. This is absolutely NOT technically stealing as they have done this to you before, and you to them, and them to you etcetera. Besides, it's all your parents' money anyway. So, basically, you're recycling, you hippie, you. To cancel this act of goodness out, you'd better smash on your friend's nostrils with your medallion ring.

How To Enjoy Any Grandparents Who Are Vaguely Still Alive

If all the above **fail** to generate enough loot to fund your expensive loafstyle, there is one desperate measure you can resort to... but only if you're hardcore. Visit your doting grandparents. They're *desperate* to make you stay with them for a little but longer, so will give you some of the cash from under their piss-stained mattress. However, do NOT attempt to endure these visits if you can't stand other people's wet farts, the singing of war songs, and multi-orifice dribblings.

If you don't have any grandparents still alive (how selfish of them to snuff it and leave you alone with your moaning parents... mind you, that's probably why humans have evolved to die in old age, to escape having given life to such annoying idiots), then visit an old people's home. They'll leave you *everything* in their will to spite their children for putting them in an old folks' home and not lovingly caring for them at home. Again, this amazing act of kindness will probably get you an automatic pass to boring heaven - this is to be avoided at all costs, so whilst you're there, rub the polyester entombed O.A.P.S. with a balloon and stick the grannies and gramps to the ceiling. Don't stand underneath, though.

7 BIRTHDAYS

How to have the Worst Birthday Ever!

Huh! What? Eh? Why, oh why, would you *want* to have a dreadful birthday??! Surely, you'll be enjoying your special day because you get to receive all the presents everyone couldn't afford to get you at Xmas; plus your birthday takes you *one year nearer* to forcing your parents into buying you your own pad!? No, have a Crappy Birthday instead… ahhh, the cunning is inspirational. You see, your parents are becoming increasingly aware that, with every passing birthday, they're *getting closer and closer to snuffing it…* so trying to enjoy *your* birthday is just one of their futile, desperate attempts to make the most of whatever time they have left. Ruin it.

Also, your parents' efforts to make your birthdays fabulous have nothing whatsoever to do with them showing how much they love you. They don't. They are simply trying to erase the bitter memories of their own rubbish birthdays given by *their* parents; furthermore, if your grandparents are still alive (just), your parents' lavish birthday celebrations are also spitefully aimed at showing your grand-parents how emotionally cold and - more importantly - materialistically mean *they* were to *your parents*.

How To Spot The Warning Signs Your Parents Are Planning To Hijack *Your* Special Day For *Themselves*

1. They don't 'accidentally' wake you up before midday by having the audacious cheek to noisily tip-toe downstairs.

2. Your Mum'll bring you a grease-fest of breakfast in bed (actually, she's hoping the fatty glory will give you acne so you'll be as unpopular as her when she was your age).

3. They'll give you the extortionate presents you actually requested, instead of their usual fungus-inducing slipper socks and creepy craft kits.

4. They'll let you invite as many friends as you like to your birthday shindig (just be wary of their attempts to flirt with your pals… your parents will each likely pick on your uglier friends because they think it'll increase their chances, therefore, dump your uglier friends).

5. They'll attempt to pay you lavish, flattering compliments like, "You're not as stupid as your Dad," "You're not as ugly as your Mum," or "There must have been a mix-up at the hospital when you were born."

How To Help <u>Your</u> Parents Show Up <u>Their</u> Parents
This is the **only** time in your life when you should help your parents… in fact, the ***only*** reason you're assisting them is because *you* need retribution on your grandparents for all those wet farts they've let out in front of you. (Incidentally, you're only angry with the 'grands' due to jealousy… you're not old enough yet to make your own wet farts, despite your attempts to foster the perfect digestive environment with beans and fizzy pop).

However, it is *most unwise* to let your nana and/or gramps become suspicious of you because they'll be snuffing it soon and it's not too late to have *you* written out of their will. Hopefully though, successfully helping your parents annoy their parents will probably result in *them* being written out, so all your grand-parents worldly goods will be left directly to you. (Ebay). Consequently, you should submit a birthday itinerary to your 'obliging' parents and empower them to spend the maximum amount of money and effort on sweet, kind you.

Again, as always, why bother writing your own grasping birthday schedule when you can rip out this all-encompassing template using your idle fingers (save your teeth for precious burger wear and tear).

Birthday Itinerary for

_____

(they won't remember your name)

on

_____

(they won't remember when it is)

12.01am - 12.01pm **Sleeping**

12.02 - 12.03pm **Breakfast in bed - Burgers only**

12.04 - 1.45pm **Presents**
~~One~~ all of the following choices to be selected: a *non-eco* car
(too chuffing ugly), a loft conversion (it's in everyone's
interests for you to be as far away from everyone as possible),
teeth whitening (stains from coffee, red wine, nicotine and
gobstoppers are so career-damaging), overseas apartment to
be used only by you and your pals (hey, it's *definitely* in
everyone's interests for your entire family for you to holiday
separately), and your own novelty doorbell (that way, you'll
know when it's your friends and, therefore, in your interests to
get to the door first).

1.46 - 1.47pm **Lunch in bed - Burgers only**

1.48 - 6.35pm **Afternoon Birthday Activity**
~~One~~ all of the following items to be selected, with unlimited
number of friends and hangers-on invited to make me look
really popular: Alton Towers, Thorpe Park, Chessington
World of Adventures, Legoland, Drayton Park, Pleasure
Beach, that Thomas Tank Engine ride at our local Asda.
Helicopter limo ride to be provided for transportation.

6.36 - 6.36pm **Dinner - Burgers only, followed by E-
number heaven cake** *(under no circumstances is cake to be
home-made or joke candles to be used).

6.37 - 11.59 and 59 seconds **Mind your own sodding
business**. I've made you *look like* you're amazing parents in
front of your own, so now it's ME ME ME time. Nah nah.

How To Blow Out Your Birthday Cake Candles
Traditionally, when you blow out your candles you're supposed to make a secret wish which will, of course, come true... But, you don't need to waste this wish on begging to become rich and famous, *obviously* you're going to be a 2-bit celebrity, anyway. Instead, you should wish for:
* Not to smell.
* Not to be unpopular.
* Not to be fat (or hey, settle for *not so fat* - that cake fairy aint no miracle worker).
* If female, the padded g-string to be invented.
* If male, the self-cleaning g-string to be invented.
* World peace, because then there's a greater likelihood that sweets from war-torn countries can be imported into the UK/your face.

Alas, you're at an age when you're supposed to pretend that silly candles are for children or the pretentious offspring of parents who still love them enough to go to the trouble of actually buying candles, but there remain many advantages to letting your mum continue to put candles on your novelty 40,000 calorie cake:
* You can blow them out in the direction of the person you like least - the smoke in their eyes will really sting.
* You can also slyly spit a bit when you're blowing so your secret enemy gets a phlegmy shower.

- Successfully blowing out your candles in one huge puff will prove to your parents that your smoking hasn't damaged your lungs. Yet.
- Your Mum'll burn her fingers trying to light them. So will your Dad when he takes over in his usual sexist manner. HA.
- Encouraging a friend with a monobrow to help you blow them out can result in their werewolf appendage becoming horrifically singed and, therefore, aesthetically improved.

However, now you're supposed to be a coolio Teenager there'll be that annoying moment after wheezing out your candles when your parents blatantly hurry to the cake cutting in a vain attempt to stop you making your wish. Cheek. Maybe you'll actually want your wish to be a *reward* for them looking after you... morbidly obese chance. Actually, they're **dreading** what you'll wish for, knowing that you'll be incapable of keeping it a secret and will promptly tell everyone what you greedily desire; this, in turn, will force them *to cough up again* in order to further annoy their stingy parents. But what on earth can you wish for, seeing as you've already got *whatever* you've *ever* asked for, surely there's *nothing left*? Not true, so not true...

How To Make The Bestest Birthday Wishes Ever Wever

1. Wish to adopt an orphaned black child from a foreign place - it's the latest fashion accessory. Better get its moanie parents to agree to this first.

2. Wish to adopt a monkey that's been cruelly kept as a performing pet - they're well funny.

3. Wish to be cryogenically frozen - *now* - because you're looks are definitely in their prime; also, your future distant relatives are bound to better than the one's you've got now, so you'd rather live with them.

How To Cut Your Birthday Cake Unfairly

It goes without saying that you have no intention whatsoever of sharing your cake with any of your party guests. After all, it's the only time you eat a balanced meal so it would be selfish of your guests to want to thievishly take that away from you: cake has Carbohydrates (flour), Protein (egg), Fats (hydrogenated cancer oil), Minerals (salt) and Vitamins (orange food colouring). However, some of your guests may evilly withhold your presents until they've received their cake, so you'll need to know how to cut the cake - you've never held a food knife before. (To avoid actually letting them have their cake and eat it, attach invisible string/ snot to their paper plates and whiz the cake away as soon as your hand makes contact with your present).

The cake should be *cut in direct proprotion to their BMI* (that's Bonking Mating Index). So, if someone has a *large* BMI give them a **huge** piece (to try and make them fancy you), and if they have a *small* BMI give them a **smaller** piece (to try and *stop* them inevitably fancying you). But if you have any-barely alive grandparents present, give them the **largest** piece of cake as this may predispose you to them in their will (don't worry, they won't fancy you).

The Stinkybunkle Hidden Cost of Teenage Birthdays

There is one heinous, monstrous issue you'll have to deal with as a Teenager… no, not that you'll secretly fancy naff celebrities (actually, you'll fancy *everyone*), but that you'll no longer receive any more really wicked cards with cool age badges on them. AGHHHHH. You never know when you might need a sharp pin to defend yourself. Luckily, the benevolent greetings card industry - anticipating your sadness - has wisely foreseen to invent "coming of age" merchandise to help you celebrate those important teen birthdays… those plastic gold keys can actually hurt quite a bit if you aim for the eyes…

How To Ruthlessly Exploit Your 'Coming Of (R)Age' Birthdays

Eh? What does *coming of age* mean? Is this a sexy-wexy reference? Nah, according to the modern bible, Wikipedia, it's a "rite of passage that marks a change in a person's social or sexual status. The term was popularised by the French ethnographer Arnold van Gennep (1873-1957), in the early part of the twentieth century. Further theories were developed in the 1960s by Mary Douglas and Victor Turner." Huh? You wot?! In plain Estuary, that means you'll suffer from:

- Zits, greasy hair and general ugliness from hormonal imbalances (you'll deal… just surround yourself with fouler 'friends').

- Violent mood swings due to excessive e-number consumption. Silver linings.

- Sudden 'growth spurts' that make new clothes purchases somewhat tight (not that the garments being too small will stop you wearing them; and of course the tightness has nothing to do with burgers.)

- Eating disorders (hopefully bulimia - at least you'll get to eat).

- An unquenchable thirst for fizzy drinks that may make your hair go curly/frizzy due to the build up of bubbles in your body.

- A penchant for street corners.

To help you survive these, ironically satisfying, events in these formative years, the greetings cards industry picked as many of the years between 13 and 19 as they dared, to help you turn these landmark birthdays into hilariously expensive excuses to milk your parents for all their worth. And then some.

Firstly, there's the becoming a teenager at **13**. Then, there's the **16th** and **18th** birthdays. Ker-ching-ching… *you get to ask for some seriously big presents on these special occasions*. (And let's not forget the 14th, 15th, 17th and 19th birthdays). These landmark gift opportunities don't *even* have *anything* to do with your parents trying to show up *their* parents; **this** is entirely because your parents' social standing **depends** on what they give you for these milestone birthdays. So hopefully, your birthday's at the *end* of the school year (if you're having trouble working that out - it's August) which gives you a *whole year* to tell your folks what all the other parents' have lavishly bought your peers. Then, when it's your birthday, your present will have had to escalate into something major. If your birthday is unluckily in the autumn (September+), it's certainly worth doing a bunk, faking amnesia and reinventing yourself, so you can move your birthday to the *end* of the summer (June+). Although, because you'll be the 'youngest' in the year, expect to be bullied and have all your great presents nicked off you.

How To Milk Turning <u>13</u>
When your parents reached this important milestone back in the last century, life was easy. *All* new teenagers had to worry about was changing their middle parting into a cooler side one and getting short socks instead of long ones (actually, many Teens simply stretched their legs on a torture rack to give *the illusion* of longer legs/shorter socks). Nowadays, you can get stabbed with a sharp crispy French fry for simply having a naff ring tone. Naturally then, your parents are terrified for your life... not because they'd miss you when you're gone, but because the thousands of pounds

worth of kit in your room will only fetch peanuts second-hand.

Consequently, on this important birthday you can demand *anything you fancy* - especially if it's for your room - because your parents will hope that this will entice you to permanently stay in there, and, thus *avoid being murdered.*

But where's the fun in so easily getting your heart's desires?! Think smart... now you're officially a Teenager, it's notoriously known that your sexy hormones start going bonkers which gives you legal permission to be as embarrassing as you like to your cringing parents. They're not to know that - due to them letting you watch too much grown-up TV - you started puberty at seven... they thought you were just being a little shit back then.

How To Humiliate Your Parents Effectively
So, unlike your usual birthday and Christmas list summons which are more effective when written (besides, they're much too lengthy to memorise), *13th birthday requests* are best *spoken* directly to your parents as this'll massively intensify their mortification. Also, break with tradition and don't stomp off after yelling at your parents... instead, remain glued to the spot and cook eggs and bacon on their faces as they slowly die of embarrassment (remember to check they have a will first). Try asking for:

1) A book on human reproduction - illustrated with real photographs ... 'humorous' cartoons won't cut it.
2) If you're a girl (regardless of your actual size), a trainer bra in 34DD. Picking on Dad when he's alone will reward you with the funniest, most horrified response and biggest gift voucher.
3) If you're a boy, a jock strap in extra large - again, use this sting on Mum when she's alone and expect a large envelope stuffed with her secret housekeeping.
4) An empty wine bottle (seeing as they have *so* many) so you can play spin the bottle in break-time, bunking off, lessons, or arcade.
5) KY Jelly. Requesting this is more humiliating to your parents than asking for contraception because it suggests that you're quite advanced. UGH, of course, you're not - rumpy pumpy is disgusting. However, walk around with a smirk on your face anyway to intimidate your frigid parents. You can actually use the stupid KY jelly on your feet to pretend you're an Olympic ice skater.
6) A series of sessions with a psychotherapist (if your wearied folks actually agree to this, don't worry, you'll be able to moan - lying down - for a whole hour).

How To Maximise Turning 'Sweet' 16

Sweet 16 and never been pissed? Ha, that's what you're naïve parents think. You're now *illegally permitted* to frequent pubs in inner cities and the rural countryside: inner city publicans need your large amounts of pocket money to pay off the gang warlords and police, whilst the countryside landlords desperately need to lure young folk back to their dying community. So in a way, becoming embarrassingly paralytic in these dens of iniquities is a selfless act of charity because you're helping them stay financially afloat. Furthermore, when you tell your parents that you're going round to Neville's to do your physics homework they're only *pretending* to believe you - they couldn't care less where you are, so long as you're not at home getting in the way of them arguing over who had the chicken sandwich at the Keele service station on June 14th 1973.

But the niftiest thing about this pivotal birthday is that you are now *legally allowed to marry with your parents' permission*. Stuff your birthday. Think of the wedding present list!!!!

How To Get Even More Presents Than A 16th By Getting Married

In fact, your folks'll be trying to find you a spouse faster than you can say "Pakistani arranged marriage"... after all, you could be out of their hair for good! Well, more like a year... before your 'marriage' goes hideously wrong. (**Warning**: pre-nups, pre-nups! You don't want your 'spouse' to get your I-pod, limited edition Hi-Tech trainers or Dairylea stash.)

Similarily, if you're working class your parents'll be only too happy to chuck you down the aisle as they just love a wedding reception - all that booze to drown their many sorrows. Then, if you're middle or upper class, they'll *also* too eagerly agree: your ooh la la education has *only* been grooming you for marrying above yourself so that you'll be quids in after the divorce - your parents then intend to successfully sue you for reimbursement of education/lifestyle fees. (Therefore, abduct their family heirlooms now).

How To Really Cash In On Your 16th

To thoughtfully and selflessly help you parents show up all your friends' parents, simply scream for:

1. A Lamborghini. Well, you're almost 17, and you're legally allowed to drive it on private land like car parks at night, or pavements. It's also scientifically obvious that you're far more likely to look after a *really* expensive car as uncool dents and scratches will make you look like a clumsy, can't-drive-for-toffee oldie.
2. A motorcycle. Suddenly, your request for a sexy car will seem like the sensible option to your parents.
3. A sex change. Temporarily pretending you want this time-off-school op will make your parents suddenly realise just how lucky they are that you're really quite a normal vile teenager.

4. Guitar/drum/piano/singing lessons - it's not too late to become Robbie Williams/Madonna/Same Difference.
5. Or, this next option is *far cheaper* than all the above ideas *put together*: fees to a London stage school. After all, it's not talent that takes you to the top, just going to the right school. Or having #good hair.

How To Make An Absolute Killing On Your <u>18</u>th (without even using your blade)

Apparently, you're now legally entitled to vote. Whatever... those politicians are all the same: ugly, badly-dressed, and over twenty. *However,* if you now **pretend** to become interested in politics to your parents, you can manipulate them any which way you please (including present demands), because:

- They'll be terrified that you're showing signs of intelligence which will make arguing with you even more impossible than usual.
- They'll cleverly be hoping that *going along with you* in your political awakening will actually *put you off* becoming one of those embarrassing political activists who ruin zombiefying shopping centres at the weekend... nothing spoils a teenager's cultish tendencies than parents showing unconditional support.
- They'll be able to start bragging to your family and neighbours that you know how to write an "X"... on a ballot paper. (An "X"

is one of those things you put after you've scrawled the name of the person you fancy.)

- They'll start fantasising that you'll eventually become an MP so spoiling you *now* may later influence you to pass a law that means parents of MPs get extra large portions from the takeaway. (If you do accidentally become an MP*, *pass* this law as this will speed up your receipt of the contents of their will). *It's defo worth becoming an MP: they get whopping salaries for doing bugger all, they receive backhanders from big business and scoff lots of fancy buffet platters for lunch.

How To Scam The Most O.T.T. 18th Birthday Presents

In your *pre-teen* years you could happily rely on the Argos catalogue to satisfy all your birthday pressie needs. Then, for your *pre-18th* birthdays, you could trawl the internet for expensive, ludicrous exotic purchases. Technically, there's absolutely *nothing* left to ask for. When has that ever stopped you before? Demand:

1. A round the world trip: how else will you know about the political, cultural, economic, social bio-geographical and sexy workings of the adult world?! After all, your parents have clearly been too ignorant to impart any worldly knowledge on you. Your folks will begrudgingly cough up, hoping that you'll

fall in lust with someone oversees who'll keep you captive for the rest of your life.

2. Your own personal TV company: then it can make programmes all about *you*, thus *guaranteeing* you fame and misfortune. For example:

    a) 'I'm a Celebrity, Get Me Into Here": how to gatecrash showbiz parties around the world (not India) (or Africa) (Or Asia).

    b) "Big Boozer": a fly on the wall reality show featuring y o u on the razzle.

    c) "Strictly Come Shopping": a dance series showing your n i f t y f o o t w o r k when hunting for clothes and accessories.

    d); "Britain's Next Top Hangover": a competition featuring y o u a n d y o u r friends in the pursuit of the biggest headache...

3. Never mind your parents buying you your first home, that's way too easy. If they *really* want to make a sound investment, they should build you a prison... you'll make a fortune hiring out the suites to the government now that there's a prison space crisis. Alternatively, it's a wicked party venue.

4. A franchise to your favourite fast food outlet that only employs people with obsessive compulsive disorder: the food may be slow, but at least you know it will be clean (that's polite talk for not being spat in.)

5. Shares in the slave gold mining industry - not only will this entitle you to cheap, cheap gold bling but you'll be able to go on holidays to these slippy canyons where you can go mud-tobogganing.

How To Shrewdly Capitalise On The In-Betweenee Birthdays

But, boo hoo, what if you're turning 14, 15, 17 or 19? Surely your parent's second mortgage can't stretch as far as supplying extravagant presents here too?! Tell them about third mortgages. On these birthdays, you simply ask for goods that **don't** depreciate in value like the stereotypical TVs, DVD players, games consoles and liver donation... besides, your parents' will *automatically* give you these items *between* birthdays to try and get you out of their hair. In fact, almost impress your parents by wisely demanding items that'll only ever *increase* in value:

- Diamonds: and none of this high street flawed tat, your ice must come from Hatton Gardens, Londidium.
- First editions of Harry Potter (don't panic, you don't need to read them - they'll be much more valuable if pristine).
- Fifty acres on the moon, well, enough for the world cup to be held here in 2763: this investment will be inherited by your future relatives and make them so rich they'll be grateful enough

to unfreeze you from your cryogenic state (then, of course, you'll steal all this money back).
- A Lloyds bank safety deposit box so you can stash *anything* you ever touch because when you're mega famous these artefacts will be ***priceless***.

How To Have An Showbizzy Birthday Party

Just as your parents social standing depends on the presents they supply on your coming of age birthdays, ***your social standing*** also unfortunately ***depends entirely*** on the parties you throw. Just supplying food with enough e-numbers to bring someone out of a coma simply won't impress your peers anymore. Nor will employing a scary 'fun' clown whom you can taunt with perv/failed actor jibes when the adults' backs are turned. Neither will swopping the fizzy pop for ancient bottles of alcohol from the oldies drinks cabinet. And unless your party bags are stuffed with Prada, Burberry or fairground thinning mirrors, forget them. You may not have exactly the same budget as the Beckhams or Elton, but that's not going to stop your peers expecting a lavish showbiz affair. Indeed, it's probably easier to become one of the 1,376 Teens who go missing ever year.

How To Host The *Early-Teens* Birthday Bash
You may well be a very advanced Teenager for your early Teens: quite the little grown-up in

stropping, sulking and stomping, but your patronising, suffocating parents will probably still *insist that you must have your party in your very humble hovel*. Ughh. They may also unreasonably argue that you're *still* too young to stay out until 3am with your friends. Patriarchal oppressors. Stinky meanies.

Their embarrassing house party stance **isn't** because they're naively reluctant to accept you're no longer their little child (although, of course, you're getting harder to throw upstairs); or that they love stuffing their faces with your additive-trippy, party food… No, your parents are just plain tightwads; they're deliberately avoiding treating you to the modern birthday party option favoured by the better parents of your peers: Ten pin bowling, skating, theme parks, or Disney, Florida (not Paris). Your abusively neglectful parents know that these *out-of-home* birthday parties are a financial snowball. *Wehey, that's the point.*

But the cleverererer amongst you will realise that the extreme expense of these birthday celebrations will ultimately be funded by your inheritance… you're potentially squandering your only future source of income… not to worry - due to your unhealthy lifestyle, you'll snuff it *long* before your parents. Ironically, though, it's actually *in your interests* to willingly agree to have your early Teen parties at home… so by the time you turn eighteen, your parents aren't morally entitled to stop you demanding that you deserve to go to Ibiza to celebrate.

How To Host Without Looking Like A Stupid Kid Loser

Of course, you're going to need to be extremely cool and smart if you're going to stop your peers wedgieing/stoning you for having a crap house birthday party.

A) Pretending To Play Traditional Party Games

For starters, if you ever-so-slightly adapt the following traditional party games your Mum's always embarrassingly keen to start, your parents will at least retreat to the out-of-date kitchen… leaving you free to play Frenchie chase:

- *Pin the Tail on the Donkey* - turn into 'Pin the Poop on the Donkey' by swopping the tail for a cut-out turd that you've made lovingly during double maths. Why not make it scratch and sniff by guffing on it.
- *Pass the Parcel* - becomes 'Pass the Barbie'. Each time the music stops, a layer of clothing is removed from the doll. If a player giggles childishly they have to do a forfeit… like down a bowl of jelly in one. If you suspect your guests are giggling deliberately, give them a wedgie.
- *Hide and Seek* - this is adapted into 'Hide and *Reek'*. When you're in your hiding place and just about to be discovered, you let out one almighty fartypops… then, when the Seeker opens the door, they'll be hit by an almighty deadly waft. The nauseous Seeker

gets a bonus prize if they can guess what you've eaten.

- *Musical Chairs* - make your own music: fart music. If, when the music stops, a guest fails to fart on command upon sitting down they're eliminated... farts sound *even more* hilarious when you're sitting down, especially if you're posh or chav enough to have leather chairs. In fact, if you *are* posh, your guests *only* came to your party because you *do* have leather chairs for guffing on.

B) Providing The Perfect Birthday Spread

This is a piece of cake. Literally. You just need loads of cakes, supplemented with biscuits and salted snacks like butter. Your guests will also be happiest if you also provide novelty tableware, say, like a trough.

C) Issuing The Blingest Party Bags

This is obviously the most important part of your party your guests, as this is a reflection of how much money you've spent on them. Forget bubbles, jokes, puzzles and a slice of cake wrapped in soggy napkin, you need to fill the bags with large sums of cash (pilfered from *their* parents' purses/wallets) to avoid having your head dunked in a toilet the next day. (This'd be annoying because you deliberately left a floater there earlier).

How To Host An Ace Party In Your *Late Teens*

Opposite sex. Smuggled alcohol. Loud music. Crisps. Dips. Alcohol. Dark room. Enough said.

8 CHRISTMAS

How to Write a Truly Touching Father Christmas* Letter (A.K.A. How To Make Sure You Get Exactly What You Chuffing Well WANT)

Ahhhhhh, Christmas is a time for receiving and receiving - and, in particular, receiving *exactly* what you demanded. People should be treating you with the love, respect and fear that you deserve by showering you with the expensive and unnecessary goods you jolly well screamed for. Now *that's* the real meaning of Christmas. But, let's acne-face it, in the past, shouting your festive material desires at your parents and threatening them with abusive behaviour hasn't really worked (they've only given in to 97% of your demands), so wise up, you'll need to take a fresh, genius approach if you're going to get that platinum zit picker on Crimbo morning... You're going to need to write the *perfect* Father Christmas letter...

How To Convince Your Oldies That You <u>Do</u> Believe In Santa, 'Onest

Before you even put finger to keyboard or mobile, though, you'll need to be truly crafty - you're parents will be well suspicious of your letter-writing motives. After all, when you were *just three* years old, you informed your parents that:

a) Santa doesn't exist: he was simply a clever marketing invention by Coca-Cola to sell their sexy shaped bottled beverage; before adding, that it's Coco-Cola's fault that no wonder Teen Boys have a penchant for holding their hand in this shape.

b) They should just grow up and stop mentally abusing you with this Santa lie in order to try and relive their sad, underprivileged childhood through you... then, taunting them with this number - 0800 1111. (Don't forget, Childline's number can be quoted *not only* through your childhood and Teen years, but well into your thirties because you'll still have the mental and emotional age of a 7 year old).

c) You're going to get up at 3am regardless of a fictional fat git coming down the chimney in the night, just to annoy them.

d) In this day and age, they should be much more responsible about you sitting on strange men's laps.

How To Sweet-Talk Your Folks Before You *Even Write The Letter*

1) Inform your parents that you only pretended you thought Santa didn't exist because you'd heard on the toddler milk-vine that the Santa in the local garden centre was a paedophile so you were just trying to protect yourself from molestation and lifelong psychological scars.

2) But more importantly, you were *protecting them* from the entry fee which was an evil rip-off because the present was crap - *and* a death-trap. (Hmmm, ask yourself if they had an inkling of the Teenager you'd 'blossom' into and was this lethal toy *their* cunning plan for getting shot of you? Store that gripe up for their deathbed inquisition).

3) Eat all your vegetables during the week prior to submitting your greedy demands (cover broccoli with bogies to make them more bearable)... this'll put your Mum in such a good, pushover mood that she'll also give in to you eloping with your art teacher.

4) Absolutely, don't write next year's Father Christmas letter on the *26th of December* as this look a tad like you're really hacked off with what you've just got (of course, you've every right to be outraged that they didn't give you a car, boarding school fees or a ratoodle (that's a cross between a rat and a poodle), but button it, think smarter - wait till the 27th).

5) Ask your Dad if you can make a gigantic Christmas paper chain with him - he'll agree to this tedious chore only to avoid spending his free time with his wife. Then, during this loving and festive charade, slyly cut off all your fingers with a billion paper cuts. Your blame-game-happy mum will be a bit annoyed with your negligent Dad and she'll buy you whatever you've put on your Christmas lists to make him look even more rubbish. (Secretly, they'll both be chuffed that you're fingerless because it's now much more difficult for you to make rude hand gestures at them... ha, you'll find a way round this.)

6) Volunteer to lick all the envelopes for your Mum's thousand Christmas cards... when your tongue drops off through hyper-dehydration, your blame-game-happy Dad will be a bit miffed with her and buy you whatever you've put on your Santa letter, *and then some*, to make your Mum look even more neglectful. (Secretly, they'll both be *really* chuffed that you can no longer speak because you'll won't be able to hurl profanities at them... ha, oh yes you can, with one of those weird-sounding cool voice box simulators like Stevie Hawkins; plus, ironically, it'll make you sound dead clever and, more importantly, evil).

How To Actually Write Your Father Christmas Letter

So, now your frazzled parents are putty in your grasping hands, it's time to create your 'charming' Father Christmas letter. However, as part of the I.T. generation, you won't actually know how to even hold a pencil... you could try pretending writing a letter is like doing graffiti can but you'd need a bloody great piece of paper. So, instead, simply photocopy the following letter template and ask an elderly relative or doddery neighbour to fill in your demands for you. They'll be thrilled to help because not only will it break up the endless lonely hours before they snuff it, but the action of writing also creates friction and, therefore, heat which stops the impoverished shivering creature from dying of hyperthermia. If your unsuspecting accomplice suffers from shaky Parkinson's, be careful that they don't wobble too when writing as this could easily start a fire and burn their freezing house down... well, at least, not before you've read their will.

Dear Father Christmas,

I've been really rather saintly this year:
- when I've sworn at my folks I've sort of apologised within the year.
- I've removed *only* a minimum amount of large notes from my Mum's purse.
- I ate a portion of vegetables on the 16th July (baked beans).
- I've reduced my bitching/sulking/ moaning to just six hours a day.
- I've only slept 18 hours a day.
- Anything I've "borrowed" from friends I've returned broken instead of selling it.

Therefore, this Christmas I'd better get...

ITEM SHOP PRODUCT CODE   COLOUR/ SIZE/STYLE Minimum R.R.P.

How To Be Cleverly Greedy: <u>Under no circumstances</u> put the most expensive item you must-have-or you'll-die-or-worse-cry ***first***... it'll look like you don't care at all that 7,9983,773 poor children in the third world get naff all on Christmas day. Put that item second.

How To Stop Your Present Giver From Making Moronic Stuff-Ups:

Supplying such kind and thoughtful information as product codes, minimum recommended retail price (you don't want any dodgy car boot sale versions - it's impossible to get a refund), or attaching a phone photo of the desired items will help eliminate any selfish mistakes on the present giver's part. Also, indicating the price up front doesn't actually reveal sheer greed or cheek on your part, it simply demonstrates how much they should love you. Besides, they'll naively believe that because your gift requests are so ludicrously expensive that:

- They'll receive a present of equal value in return - hahahahhahaha, you're not *that* good a shoplifter.
- You won't make their life a misery for the following 364 days after Christmas (they clearly suffer from a delusory mental illness).
- They'll hope you'll get mugged by a peer group member which will knock the confidence/horribleness out of you (tcha, you *are* the peer group mugger).

When To Send Your Father Christmas Letter: the most thoughtful time to submit your greedy seasonal thesis is exactly three months before December 25th, because this gives your gift donors' sufficient time to apply for a second mortgage, take out a house-repossessing loan, or flog their organs on the internet to finance your really quite modest desires.

How To Send It: Father Christmas letters are traditionally posted to Greenland, but you should inform your Mother that you're deeply worried about the environmental carbon damage that will result from the air miles, and, instead, suggest that she walks there and delivers it by hand. The majority of Mums will actually *jump* at the chance of a 2,865 mile hike - largely because they know that they've seriously let themselves go since having you and know that their husbands will run off with a younger, slimmer woman if they don't shape up (and then they'll lose the house), but the trek will also mean spending less time with you. If your Mum refuses to go on the hike and insists that Santa's got a fax, it's because your Dad has seriously porked out so she couldn't care less if they get divorced (she's already got a solicitor who knows how to make sure she gets to keep the house anyway).

How To Behave When You Hand Over Your Letter: Act natural (i.e., ungrateful and moody), despite you both secretly knowing that your Mum's only going to photocopy your Father Christmas letter a thousand times and circulate to all your relatives, friends, teachers, neighbours, probation officers, enemies and, indeed, anyone *you've ever met* in the hope that it increases the chances that you get *exactly* what you asked for so you won't bother speaking on Christmas Day. Or, more likely, she'll be crossing her worn-out fingers that you'll be so overwhelmed by the sheer volume of presents that you'll drop down dead.

And How To Guarantee You'll Receive Every Listed Present Demand:
Add a handwritten note on your letter to Santa saying that you're the victim of bullying at school and having some cool presents might make the bullies like you, (this clever strategy will also work on *any* present-giving occasion like birthdays, Easter and Monday mornings).

When Christmas Presents Go Baaaaaaaaaaaad

Despite your best and kindest efforts to help your present donors give you exactly what you want by issuing this very clear wish list, some of these jerks will *still* stuff it up. Either because they're poor/ cheapskates who'd already bought this year's pressie for you during last year's New Year sales of un-shiftable cheap tat (what makes them think they're above getting credit debt like everyone else?). Or because they're deaf, dumb and blind. Or they have a death wish. Or they are terminally ill and hope that acting against your wishes will result in you putting them out of their misery.

How To Teach Them A Lesson They'll Never Forget (though they'll try to with a lobotomy)
Naïve Idiots, they should really know you well enough by now to know that if you don't get on them... who says you don't join in with games at Christmas:

a) Instead of the sixpence, put six-week old bogies in the Crimbo pudding... if you *already* add this textural delight for larks (this is the *real* reason you never want any Christmas pud), then why not also add your cute collection of nine-month old scabs.

b) Remove the air freshener from the loo and seal the window with superglue: when these bad present givers visit the powder room after their turkey and sprout dinner, they'll be horrified at their inability to get rid of the stench, and promptly leave your home (help them evacuate faster by hurling the gift at them as they leave).

c) Put disgusting carrot juice in the Christmas bottle of advocaat, so when they have a seasonal tipple/binge you can giggle knowing that they'll see all the spiders in their room at night whenever they wake up (if you're house is sadly lacking in spiderage, take your scab collection and attach pipe cleaner legs to the 'bodies').

How To Give That Has-Been Santa The Sack
(E.G. Be 100% Sure You Get Your Heart's Desires)
You've long known that the fat git in a red suit dumping presents under the tree is your Dad... you'd know that whiff of B.O. anywhere. If, now in your Teens, your Dad is *still* pretending to be Santa it's only because your Mum is kinky and likes him to dress up for her - your Dad *only* agrees because he mistakenly thinks that she may eventually give it up. Knock this farce on the head by telling your Mum that you're worried that all those mince pies and whiskey for 'Santa' is a recipe for a fatal heart attack. Your Mum will suddenly panic that she'll be left a widow and have to fend for herself. Oh, and you.

Consequently, your Mum'll knock your Dad being Santa on the head faster than OJ Simpson swings a golf-club/hammer. In fact, she'll have to find a way for your idle Dad to do *even less* than he already does at Christmas to try and keep him alive a bit longer. So, for starters, she'll stop deliberately sadistically dragging him round the shops to do Christmas shopping... instead, she'll ***immediately*** lobby all your favourite retailers to start a ***Christmas Teenager Gift List Service***. This *will permanently remove the chance of human error regarding your presents*. Clearly, this service can then be rolled out to include celebrations like Birthdays, Bar mitzvahs and School Suspension Days. Here are the Head Offices of all the relevant retailers your Mother should enlist:

Dixons - Maylands Avenue, Hemel Hempstead, Herts, HP2 7TG

Harrods - 87-135 Brompton Road, Knightsbridge, London, SW1X 7XL

Gucci - Rembrandt Tower, 1 Amstelpein, 1096 HA Amsterdam

Transform Cosmetic Surgery - 22 Wimpole Street, London, W1G 8LD

Weightwatchers - Millennium House, Ludlow Road, Maidenhead, Berkshire, SL6 2SL

Rolex - PO Box 430, 7211 Geneva 24, Switzerland

Ferrari -

H Samuel -

Poundstretchers -

Prada -

Primark - Shit House, Shit Avenue, Shitsville, SH1 TYY

How To *Appear* Grateful When You Receive Your Presents

On Christmas Day it may actually be surprisingly easy to appear happy and grateful for your presents... thanks to all the sneaky drinks you've downed behind your parents' back; but, if you really *are* too young for booze (e.g. you're just 13 and still smart enough to realise that alcohol tastes gross), then you can still achieve 'joyfulness' from a sugar rush off the Crimbo tree's nasty chocolate decorations. So, pretending to be pleased when ripping open your gifts should be a tipsy doddle, but *if* you perform the following routine of *delirious gratitude* on Christmas morning, or whenever you get round to it, ***you'll be allowed to stay out really late on New Year's Eve - say, past 7.45pm.***

However, if you're too young to go out (and get violently sick) on this hallowed night, you can expect your suspicious but proud parents' to reward your impressive display of 'present gratitude' with letting you gobble all your chocolate stockings before Christmas dinner; though when you hit the sugar withdrawal at 7.46pm, your parents will be unjustifiably angry... just remind them that they were your pushers.

How To Give The Xmas Present Opening Performance Of Your Life

You're *already* a skilled actor, having learnt how to pretend to appear devastated when you and your current boy/girlfriend split up (after all, appearing suicidal means your parents give you more chips at dinner, lunch and breakfast). So, you can expect to be awarded an Oscar for performing this sham of a Routine... ***Pre-performance Warning***: Don't, whatever you do, rip off your wrapping paper in a salivating frenzy. You may receive a fatal paper cut.

a) Firstly, you must *gently* unwrap the naff paper, *without tearing,* so it can be used again by your skinflint parents... this paper will *never* actually be used again, but gather dust just like your Mum's 'sexy' underwear. Your tight folks will be most impressed by your ecological thoughtfulness and sudden, gracious maturity. Besides, taking an excessive amount of time may also result in Christmas dinner getting accidentally burnt and having to get a kebab instead.

b) Open your eyes to their widest point (imagine you've just been caught in a man-trap, or worse, been given the finger by E.T.) - this'll look like you're overwhelmed and delighted. Tcha.

c) Blink rapidly as if trying to fight back the tears (try pulling all the hairs from your nostrils)… being hair-free here will also make you marginally more attractive for sexy stuff. And less attractive to evil static balloon attackers.

d) Look the present donor in the eye - this'll freak them out and disorientate them as you haven't looked them in the eye since you were four. Then, brace yourself, say "Thank you"… not only have they ***never*** heard this word uttered from your lips, if you add a break in your voice, it'll really pull on their heartstrings (boys have an unfair advantage here, being late, retarded developers).

e) Finally, if you can bear it, give them a cuddle, but avoid actual contact between chests as this is pervy.

Of course, this dazzling, heart-rending performance is only worthy of bestowing upon your audience if they've bothered to *obey* your Christmas list. What if a gift **sucks**?! What if some masochist has flouted your orders?! YOU MUST TAKE ACTION. Employing the following tactics after opening the vile present will ensure that, at least *next year*, they'll give you a gift token. (Incidentally, if you ever receive a gift voucher for a pointless bookshop, show your appreciation by using the said voucher to give the donor a paper cut... on their eyeball).

How To Make Sure You're Never Disobeyed At Christmas AGAIN

Even before opening, you'll be able to tell if the gift giver has broken your Christmas commandments by the presence of pouring sweat on their stupid, ugly, worried face. Therefore, why not milk the slow unwrapping with lots of squeals of delight (imagine you've finally discovered your grannies savings under the lacey dolly toilet cover), then choose from:

    a) Laugh sweetly, then add - embarrassedly, "Silly me, this can't be *my* present. I've opened it by mistake - this must be for your elderly dying relative who can't see, smell or feel. Sorry!!"

    b) Stare them out: try waiting till the 12th day of Christmas if need be.

    c) Say **nothing**. Then leave the room with a minimal of bounce... as if you're floating like some evil presence. They'll poop themselves. Call it a Christmas log.

d) Scream "Noooooooooooooo" until their ears bleed and they'll be reaching for their purses/wallets faster than you can say, "A snowball is basically alcohol free". Everyone carries *extra money* at Christmas to bail themselves out of jail when they've been naughty after too many liqueur chocolates.

e) Declare "I could die from some tragic accident next year, and you want *this* to be the last Christmas present you *ever* give me!?!"

Hopefully, you **won't** die before next Christmas because you only qualify for the really extortionate presents *the longer you live*, say, into your twenties. For example, at 21, you should expect your parents to give you a house... this is a shameless and transparent, desperate, and futile attempt to try and make you leave home. So what - it's rent free.

How To Cope If Your *Birthday* Is At Christmas

If the two most important dates of the year - your birthday and Christmas - are close together, like within days of each other... oh let's not split hairs, or are a couple of months apart, you're morally entitled to demand *one* almighty, ginormous, extravagant present. (Obviously, if your birthday and Christmas *are* a couple of months apart, you're still legally entitled to a *second* massive gift on the second occasion, denying all knowledge of receiving the supposed combined present.)

Surprisingly, your parents will readily agree to your outrageous request. Hmmmm, why?

1. They may be heading for divorce - both are secretly trying to squander whatever paltry savings they possess to stop their soon-to-be-ex spouse getting their half in the financial settlement... for poorer or for poorer, who cares, you'll be blinged up, having siphoned off money from their secret stashes from the day you were born (they gloatingly thought you were just a genius baby, crawling about... in a way you were, you were actually thieving).

2. They feel bad about mis-timing your conception. Not because it's a shame for you but because buying two presents is a lot more faffing hassle for them than buying one.

3. Giving you one huuuuuuge present gives them the chance to show off to friends, family, neighbours and shop staff about how much disposable income they have (e.g. dodgy credit limit).

4. They're about to tell you that you've inherited a genetic disease from them. Oh well. That'll get you a car.

How To Survive Boring Boxing Day

Historically, Boxing Day is the Worst Day in the World. Worse than the bombing of Hiroshima on 6th August 1945, the discovery of Auschwitz by the American troops on 11th September 1945, the death of Elvis on August 4th 1977, the collapse of Ratners on 23rd April 1991, Busted splitting up on 14th January 2005, and the invention of smoothies on 23th June 1968 (grrr, a hideously and annoyingly nice way to ingest veg and fruit). Without a doubt, Boxing Day - even with the start of the Sales (which is actually a government initiative to stop families divorcing) - is the dullest day in the universe.

Why Boxing Day Is A Stinky Anti-Climax:

- Your parents are no longer drunk - their embarrassing Christmas day inebriated stupor just about made their company bearable.
- Whilst your own sprout fart tidal wave is hilarious (the only reason you ate any yesterday), walking accidentally through someone else's gaseous tsunami *is not* funny.
- You won't be able to find *all* the receipts for your presents because your Mum has secretly and spitefully burnt some to annoy you.
- You're supposed to put your presents away. Where oh where for sweer Jesus's sake!? Your room is a floor-to-ceiling pigsty. Remember to put an

illegal maid on your Christmas list next year.
- There are no more advent calendar doors to open. Restrict crying your eyes out to your room.

Consequently, getting through Boxing Day will be tough, particularly because you're likely to be visited by dribbling, incontinent relatives you can't possibly be genetically related to. You must devise a strategy that will entitle you to take to your bed all day… select one/all of the following options:

1. Eat *all* the liqueur chocolates: despite being more gross than sprouts, after scoffing the 3,754 foil-wrapped "delicacies" you will actually be terribly drunk and your parents, fearing the NSPCC, will boot you upstairs.
2. Pretend you've been visited by Jesus, and start evangelically trying to save your family from damnation. They'll strap you down on your bed till you come to your senses… you know that'll never happen, so you may never need to get up again.
3. Put your head in the freezer for several hours… claim that because it hasn't snowed you're really sad and this is the next best thing. Your ears may drop off through frostbite but your Mum'll tuck you up in bed to defrost. Actually, she'll be more angry with you for ruining the freezer contents and not want to see your stupid, icicled mug.

4. ***Really*** annoy your parents by saying your New Year's Resolution is to learn the violin. They'll lock you in your room till you admit you were lying. Many weeks later.
5. Put "The Sound of Music" on the telly - you'll be sent to bed within a nanosecond.

*If you are not a Christian or normal non-believing white person, it *doesn't matter* if you feel this chapter isn't relevant to you. This seasonal holiday is purely about getting stuff you want, and stuff you can easily exchange. You don't think Jesus kept that Frankincense, do you?!

9 POLITICS

How To Make The World A Happier Place To Live

Don't panic. Stop faking your look-at-me-I'm-so-special asthma attack. That title was just a hilarious cunning joke to give you a heart attack slash cool cheap thrill. Obviously, you're *not* going to have to come all over Ma Teresa, Martin Loofah King or Trisha Goddard - self-promoting B-listers, the lot of them. This "Equality" isn't about political nonsense like going on patronising, sexist demonstrations for equal pay for women (that's ridiculous - working women spend 14 times longer in the loo than their male counterparts); or condescending, tediously slow marches for decent pensions for old people (why? they don't eat much, they live in one room because they can't get up the stairs which makes their heating bills really cheap, so they don't *need* much cash. Plus, they can't get out and spend it anyway!!?!).

This Equality is well important. This is about fighting (cool, bring it on) for the equal rights of a silent oppressed majority… yours.

'Snot fair. Adults get loads of special celebratory days: Mothers Day, Fathers Day, Grandparents Day, Employer's Day, Prostitutes Day, even Wicked Step-Parents Day. Talk about needy. What about the Teens? When's your special, honouring day? More importantly, where are *your* presents?! Stand up (if you're feeble, underused legs can hack it) and fight for your greedy rights. NOW is the time for a "Teenagers Day"??! After all, you have *a lot* to put up with being a modern Teen living in a highly pressurised, wonderfully narcissistic, danger-filled culture.

Life As A Poor, Down-Trodden, Abused 21st Century Spoilt Teenager

- You have to live with the knowledge that if obesity isn't going to kill you, cancer will. What's better? Dying fat and relatively wrinkle-free due to skin stretching or dying emaciated with amazing cheekbones?
- You're at serious risk from B.S.E. (that stands for Burger Stuffing Explosion - it's a veritable Russian roulette. Well worth it though).
- Teenagers are being shamelessly exploited by authors writing multi-book epics that are made into endless movies… this costs you (via your parents) a fortune in popcorn and smuggled-in alcopops on cinema dates.

- There's the extortionate cost of sun-beds, or even more expensive safe fake tan... jaundice isn't easy to self-inflict (you'd need a dodgy liver so try alcoholism or chilli kebabism).
- There's the psychologically scaring, once-in-a-decade devastating experience of hearing your parents having drunken sex - with each other. Or by themselves.
- You have to survive the realisation that you won't be a pop star, footballer or marry a member of the royal family (although simply sleeping with any of these 'individuals' will make you much more money, *and* more famous).
- The excessive use of scrumptious food additives makes you twitch somewhat embarrassingly in public. Mind you, this is perfectly OK whilst you're clubbing because the jerky spasming makes it look like you're a professional hip choreographer.
- There's an abusive increase in the variety of vegetables in supermarkets for your Mum to buy - as if broccoli and carrots aren't torture enough. Indeed, she *only* buys mange tout in the hope that it'll force you into leaving home.
- The agonising increase in fast food options renders decision-making nigh impossible. Did you know that dithering actually leads to self-implosion and is the fourth biggest killer of Teens: the first is cars, second is listening

to Avril Lavigne, and the third is bogie choking.

- The endless variety of jeans styles: it's positively soul-destroying picking the denims that *least* suits you. No wonder you're permanently - and rightly so - angry.
- Finally, there's the 'unbearable' choice between welfare benefits, working for a living, or waiting for your parents to snuff it and living off your inheritance. Tricky. Alternatively, it's much easier to just become a WAG. To achieve this, simply move to Cheshire and get dodgy hair extensions; if you're a guy it's seriously worth having a sex change because becoming a WAG will mean you get to see free footie games.

In conclusion, being a spoilt, selfish Teenage in today's world is just plain aggravating... Having a pampering 'Teenagers Day' would at least give society a day when you were slightly less vile. In theory...

How To Establish A 'Teenagers Day'
Erm, you'll need to lobby (that means "to whinge at") the relevant government thingummy (that's this geezer called Bono) to officially recognise and celebrate your oppressed, disadvantaged minority, and thus get *them* to establish an official 'Teenagers Day' for you. Bono's private number is 07797 735822. Just text him. A hundred times. He's right on. He won't mind*.

How To Create 'A Teenagers Day'... With Even Less Effort

Why not take the shortcut to national support... like all politicians you'll need to go on GMTV to achieve *instant and automatic* public backing for your humanitarian cause (and 'accidentally' achieve personal fame). Sadly, however, going on morning TV will mean having to get up in the morning... but, it *will* be worth it because they have proper make-up artists who can make you look like an "OK" wannabe. Plus, they'll have a free greasy-heaven canteen ("free" as in run past the cashier), and it'll be full of fading TV stars for you to hilariously blank.

Be warned, though, that the director will sit you on a settee that won't be facing the camera *straight on* and that just isn't flattering to your bulbous face shape. You could solve this dilemma by - at the last moment - suddenly sitting, uninvited, on the presenter's knobbly knees (only weather girls have good knees because they have to be shot standing up)... Nah, forget it, they all look like they smell of lily of the valley air freshener.

How To Waffle Whilst On GMTV And Look Really Cool And Sexy

Some adults will foolishly expect you to have life-enriching ideas about what a Teenagers Day will involve. Isn't it blinking obvious!? It involves **naff all**... You - doing **naff all** absolutely all day long (yes, even less than usual). However, some annoying grown-ups may need persuading to your banal way of thinking. Fortunately, to achieve this you simply need to:

1. Talk a lot, and ***without swearing*** as this'll make them think you've had some kind of admirable, coming of age epiphany.

2. Look the presenters being conned ***in the eye*** as this is very strange behaviour for a Teenager... the effect is truly disconcerting and they'll mistake your blank stare for intellectualismish and sincerity.

3. ***Wave your hands about randomly*** as you recite your verbal diarrhoea: this is pure politician and will make you sound dead smart - particularly if you don't accidentally smack yourself in the face.

4. Adults are easily impressed and intimidated by ***the use of certain words***, so to win your imbecilic argument bung some in your 'Teenagers Manifesto'. For example: for example, agenda, notwithstanding, diatribe, proportional representation, salmon fishcakes with dill, economic migration, Euro, spirogiro.

5. Simply drone on using authoritative, emphatic, hypnotic ***bullet points...*** (bullet points are easy for a Teen to remember because you can pretend you're firing them from a handgun).

The Teenagers Manifesto (Well, More Like, Manifest-ering, Tee Hee)

- On 'Teenagers Day', you will all be entitled to lie in bed, un-nagged, all day... this will last for 364 days.
- Only fried or fast food may be served to them... by a parent who isn't allowed to make eye contact, speak or breathe whilst on the teenager's property. Ideally, a sexy au pair should serve the grub.
- Large amounts of money should be deposited in your bank account - uhuh, even more than usual. To provide sufficient funds, parents should prostitute themselves (ha, a pittance will be made), rob a bank or pensioner, or empty your neighbour's child's piggy bank who's saving to go to Disney or your granny's bed who's saving for a life-saving boob job.
- Music must be played loud enough to make your parents' ears bleed: if permanent deafness results, your oldies will actually be eternally grateful as they'll no longer have to listen to each other's incessant bickering. Or yours (in fact, if you become deaf too, this is a bonus because when you then learn sign language you can have a real laugh in public by throwing in rude hand gestures).
- Any siblings must be dragged kicking and screaming to your bedside and be positioned at your gluteus maximus for the passing of wind.

How To Achieve International Awareness And Immortality

To clinch global success for your noble U.N.-ish humanitarian cause, you should support your campaign with a *petition*... obviously not a real one, *that* would require you to speak to people. Instead, simply download lots of handwriting fonts off the internet and cobble your petition together using hilarious names like "Ivor Smallone", "Hitler Ghandi" and "Jade Goody". Or, better still (because your parents illegally spy on your internet activities), make that left-handed kid at school or college - whose handwriting is hilariously rubbish - write the petition... they'll welcome the chance to practise their shambolic, never-get-a-job scrawling. But *don't* ask the school forger to fake the petition... it'll be *too* good, and thereby rouse suspicions - petitions are supposed to look home-made and illegible. *Even better still*, just cut out this petition and shove it on the top of a huge pile of blank paper... no-one *ever* reads a petition.

GENUINE PETITION FOR
NATIONAL TEENAGERS DAY

NAME	ADDRESS	SIGNATURE

Nelson Mandela   Ghetto Town, South Africa, The World

Pope John XXth   The Vatican in, er Paris in, ahem, Spain

Nancy Drew   Mid West, America

Roger Rabbit Warren Road, Bucktoothshire, or a road - squashed... bright eyes, burning like fire.

Jesus 2nd   Abergevny, Wales (shh)

Jimmy Savilon   Stinky old caravan, so could be anywhere

Limahl   Too shy, shy to reveal whereabouts

Daddy Long Legs   Currently residing in every lampshade in UK

Brussel Sprouts   Hell

Lord Lucan   13 Mortain Drive, Berkhamsted, Herts, HP4 1JZ (honest! It's definitely him)

Tony Blair   Unemployed, of no fixed abode

Shellsuits   'Oop north, still

Loch Ness Monster   My husband's pants (tee hee hee hee hee)

Running out of jokes STOP reading this, Now-shire. Grrr.

Blah blah   Blah blah blah

Blah blah   Blah blah blah

Blagh blaAGH   Blah get a life blah

***How To Make Yourself More Famous Than
Shilpa Shetty*** *(wasn't that a crafty plan to be so
annoying that you incite racial hatred amongst
your housemates and thereby achieve international
fame and fortune?)*
Establishing a world 'Teenager's Day' is going to
make you the most famous Teenager since James/
Lauren Harries. But just in case Bono's too busy
getting a hip replacement or hair weave fitted to
read your petition, you'll need to deliver you
mighty petition to his second-in-command, the
Prime Minister. Try popping by at No.10 midweek
so you can take a day off school/college/uni/
nothing; and, *more importantly*, so you can visit
Oxford Street when the shops are quieter (thus
making shoplifting harder and, therefore, more
enjoyably challenging). You'll be able to just waltz
up to Gordon's front door - being as good-looking
as you are, all the coppers will be transfixed by
your stunning looks and not bother with any
security checks. Unless you're a Muslim.

How To Fight Your Own Ageist Discrimination
Mind you, don't be surprised if Gordon slams the
door in your sulky, snarly face... he most definitely
will, if the TV cameras aren't turned on.
Outrageously, many Teenagers have a reputation
for being lazy, apolitical, un-environmentally-
friendly, wasters. What!? Is that all? You're *also*
aggressive and relentless in your greed and self-
interest; so, don't be put off, you'll simply need a

back-up plan for making your whiney voice heard as the Messiah for the Teenage Oppressed:

- Knock and run on his door repeatedly. After the 3,835 time, it'll be so annoying that he'll grant your every wish... including the vote-winning replacement of physical education for hair straightening iron lessons.
- Whistle really badly (or brilliantly) it makes no difference, because the screeching noise is well hideous and is actually employed by the British army as their hush-hush torture treatment in Iraq.
- Put your hand under your armpit and make farty noises. It's totally historically documented that all Prime Ministers *love* doing this so the P.M. will invite you in for a fart-off faster than you can say hydrogen sulphide gas. However, you **must** remember to let the P.M. **win** or he'll have you thrown in the Tower of London. Goodie goodie gumdrops: no college, parents, or vegetables. Plus, there'll be plenty of cockroaches to either: a) if you're male, operate upon; or b) if you're female, dress up in cute clothes.

How To Exploit Becoming An Imprisoned Nelson Mandelson Icon

Firstly, rub your hands with glee because when you *are* finally released not only will you make a bundle from your sordid Kiss-the-Beefeater-and-Tell, but due to not being served junk food you'll also be acne-free and thinner; the snag is, you'll have wrinkles instead. Luckily, whilst you're imprisoned in the Tower living it up doing nothing, your 'Teenagers Day' cause will be adopted by Amnesty International and they'll do *all* the hard work for you. So, thankfully, your 'Teenagers Day' won't stay a selfish pipe dream, but a selfish reality. Don't fret, you'll still be seen as the original instigator and receive a Nobel Peace Prize which you can later sell on ebay for fifty million quid.

However, to avoid being sent hundreds of boring, 'morale-boosting' postcards from Amnesty members who'll be campaigning for your release from the Tower, you can actually by-pass **all** the above falderal trying to start a 'Teenager's Day' by simply appealing to a ***higher power***. Nope, not the Dally Llama. Just contact Clintons Cards, The Crystal Building, Langston Road, Loughton, Essex, IG10 3TH.

*If, by the time you call Bono on this number and it no longer exists, that's because he's a grumpy, two-faced saint wannabe.

10 LIFESTYLE

How To Eat (More) Disgustingly In Public

Naturally, you avoid eating *at home* as much as possible as this reduces the amount of rancid time you must spend in that naff hell-hole. Similarly, eating with your family is even less appealing than having din-dins with Armin Meiwes*. In fact, the **only** food you regularly and willingly ingest whilst at home is:

- Your belly button fluff. It's like free candy-floss. Without the taste. Cool e-colour. And stick (though there *was* something quite nice and chewy in there).
- Your very runny snot (probably the result of you manually extracting your nasal hair instead of secretly using your parent's hair trimmer - god knows where that's been). Streaming noses is actually the reason why the body evolved a tongue, and *not* for articulating swear words as Darwin previously claimed.

- Your knee scabs. Luckily, these can still occur in Teenhood: if you're female it'll be due to wearing ridiculously high shoes and falling over, or if you're male, from carpet burns as you pretend to be an Action Man. You don't *intend* to eat your scabs but after you've prematurely hacked them off your knees they accidentally fall in your mouth after you stick them to your lips and pretend in the mirror that you're a zombie with cold sores.
- Your ear wax. Apparently, ear wax is actually brain poo* and is amazingly high in clever-making omega 3, so consuming vast quantities of your own ear gunk can help prevent you from catching Pushing A Pull Dooritis In Publichondia - the biggest cause of Teenage suicide. *see Wikidpedia for scientific proof.

How To Imperfect The Art Of Table Manners

The older generations (i.e. anyone more than a week older than you), think the youth of today have no table manners or etiquette. And? Don't they realize that your lack of politeness when eating is a blatantly obvious attempt to get them the f*&! out of your dribbling face. However, a serious sociological problem has arisen because these pretentious 'middle-class' moaners have become so saturated by your peer groups foul eating habits in public that they now *barely even notice when your deliberately spit your sweetcorn cob bits at them* (obviously you don't *really* eat this vegetable - you simply suck off the butter they come drenched in and then pretend to do a typewriter on the cob... just long enough to get some bits stuck so you can gob them at your fellow diners). Consequently, you'll need to up the bad manners ante when it comes to 'dining' in any of your fast food dining establishments:

- *The wrong use of cutlery*: it goes without saying that you haven't used a knife or fork since you deliberately poked/stabbed your Mummy with it when you were weaning; however why not now attempt to master the art of eating with various non-cutlery items, like eating chips off the tip of a flick-knife, or a burger balanced on your shooter, or ketchup off your electronic tag.

- *Eating with your mouth open*: instead, now try eating with your shirt open. Regardless of being a boy or girl, trust me, there'll be nothing more revolting to your fellow diners to witness than this. Seriously.

- *A simple "Please" or "Thankyou"*: come off it... if you muttered either of these pleasantries to the plebs serving you behind the counter they'd think you (wrongly - obviously) fancied them. Besides, they probably wouldn't understand these words *anyway* having come from under-privileged backgrounds. Instead, you should inform them of true facts regarding employees in the fast food service industry:

a) The average fast food worker's life expectancy is 20 years less than the national average.

b) They earn 55% less than their peers in any other professions - i n c l u d i n g dustbin men and nurses.

c) 94% of employees suffer from the industrial disease of Greasyhairitis... currently, though unlike asbestos lung disease, y o u c a n ' t m a k e m a s s i v e compensation claims against your employer. However, Julia Roberts is currently trying to fabricate a case in order to star in an oscar-winning film.

- *Belching*: sadly, it's not worth moving to Eskimo land where mouth farting is a sign of appreciation of the meal... but only because Santa lives at the other pole. The modern-day tragedy is that belching during and after meals has become as commonplace as Britney showing her pimply bum in public. Consequently, you should stand on the table and guff one off; amazingly, despite your absolute lack of vegetable intake, you can still fart as handsomely as any goody-two-shoes vegetarian... thanks to a deadly combo of kebab sauce and fizzy pop.

- *Not washing your hands*: actually, the only people who *do* wash their hands before eating are morticians - and only because the grieving relatives have been wiping their snotty noses with their hands and shaking the funeral directors' hands... it's got nothing to do with them handling rotting corpses. So, in your fast food joint you'll need to make a big show of going to the toilet before you commence gorging and returning with your hands dripping in poo and piss. (Clearly, not *real* poo and piss - you already know that they taste dreadful - no, you've doused your mitts in chocolate sauce and lemonade, you genius you).

- *Leaving the table a mess*: traditionally, Teenagers have <u>never</u> cleared up after themselves following a meal, so leaving the table looking like there's been a rabid chimpanzees tea party is nothing new...so, once you've finished bingeing, to this mess you should add: a shopping trolley, a road cone, a snoring tramp and your friend's underwear.

- *Deliberately showing the barely-chewed contents of your mouth*: this is *so* old hat, and *further* spoilt by your doddery parents' generation trying to get in on your act now they're losing their teeth and marbles. Alternatively, why not show your dining companions... the contents of your gross colostomy bag! You can buy one of these from Ebay and attach it yourself using a cool curly straw and brut force.

How To Excel At The Physical Act Of Scoffing

Fortunately, fast food requires little effort to eat... in fact, possibly the *only* food that may *ever* require chewing is a dubious 'meat' kebab. However, despite the lack of chewing necessary you should still treat your fellow-diners to ***plenty of open-mouthed mastication*** (hee hee - a lot of you will think that word means something *entirely* different) ... approximately 15 minutes per massive mouthful. In addition, don't forget to:

a) Make more slurping, dribbly noises than a rabid dog having a drink after chasing a cat on a summer's day.

b) Allow lumps of food to fall from your gob, preferably into your fellow diners mouths.

c) Between the above actions a) and b), spit out the semi-chewed food   to re-eat over and over. Not because you're pretending to be a fly - as cool as this is, but because it's bloody gorgeous and you want to get   your ('borrowed') money's worth.

In fact, what you *really need* is ***a big pelican throat*** for you to chuck whole items of 'food' into, like a chip or rotisserie chicken. This massive, sexually-repellant mutant turkey chin is a tragic, inevitable part of the ageing process and getting even more fattybunkle... it'll suddenly appear overnight in your mid twenties. But you may as well get yours now because it'll also be really handy for secretly stashing and smuggling your illegal booze into nightclubs in your early twenties. Luckily, you can easily make one of your own *now* by attaching heavy bricks (not Lego ones, they won't work, plus you'll just look silly... because you still *have* Lego) to the dirty skin under your chin using rope and clothes pegs; or if you don't know what clothes pegs are, with a stapler (your Dad'll have one - nicked from work in bitter revenge for being so underpaid but too wussy to do anything grown-up about it).

How To Avoid Lifting Your Feeble Arms To Eat
When you are reincarnated you should cross your fingers to come back as a dog, or a whoopee cushion. *Dogs have it all*: they can lick their own privates in public, hump the legs of embarrassed, frigid relatives, they make wicked stinks, dog breath is socially acceptable, they can destroy the home without being put in youth detention, plus they get to eat from a bowl... no paws necessary. Mind you, for every year that's seven in dog years so you'd look hideously haggard by the end. Get run over. Do it on a motorway to guarantee death... local roads may just result in you becoming deformed.

However, you can *still* eat like a dog without using your un-exercised arms by:
- Making your Mum lift the food to you - she'll willingly agree because not only is she depressed and desperate to get out of the house, but she can scavenge any on the delicious junk food that falls from your gob.
- Pretend to be a quadraplegic - fellow diners will jump at the chance to feed you because they deludedly believe that not only will this get them into heaven, but better yet, free fries from the uncomfortable manager. You can make a quite convincing wheelchair

from large cereal boxes and an old-fashioned computer mouse. Just remember, don't jump and run if your friend does a real bad eggy duff.

- Can't think of a funny third point (apparently that's not as funny as I thought it was).

*It's highly likely that you haven't the foggiest idea who Armin Meiwes is because the only 'current affairs' news you're interested in is accompanied by fish and chips. And I'm not telling you, you thicko... Um, oh well, yes I will, otherwise this great joke falls flat on its face: he's the German guy who met a guy on the internet and ate his knob.

-o-

How To Fart Silently And Really, Really, Really, Really, Really, Really, Really, Really Violently

Clearly, every Teens natural instinct is to want to fart loudly, crudely and victoriously. But this is a double-edged kitchen knife as it gives your immediate audience *far too much warning* to immediately vacate your vicinity. Although, if you're surrounded by decrepit old people - like at a funeral, *fart away* as they'll all fall hysterically over trying to escape and be stuck there for hours, slowly suffocating on your impressive toxic anal gases, whilst they wait for their relatives-who-desperately-want-their-inheritance to come very slowly to their aid.

Ideally then, you should practise the ancient Chinese proverb's wisdom of the "silent but violent" approach to methane bum-blasts. By the way, talking of China, did you know that Hiroshima was *not* actually a nuclear bomb, but the aftermath of a vegetarian's curry dinner party... you just should *not* curry sprouts.

What To Eat To Guarantee You'll Fart Like A Trooper

Of course, being a Teenager you can fart on command - this comes more naturally to you than chasing pigeons, an ex-soap star in a shop, or even a one-legged tramp with a can of Special. But these everyday, run of the mill farts *lack* their potential full impact in flavour and stench: **your *chief goal in guffing toxic fart clouds is to force your victim*** *walking through it to accidentally taste your pop-off as they breathe and, consequently, GAG.*

Joyously, it's well known that certain "foods" can create excessive wonderful putrid, rancid, rotting flatulence: sprouts, cabbage, broccoli, lentils and any other pulses (that doesn't mean eating your wrist - a 'pulse' is a Chinese purse)... So, this is therefore a truly epic, "Eastenders" scriptwriter dilemma: *To eat or not to eat, that is the question*? After all, you've spent your **entire** meaningless life impressively avoiding these vegetables - you've even got the scurvy to prove it - so can you bring yourself to swallowing Satan's offal? Well, you've eaten worse, phnar phnar.

How To Stomach Satan's Offal
- Smother the g-agh-srtonomic items in snail jism, not only will this savoury sauce take your mind off the evil greeniness, but afterwards, you can throw rice crispies onto your face for fun.
- Slather bogies on the vegetables - if you run out, visit a local school and bolster your nasal supply with scrapings from under the desks. Or from behind the disliked teacher's ears.
- Imagine that you're a cannibal and believe devouring your victims will help you metamorphosis into them, i.e. the veggies are the bodily and

facial items of beautiful celebrities you'd like to be. To avoid disappointment, please remember that this probably won't come true.

- Cut a gaping hole in your belly with a nail file (if you're a girl) or bottle opener (if you're a boy) or nail file (if you're gay) and insert the v-ugh-tables directly into your stomach to avoid them coming into immediate contact with your mouth, as this is where your taste and swear-buds are located. This gangrenous, bleeding gash will also prove très useful:

a) you can hide stolen or permanently borrowed items
here, although they'll stay here forever because you'll be   too chicken to fish them out.

b) You can make people laugh by pretending to making   t h e pussing hole talk.

c) It's guaranteed time off school/work in hospital, or a
longer stay in a hospice.

d) Blag £300 easy money for selling your story to a   crappy women's magazine. Sure, it's not "Heat" but
you've got to start somewhere.

- Alternatively, drizzle your e-number ridden sweets over them… *nothing* will get in the way of you and your self-induced hyperactive stupor.

HANG ON! KEEP YOUR G-STRINGS AND TANGAS ON (mind you, *real* celebs don't wear knickers any more), YOU DON'T NEED TO EAT ANY OF THIS DEVIL FOOD.

How To Fart Without Ever Touching A Poisonous Vegetable

Baked beans!!!!!!!!!!!!!!!!!!! And the cheaper and nastier the brand the better. It's not well-publicised but snobby Heinz have spent a fortune removing the part of the bean that causes the heavenly stink, and all because the killjoy M.D. of the company once accidentally walked through his own fart-cloud which was sooooo bad it singed off his eyebrows…and his pubes (this is most handy to know if you can't afford a Brazilian or a back-sack-crack wax; or if you're Italian, the back-sack-crack-leg-feet-arm-neck-hand-tummy-eyelid wax).

How To Maximise Your Victim's Displeasure
For the utmost impact, you should also only ever eat baked beans *heated up* because there's nothing more disgusting to your victim than walking through a *warm* fart cloud. Cold fart clouds can often be quite enjoyable. But of course, it's not as if you're ever going to go near a cooker and make your own meals, so simply place the can between your fat, chafing thighs and let the natural friction heat the beans.

In conclusion, praise be-eans, to a Teenager, baked beans are the *perfect food*: it's fresh from a can, it doesn't require chewing, and it's orange - so if you run out of fake tan, you can convincingly bronze yourself up by merely smearing yourself in the sauce... as Sam Fox once sang, it's a wonderful world.

How To Train Your Botty To Fart On Command
Of course, you mistakenly believe that you already fart to order, when in fact, what you're really doing is - thanks to your atrocious diet - farting more or less continuously. This is okeedokee, but imagine the catastrophic fun you could have if you learnt to *control* your botty hole. After all, *your arse is a muscle* and not just a flabby, disgusting and embarrassing disfigurement that you spend your entire time trying to hide by walking with your back against the wall (aha, it's got nothing to do with worrying about getting stabbed in the back).... with a little bit of exercise and effort you can actually train your skiddy arsehole to **keep the fart in** until you're surrounded by **a minimum of six victims**.

Simple Sphincter-Strengthening Exercises
1. Imagine that you're about to get the squits in front of the Queen, Davina McCall. You'll then feel your sphincter *naturally contracting* because Dav'll *never* interview you if she suspects she's about to get sprayed in doo-doo (her detractors are starting to say she's shit already). Mind you, do you *really* want to get interviewed by someone so uptight?
2. Pretend that your arse is a bubble blowing machine: wobbling your sphincter in and out will

create an imaginary gazillion bubbles that you can run around and pretend to pop - what larks. In fact, why not literally pour bubble solution into your backside and make a fortune hiring yourself out as kids' parties?

3. Kid yourself that the tighter you can squeeze your sphincter, the smaller and more sexy your bum will become as it sucks itself inwards. You may find, however, that you'll soon be able to squeeze hard enough for your bum-hole to suck in your *entire body...* this is extremely handy if you need to disappear in a hurry. Only do this once, though, because you will never reappear.

Alternatively, just take a cork (your Dad'll have hundreds stashed in his secret place) and shove it up your bum - this'll keep the nauseating fart cloud up there until you need it. Also, the resulting protuberance is incredible useful: horrified onlookers will think that it's a turtle head so you'll always be guaranteed plenty of personal space in the bus or changing room or pub or defendant's box.

How To Fart On Command: The Lazy-Arsed Method
Of course, the above exercises may be quite dangerous for someone as unfit as yourself to attempt. Ho hum. Good. Instead, rely on the fact that your arse is just like a silly toddler/Teenager/ Politician - you can persuade it to do **anything** you want if you **bribe** it well enough. Therefore, try

promising your sphincter any of the following bribes:

- Butt surgery. But forget liposuction, uplifts and implants - the latest craze is tattooing your favourite celebrity's face across your butt-cheeks, your hairy hole being their mouth.
- 'Polyfiller' to fill in all the dimples, but if this means you'd have to go to a DIY shop and smell the working class shoppers' compulsory B.O., use peanut butter instead - smooth, obviously.
- Threaten your jacksie with a pair of unsexy 'Primark' jeans if it doesn't obey your controlling commands. Or worse, your parents' jeans.
- Vow to your down-trodden bum-cheeks that you'll stop sitting on it and squashing it for the rest of your life (naturally, this is a blatant lie... but it's not as if your bum is going anywhere. Although, it's wise to remove any cheese graters in your house in case it tries to de-bum-itate itself from you).
- Inform your butt that if it doesn't comply with your fart orders you'll put yourself down on the National Bum Donor Scheme should you be (quite possibly) killed crossing the road - after all, your poor bum may end up on someone *even more ugly and fatter than you.*

Where To Fart Silently And Violently

You may well be tempted to savour your fart whilst on your own... after all the hard work you've put in fermenting the most toxic stench, why share it? As understandable as this is, fart-depriving it's quite a selfish act: farting is the **only** thing you'll willingly enjoy sharing in your entire life, so make the most of this charitable act, you do-gooder you. Besides, it's not as if you're going to leave anything else of any value on the planet: farting is your legacy. So, give your windypops the chance to permeate *as many* people's clothes and hair as possible... did you know that the aroma of fart gas is actually harder to remove from clothes than nicotine and nepalm.

So, the best places to let rip are situations where your victims can't easily escape:
1. *Funerals* - they'll look pretty darn rude to the bereaved if they try to scarper.
2. *Weddings* - they'll all look like they've slept with the bride or groom if they do a bunk.
3. *Christenings* - the trouble with this venue is that the baby may try to take all the credit for the terrible smell. Make sure everyone knows it's *you* by guffing at the altar - whilst mooning.
4. *Public transport* - most people won't want to jump from a moving vehicle in case they land in a dog poo, road kill, or tramp.
5. *Changing rooms* - they've probably had to queue for hours (e.g. in Teen world, that means anything over three seconds) so they'd

rather stay put and inhale your vomitable stench than queue again.

6. *Airport security check-ins* - not only will the queue-ees not want to re-queue, but if they start running frantically, they'll probably get mown-down by terrorist-prevention gunfire.

7. *In bed with someone* - the infamous **'Duvet-Waft'** N.B. will probably be your happiest memory in life… your choking victim won't be able to leave the bed as that will result in you actually seeing their hideous naked body.

How To Give Yourself A Special Birthday Treat
In addition to the 1000+ presents you'll receive, you should celebrate turning another year older and less wise with a priceless gift to yourself: one of your very own farts. To honour your fart's prowess, you should fart directly in to your excited hand and lift it to your begging nostrils. Nirvanaaaaahh. Or if lifting up your own arm hurts too much, make the local friendless geek use theirs.

N.B. The first recorded historical account of the Duvet Waft is attributed to Cleopatra who after eating a dodgy goat's cheese kebab, had the farts big-time. She ordered her slaves to hold down her papaya bed linen whilst an unsuspecting Anthony lay gasping for air - one of the slaves even used a big palm leaf to further waft the stench over him. Accidentally, Anthony snuffed it due to lack of oxygen and an embarrassed Cleopatra set up XXX to take the blame.

How To Perfect The Modern-Day 'Duvet Waft'

- A 'duvet waft' occurs on the planet every 1.7 seconds.
- To date, there have been 635293187640736851648305294 6720963 waftings.
- Every single person on the planet has performed at least one Waft on their bed-partner - even The Queen, Bin Laden and Julie Andrews.

So, sadly, the unsuspecting victim no longer exists. Therefore, you'll have to try a little bit harder to catch your victim out. Firstly, modern duvet covers aren't typically big enough for you to tuck evilly under the mattress, so you'll need to fix the duvet to the sides using a stapler or your heavily polluted, extra thick bogey supply. Alternatively, simply superglue your victim to the bed. Secondly, don't giggle - that's a sure giveaway, though giggling in bed at your partner won't be easy full stop, so try imagining that they've just snuffed it. Or they owe you a quid. Thirdly, it's best to wait till they're asleep - which, when taking in to account for your performance in bed, won't be long - and then position yourself so you can actually fart directly in to their nostrils. Use a nasal hair trimmer first to speed the passage of toxic death up to their nose.

-o-

How To Flick A Bogey With Devastating Effect

Despite years of pre-Teen practise, the majority of Teens are still pathetically lacking in bogey flicking expertise: the snot consistency, attack strategy and aim are sorely amateurish. Furthermore, it has been scientifically proven by CSI Las Vegas that the modern cultural explosion in texting has massively compromised the average Teens (and you're *all* average) ability to use their index finger for good-old fashioned bogey picking. So much for evolution.

How To Concoct The Perfect Bogey

Thankfully, due to the recent horrendous and deadly increase in air pollution, bogeys have massively - and naturally - improved in volume and texture. The nasal passage glands must create *huge* amounts of bogey to try and keep out the damaging allergy-inducing free radicals in the air to try and stop you from dying of an embarrassing asthma attack. So, bogies are generally now infinitely more gritty and sticky, making the rolling of the snot-bombs much easier and more fun. However, *lucky as you are* to have such large deposits of black mucuousy tar to create your bogey-missiles at your disposal, you can also *further increase* your gooey production by:

- Moving to an inner city, preferably near a nuclear power site, or better still, next to a poor family. Their doley lifestyle with 24/7 chain smoking and full-time chip pan frying hydrogenated vegetable oil has created their very own deadly carbon volcano.

- Getting a part-time job in a garage - it's actually worth the effort working for your money because the fumes from the forecourt will result in bogies of asteroid proportions. Plus, all that chocolate on sale is free to you as the only perk of the job. Oh, and sniggering at customers who 'push' the door instead of 'pull'.
- Working down a dust-filled coal mine. In the (g)olden days, you could do that oop north, but now you'll have to commute to the Ukraine. Not only does this mean wonderful time away from home (your parents'll be surprisingly agreeable to this, relieved you're not *entirely* sponging off them any more. Ha - oh yes you are), but whilst you're there you may also cop off with an eastern European... luckily, they have fantastic bone structure so, if you have a baby together their amazing cheekbones should - thank Gucci - cancel out your pudgy, moon-face.

How To Increase Bogey Production - The Bone Idle Method

Of course, if that all sounds like too much life-threatening effort, more simple options include:

1. Shoving soil up your nose will bulk out your own natural bogey stockpile. If you live in an inner city where soil

is not readily available, dog poo is a handy alternative - though clearly *not* your hand, ask a blind person to help you... they'll be grateful for the social contact.

2. If you suffer from hay fever, rub your face in the grass or tree to make your nose run, then mix up the quite liquidy snot with quick drying cement (don't mix this *up* your actual nostrils as this'll result in suffocation and death, or worse, you'll have to pull out the hardened mixture and rip out nasal hairs - boo hoo).

3. If you're female watch a sad film, 'Neighbours', or any film with Brad Pitt (him copping off with the female actresses instead of you always makes you hysterical)... once you start crying blend the streams of snot with any of the million unused powdery make up items you've bought, nicked or borrowed.

4. If male, watch your footie team play... regardless of whether they win or not, you'll start blubbing when you realise that you're not ever going to play professional soccer. Mix the torrential bogey downfall with your ear wax for wondrous soon-to-be-hard bogey balls: hey, at least you can become mediocre at bogey-ball.

N.B. Jewish Teens and the love-spawn of Barry Manilow have an enosemous unfair advantage when it comes to bogey supply, so it's always worth pretending to be their friends to hopefully avoid enduring their wrathful bogey bombardment.

How To Extract The Deadly Bogey Bomb

Simply sticking your finger up your already chasmous nostrils will just result in you scraping the tip of the greenie iceberg; after all, your nasal passages are actually quite gigantic... they go *much further back* than the average human being because there *isn't the same amount of brain behind them*. Therefore, you'll need to create a tool for the maximum extraction of bogey. Girls are lucky because they can easily use their 7" long false nail as a shovel, but guys tend to look a bit gay if they have long talons (although appearing gay could *also* be used as a clever disguise for approaching your victim who'll never suspect that you're about to bombard them with Satan snots.) Therefore, if male, why not try an ice pick instead. If you *do* dig a bit too hard you may find that you hook out your brain as well. Never mind, though, as this makes a fantastic, (slightly) larger alternative to a bogey bomb - but pick your enemy wisely as this will be your last bodily fluid catapult. Don't waste it!

By the way, did you know that a bogey bomb can be a much more harmful, and emotionally distressing than a stabbing with a minor weapon?

How To Roll The Best Bogey Bomb In The Universe

Rolling bogies is actually the modern Teen's alternative to stress management and intensive counselling... so you don't need to see a child psychologist, after all. (Although don't tell your parents that, still pretend to see your shrink and pocket their ridiculous fee for yourself. To con your parents into believing that their investment in your therapy is paying off by saying any of these impressive words at random: "low self-esteem", "debilitating panic attacks", "psychosomatic" - they won't have a scoobie but the words'll terrify them, especially "paranoid schizophrenic"... these two little words will get you whatever you want).

Fortunately, moulding the most effective bogey bomb is as easy as A, er, something. You simply need a *thumb* and a *forefinger* and once the bogey secretion is stuck between them, your digits will *instinctively* know what to do. Ahh, evolution. Then, the average bogey rolling takes just 27 seconds to dry to a consistency that can easily be flicked *without sticking* - impatiently waiting less than this time will result in the still moist bogey's refusal to leave your finger and you'll look like you're having a hand fit. Or an embarrassing "boyakasha" regression.

How To Roll Bogies If You're A Leper Etc.

If you're an annoying Duke of Edinburgh over-achiever who's, like, climbed Mount Everest and lost all their unbitten fingers to frostbite; or perhaps you've had a handy bout of time-off school meningococcal meningitis, you'll find the bogey hand rolling and flicking method a touch fiddly. No probs. You can easily use your tongue to roll the snotball...mind you, this is just too darn tempting and you won't be able to resist swallowing (who says you don't eat greens? - this is officially the worst joke in the book and should have been sneakily deleted by my husband/my agent/the publisher/the typesetter.) Instead, you should opt for an entirely different attack strategy: *The Silent Stealth Wipe.*

How To Perform *The Silent Stealth Wipe*
The impact of this attack upon your victim isn't as immediate or as obviously hilarious as a sudden bogey bomb, but the long-term effects can happily be just as devastating. Clearly, having no fingers gives you a huge advantage in approaching your target because they'll be reluctant to start running... now, you may think that your intended victim is trying to show no prejudice towards your disability/deformity, but, in actual fact, they are *frozen with fear to the spot, terrified that they may catch whatever it is that you've clearly got.* You can then, quietly, and without your target protesting, smear or stick your bogey bomb wherever you fancy: if they are *really* terrified, you can be even more brazen with your targeting as the lily-livered idiot has lost the power of their pussy limbs.
Where To Stick Your Snot-Ball:

1. Their eyelids. If you do this when your victim's asleep, they'll wake up and confusedly believe the crusty stuff to be eye shit (if you're gay, you'll call it 'eye sleep'). For days, you can chuckle away as the goo threatens to drop on their eyeball.
2. Behind their ears - yum yum - a tasty treat for their snog-partner.
3. On the soles of their feet. Why not build up the layers of snot over the course of a few weeks and sit back and laugh as the victim swears to all and sundry that they must be levitating.
4. Scattered on their shoulders - "dandruff" is even more socially degrading than nits.
5. Dotted on their thighs... the resulting pimpling will look like cellulite and they'll be sent to leper Coventry by their gang.

Indeed, it's *almost* worth chopping off your fingers so you can perform these amazing Silent Stealth Wipes. If you do decide to amputate, just please remember to leave your vital middle finger behind.

How To Flick With *Deadly* Accuracy

Bogey bombs are most lethal if aimed at your victim's *face*; therefore, to improve your accuracy you should reward yourself with stickers as a jolly good incentive. Well, not stickers exactly, more like alcopops*. The points system is as follows:

- The Forehead = 1 alcopop
- The Nose = 2 alcopops

- The Cheek = 3 alcopops (double if you land one on both - but *no more* than this as this target is quite easy because they're so fattybunkle)
- The Hair = 23 alcopops (blinking hard to remove, well done)
- The Eye = Well done you. Treat yourself with 1 Tennents Special (you could join the S.A.S.)
- The Mouth = Top marks deserves your Parents special champagne that they're saving for when you finally leave home.

How To React If *You're* The Bogey-Bomb Victim

It's impossible to live through your Teen years without becoming a crusty casualty at some point: the only way round this is to be severely allergic to life and be forced to life in a plastic bubble. Actually, this is a dream existence for a Teenager because:

a) No-one is physically allowed to touch you.

b) It'll smell like fart heaven.

c) People from all over the world will send you gifts...

However, most of the presents will be shit teddies so, on second thought, forget it.

You had better be prepared, your attacker could be *anyone*: your best friend, a parent, your religious counsellor... now, whatever you do, **don't** give them the satisfaction of flinching and being horrified as you feel the DNA-diseased, festering bogey-bomb crash land on your face. What you should do is:

1. Just take your own chewed, pussing finger.
2. Find the bombsite and squidge it around on your face.
3. Then, pop the bogey in your mouth and eat it.
4. Smack your lips in appreactiation.

Ha, that'll show them. **What**? Of course not, you'll simply be performing a slight of hand trick - you're an expert magician having already become a talented shop-lifter, Mother purse-pilferer or charity box donator con-artiste (this involves pretending to put money in the can, then - the genius - pushing *heavily down* and shaking the can simultaneously so that the collector thinks you've just out loads of cash in).

How To Reap Revenge On Your Bogey Attacker
MI5 is secretly collecting bogey samples to create a DNA database of the entire population. They then intend to use this information for fining every person who is caught on CCT illegally crossing the road without using The Green Cross Code. This money will subsequently be used to pay out compensation claims to pedestrian victims of high-speed police chases. You can call 'BogeyStoppers' on 0800 666 666 and receive a reward of £2.50 for every civilian you stitch up. Heather Mills will not be eligible for any pay-off as she will soon be due her back-pay for her care assistant work to Sir Paul.

*The author wishes to assert that in no way does she condone illegal under-age drinking as this seriously devalues the numbing effect of alcohol which should be saved for when you're an adult and your life is genuinely crap.

-o-

How To Get Famous For Doing NAFF ALL

Since time began, people have unfortunately had to rely on inspiring acts of noble achievements in order to become famous and idolised: discovering cures for terrible diseases, inventing amazing life-enriching machines; creating works of artistic brilliance or humanitarianly saving entire nations of losers. Muppets. Thanks to TV, crappy tabloids and trashy magazines, you can *now* become famous for simply being a good-looking idiot; in fact, even ugly people can also have their fifteen minutes of shame, eh Jade?

How to *Look* Like You Deserve To Be Famous

The most important qualification for becoming a celebrity is *to NOT be ugly*. Thankfully, with the humanitarian 21st century explosion in life-saving cosmetic surgery, even hurl-worthy people (that 99% of the population) no longer have to suffer from bitchy unsexual discrimination in the battle to become a tabloid tart. Indeed, Googlewhack "cosmetic surgery" and you'll discover 9,970,000 businesses to improve your diabolical physical appearance (their ads thoughtfully sponsored by various loan companies), so, there's really *no* excuse for putting up with your Quasimodo looks when buying major reconstructive surgery is now so much easier than buying a pair of jeans that fit.

So, before you hit the small time, what visual qualifications do you need?

- Obviously, *you should be orange*. Of course, traditionally this'd mean going on a sunbed every day, but that has its drawbacks. Firstly, it's well expensive - in some places it costs more than 5 pence an hour (although that's what stupid foreign coins leftover from your chavvy Spanish holiday are for). Secondly, if female, you can get pregnant from the jism left on the smeary tubes. Thirdly, it gets bloody hot and you might break a sweat and that's something you avoid doing at *all costs*.

- Your *teeth should be Chernobyl-glowing white*. This can easily be achieved with either correction fluid, sticking years worth of your collected dandruff over your yellowed gnashers, or by super-glueing those cool sweetie teeth over them. Alternatively, just paint your gums dark brown with creosote as this will make your teeth look well white by comparison.

- Your *hair should be massively over-styled* - particularly if you're a bloke. **Guys** should aim to smear enough hair products in their hair to make it hard enough to rebuff an angry bull should they find themselves in a matador ring… in fact, the bull should die on impact. Meanwhile **girls** should aim to look like every other floozy, i.e. with enough peroxide to damage any brain cells the head may still contain: this brain damage is vital as you're better off not knowing that when you enter adult life, women are paid an average of 30% lower than their male counterparts. Then again, you'll probably never have to work because you're going to be a WAG, inn't ya.

- You should *avoid buying clothes from "Primark"*: not just because the clothes are cheap crap but because you'll come into contact with rabid people in their thirties who think they've still "got it". They may accidentally touch you in their greedy frenzy and you may contract crow's feet, muffin top, or baldiness. Instead, you are far safer shopping in Dolce & Gabbana, Stella McCartney, Versace etc., because spoilt Teenagers and real A-listers are the only people who will pay for this tat.

Actually, it won't even matter if - after all this makeover work - you're still quite skanky because you'll think you're hotter than a vegetarian shitting at the top of a volcano after a cabbage vindaloo. And that's all that matters.

How To Achieve Instant Minor Fame And Fleeting Fortune

1. If you're female, simply become a WAG (it's easy - footballers are desperate to have any old sow as a girlfriend to try and prove in the changing room that they're not gay). Better still, be an Ex-WAG… e.g just before he gets old (at age 27) and is about to get ditched by his manager... you should then hunt down a pro golfer (longer career expectancy).
2. If you're male, just become a footballer. It's a doddle because you're already a closet cry-baby. Sadly, though you'll end up getting hitched to a freeloader.
3. Marry Paul McCartney - don't divorce him though, you'll get stacks more money if you wait for him to snuff it… it won't be long.
4. Shag a celebrity and sell your story for £27 to the tabloids. But, if you've been brushed with the *really* ugly stick, you can still cop-

off with a has-been like Dean Gaffney, Jade Goody or her Mum. It doesn't matter if you're rubbish at sexy stuff either, because the more you lie, the more money you'll automatically make.

5. Get knocked down by a police car or drunk-driving star… better still, a drink-driving star being chased be a police car. Ideally, the more serious your injuries, the higher your compensation claim.

6. Appear on a reality TV show…

How To Truly Stand Out At A Reality TV Show Audition

Nowadays, crap reality TV shows make up 99% of the TV schedule (the remaining 1% consists of the news and the Queen's speech - and ironically they're both *far* removed from reality). Sadly, telly is now veritably puking out copycat cheap ideas parading moronic everyday folk as "entertainment". Excellent. Consequently, the only citizens in the UK who currently **haven't** auditioned for a reality TV show are newsreaders and the Queen… (killjoy Philip stopped Lizzie trying out for "I'm A Celebrity Get Me Outa Here" on the grounds that she'd be have to wipe her own bottie). So, you've really got to be *totally* different from the lemming herds of ordinary divvies auditioning with you…

Unfortunately, there's already been an audition explosion in ***disabilities*** which automatically entitles those auditioning to make it to the very small screen: stutters, nervous tics, wheelchairs and the like have **all been done to death**. Instead, you could try:

    a) Being an anorexic.

    b) Being morbidly obese (yet still facially good-looking... obviously).

    c) Having a conjoined twin (if you don't happen to have one, try super-gluing a good-looking friend to your torso, bingo).

    d) Being terminally ill.

    e) Being dead.

How To Get Rid Of Your Auditioning Competition

Alternatively, during the audition process you could easily eliminate the rubbish competition by:

1. Eating enormous amounts of egg sarnies prior to standing in the queue - the resulting Hiroshima will mean you'll be the only one left to audition. If you're hardcore, try adding cress to the sarnies as the extra greeniness will be lethal. Even to yourself (see point 'e' above).

2. Talking excessively and excitedly about serial killers.

3. Sleep with them... they'd rather skip the audition and lose the chance of becoming a millionaire than look you in the face again.

4. **Very, very, very** slowly and discreetly placing Klu Klux Klan bonnets on your fellow would-be contestants.

How To Behave Whilst On The Reality Show

Obviously, you want to win. You're going to win. You need the audience to love you. So just be yourself. Be vile.

However, once you've appeared on your TV show, you should be prepared for the public backlash as they'll undoubtedly hate you more than Bin Laden, Katie and Peter, and The Chucklebrothers all rolled into one. Hoorah! Because that means you'll stay in the tabloids for even longer.

How To Survive - And Positively Enjoy - The Public Hating You

- *Strangers gobbing at you on the street* - you're already an expert blackboard-cleaner-hurled-by-your-desperate-teacher ducker, or bottle-throwing-in-nightclub dodger, so they're *never* going to hit you. Justifiably retaliate by throwing that morning's empty "Moet" bottle at them.
- *Passers-by hurling impressively abusive insults* - chances are you won't understand a lot of the words they use any way. Or, you'll have boringly heard them all before from your parents. However, under no circumstances should you retaliate with name-calling... as "stinky-face", "bum-chum" and "I'm going to get my dad on you" may make you *look* immature, even though you're well not. Instead, you should cry a lot in public as this will get you loads of free paparazzi coverage, which will inevitably

lead to a starring, lucrative role in a tissue paper commercial.

- ***Being hounded by the Paparazzi*** - this won't be nearly as much fun as you expected because, from now on, you'll have to try and make sure that they only photograph *from one particular angle* because you'll look bloody fat and ugly if they don't snap your 'best side'. E.g. the only position you look vaguely OK is being shot from above as you lie draped on your back on a wheel-able platform, pulled by your hanger-on 'friends', though a 'dry ice' cloud of self-raising flour.
- ***Being stalked by a deranged fan*** - perfect. Being hunted by a psycho and living in fear of your life is just what the psychiatrist ordered when your 15 seconds of fame are nearly up... the TV company behind the show will be morally obliged to provide you with a new identity - Harley Street here you come. But should you accidentally get slaughtered by your stalker, you're family will *still* make a bundle out of their misery on Jeremy Kyle; plus, you'll become immortal, a bit like Martin Luther, Lennon or that guy out of Milli Vanilli.

How To Streeeeeeeetch Out Your 15 Minutes Of Shame

Attending second-rate premieres, non-Park Lane parties, and photo shoots in 'Woman's Own' will have given you a real taste of the high life, so you'll want to drag out your notoriety for as long as poss.

Therefore, you'll need plenty of anorexic skeletons in the closet for the tabloids to squeeze every last drop of contaminated blood out of your 'popularity'. Alas, ASBOs, bedding Sven Erikson or being the reincarnation of Hitler are a bit last year, so here are some new ones... they don't even need to be remotely true because everyone believes tabloid tittle-tattle:

- You are the love child of Cliff Richard and Anna Kournakova.
- You are Lord Lucan.
- You are the separated conjoined twin of Simon Cowell; you were joined at the hips, hence Simon's strange high waist-banded trousers - a feeble attempt to distract attention from his deformed middle.
- You can play the spoons just using your bottom.
- You saw Tom Cruise kicking the shit out of Ghandi.
- You once crapped a poo that looked like "The Hoff".
- You've had the world's first brain transplant. You were given the brain of a pig. Oink.
- You're a stowaway from "The Titanic" - to pull this little white lie off stay permanently wet by throw a glass of water over yourself. You can get water from a thing called a tap.
- You saw Saint Oprah shoplifting in Harrods. And have the mobile phone

picture to prove it…er, no you don't, but the tabloid will fake it.
- You saw Osama Bin Laden working as a dancer in a strip club in Clapham.

How To Survive Once You're A Nobody Again

This doesn't bear thinking about. This will be the time to get yourself a labotomy. Oh, the irony… obviously, it's highly unlikely that you'll know what a lobotomy is, you're basically brain-dead already. DIY labotomy kits can be bought from Ebay at a highly reasonable *'Buy It Now' £24.99**.

*The author is hedging her bets that "How To Be The Most Obnoxious Teenager Ever" may not make her a millionaire, so she's subsidising her annual income by flogging these dodgy kits on the gypo auction site.

-o-

How To Pass Your Driving Test When You're Clearly Dangerous

99.8937284% of Teenager Learner Drivers are appalling drivers - the remaining 0.1946326% is Lewis Hamilton (if you checked those percentages added up, you're a loser - that'd require the writer to use a calculator and she's too thick to know how). Today's Teenagers are far more worried about checking out their hair damage in the rear view mirror than caring about mowing down a wheelchair-bound blind old lady who's having a heart attack after being mugged for her paltry pension. But it's not the Teenagers' fault… they've received terrible instructional and moral guidance from their parents who've blatantly used the claustrophobic confines of the family car to practise screaming at each other, and then used the roads and other vehicles/passengers to vent their raging marital anger upon.

Besides, today's Teens have grown up playing cool 'Colin McCrae's rally',   so it's no wonder they're more deadly on the roads than a police car in a high speed chase. Anyway, to pass your test *first time* would be positively humiliating - only special needs kids pass first go because the driving examiner is well embarrassed about not wanting to fail them and look prejudiced. But hang on… maybe passing first time would actually be really funny because:
- Your parents will be so angry that you proved them wrong (mind you, this has to be weighed up against passing first time but then keeping it a secret and pocketing all the 'extra lesson' money you're parents'll will cough up). Also, you're now legally required for them to cough up and buy you a brand new car, R.R.P £14,999. Anything less will make your parents' look embarrassingly hard-up.

- Your driving instructor will be so delighted that you proved them wrong (they'll be dreading you failing and having to spend more time with them in their learner car),
- Your friends will be so angry that you proved them wrong. They had a sweepstake on you failing so you'll have cost them that night's alcopops (approx. £276,98).

How To Pass That Stupid Written Test Thingummy

Actually, this is far easier than falling off a park bench, because not only have you already developed X-ray vision from cheating at school exams, but the tables will be stupidly close together so that the D.V.L.A. can *further* maximise the profit from the extortionate exam fees. Alternatively, it's genuinely true that the answers to *all* multiple choice questions in the world follow a simple zig-zag formation - so that's basically "A", "B", "C" then "D", followed by "C", "B" and "A"... all exam question setters are anal weirdos who like patterns.

And if none of the above work (i.e. you can't actually be bothered), you can just **loudly** ask your fellow examinees for the answers: your timid middle-class examiner will be *so afraid* of having Teenagers present in the difficult-to-escape-from-room (typically they'll be at the furthest point away from the door) that they'll happily let you cheat. In fact, why not just ask them for the answers. Wear a hoodie.

How To Pass Your Practical Driving Test With Flying Colours

Hahahahahahahahahahahahahahahahahahahahah ahahahahahahahahahahahahahahahahahahahahaha hahahahahahahahahahahahahahahahahahahahahah ahahahahahahahahahahahahahahahahahahahahaha hahahahahahahahahahahahahahahahahahahahahah ahahahahahahahahahahahahahahahahahahahahaha hahahahahahahahahahahahahahahahahahahahahah ahahahahahahahahahahahahahahahahahahahahaha hahahahahahahahahahahahahahahahahahahahahaha. You didn't actually think that there was any way in hell that you'd legitimately pass your test, did you? You can't even always steer a chip into your gob - and that's massive. And it's not as if you can get a plausible double to stand in and take your test *for you* - Brad Pitt/Jessica Alba have strong American accents (although, you *have* been known to have a pratty mid-Atlantic drawl when you're on the pull). No, there's only one way you're ever going to actually pass your test. And that's blackmail.

How To Stalk Your Driving Examiner

Of course, there are bound to be a few examiners working in your local test centre, but finding out who'd be yours is easy. The nasty looking one... they've specialised in obnoxious Teenagers.

1. You need to find out where they live, so you'll need to hang outside the test centre in disguise: the only way for the eagle-eyed meanie examiner *not to notice you* is to dress as a road cone. Don't worry about the

discrepancy in your size compared to a real cone - the nasty examiner will just put down seeing a giant road cone to the sneaky gins they had at lunchtime (how else are they going to get through taking Teenagers for their tests!?).

2. Then you'll need to follow them home - you'll have to go *fast* as they illegally speed through the suburban streets in a frantic bid to get home to their gin bottle, so why not hang on to their bumper. It'll be a bit like getting an all-over exfoliation and anti-cellulite massage. A bit.

3. Then you'll need to camp outside like a trampy gypo (this will also handily get you used to what it'll be like when you finally leave home). In fact, living in a hedge can be a most pleasurable experience because you'll get to drink all the dregs from the lager cans lazy tossers chuck in there. Similarly, there'll be rich pickings from all those discarded polystyrene takeaways. Quite frankly, you've never had it so good.

4. Plus, you can shake the bushes scarily when people walk by in the dark. Actually, these days, it's much more fun to do this to nervous, non-gang young men on their own than young women, who are *much* more likely to 'mace' you with their cheap and hideously nasty celebrity perfume.

5. Now you have to lie in wait (heaven) to catch your would-be examiner doing

something naughty. Their most likely crimes include:

i. Deliberately running over their neighbour's cat, Tiddywinkles (slaughtering innocent pets is their only form of stress relief). Besides, never mind, cats are rubbish. And this cat crapped on you in the bushes. If the examiner only clips the cat, you can always try finishing off the limping cat with your feet.

ii. Having a secret affair with one/ all of their future Teenage examinees. For you, this is not an option - you're so forgettable *in general* (never mind in bed) that they wouldn't remember you when you went to take the test.

iii.Not recycling their booze bottle in the assigned recycling box because they don't want the bin-men to see what they've downed in a week or several weeks(depending on where you live in the UK). It's not well-known but bin-men cheekily use the recycling bins to see what households spend the most on booze and then deliberately target these richer houses for their Christmas tips. If you're dumb enough to do a paper round, employ the same Christmas tipping policy.

iv. Sitting in the garage with the door down, the engine running and winding all the window up and then **farting**, letting the warm car intensify their toxic stench. Their addiction to farts is an inevitable consequence of working with Teenage learners. Of course, this is no problem for you either as you scratch a hole in the back window using your teeth to join in the fun.

v. Listening to *nothing* on their stereo. That's well dodgy. The stuff of serial killers.

6. Next, you'll need to record the damning evidence. Forget 'happy slapping' on your mobiles... that's *so* last week, your phone was actually designed for you to practise the art of blackmail.

How To Be A Dastardly Cool Blackmailer

You're now ready to confront your would-be examiner with your damming evidence... they'll do anything (including passing you on your test) to avoid having their career ruined. They only became driving examiners in the first place because they sucked at everything else they tried. Indeed, they are now at your complete beck and call (much like you Mum and Dad, but luckily your examiner doesn't live with you which makes them infinitely preferable to your M and D) and you can make them:

- Clean your new parent-bought sports car every second day. Dust on a car is a symptom of a driver owner who's far too busy working to have time to clean their car, and you want people to know that you're a proud lazy shirker. Indeed, a dusty car would also conveniently trigger your 'asthma' and result in days of school/work/ dole office.
- Scoop up your own merciless road kill and bury it in the local playground sand pit. Sand is *much* easier to dig up than soil.
- Follow you around 25/7 in their own car and distract the police from *your* terrible driving by ramming the cop car/bobby on the beat.
- Parking it for you.
- Driving it for you.

-o-

OTHER STUFF THAT ANNOYINGLY DOESN'T FIT ANY OTHER CHAPTER

How To Give The Most Painful Wedgie Ever

In today's society, just simply pulling your victim's pants *riiiiiight* up their cakey arsehole just won't cut it any more. You see, unfortunately, contemporary cotton underwear is just *too soft* to inflict any real pain, especially with the widespread use of heinous fabric softener (although poor people won't generally be able to afford it - they have to resort to trying to soften their cheap and nasty clothes by bunging a bobbling-removing hedgehog in the washing machine). Furthermore, with the proliferation of G-string wearing, the female species *may not even notice* that you've performed a skilled Wedgie manoeuvre on them. Therefore, you must select your victim with care… indeed, you'll be going near your target's derriere so you don't want your plan to ***literally backfire*** on you.

Who To <u>Avoid</u> Performing A Wedgie Attack Upon

1. Old people over thirty-five: not only are they all **incontinent**, but they also eat a lot of baked beans so that they can pretend that their fat stomach is due to a build up of gas. Indeed, overweight women call it "bloating" and blatantly lie that they have a wheat or dairy intolerance.
2. Babies: they are *definitely* incontinent. Plus, their hysterical, over-protective Mums will batter you. However, it may be worth wedgie-ing the annoying infant to experience the full, amusing evil magnitude of nappy stench (the actual reason why babies are put up for adoption). Incidentally, if you can stomach it, nappy bins in shopping centre baby changing facilities provide excellent ammunition for 'nappy poo bombs'... they're a *much more* mature Teen version of the childish water bomb.
3. Policemen: not because you're scared of them but simply because they wear tight leather belts that make grabbing the pant elastic annoyingly fiddly (did you know that the police only wear belts in the hope that it makes the cut of their boring trousers a bit more sexy, and not for illegally restraining innocent-until-proven-guilty yobbos as previously thought?).
4. Vicars/priests etc: they may send you to hell, or worse, Youth Camp.
5. The gays: you don't want to be creeping up behind these guys.

6. Chavvy pop stars and actresses getting out of cars at crappy premieres: it's a waste of your precious time because they never wear a n y knickers.

Who You <u>Can</u> Perform A Wedgie Attack, Attack, Attack Upon

1. Mothers over the age of twenty-three: they're guaranteed to be wearing big fat has-been knickers which are easy to grab. Ironically, as worn-out, new mums they're so starved of physical attention that they'll probably enjoy your excruciating Wedgie. So charge them fifty pence a Wedge.

2. Any girl/woman/embarrassing granny wearing hipster trousers: their knickers will be on arrogant display, veritably begging you to commit knicker hara-kiri on them. The trouble is, these females buy slave-labour cheap underwear and it'll definitely snap on you; this is actually how the 1p a day sweatshop children get their revenge on the western world... by sewing well dodgy seams. Therefore, you'll need to wear protective clothing for when their undies flick their crud on you, i.e. your least favourite friend's.

3. Nerdy teenage boys: they're not cool enough to know that it's a Teenage Law to wear your trousers half-way down their arse to reveal their grimy Calvin Kleins. After you've performed the Wedgie-eeeeeh on them, they'll attempt to pull their trousers back

up!!!!????!?!? Lucky for you, this is now the legally required time to inflict the **Front** Wedgie*.

4. Superman: anyone who wears pervy tights *under* garishly-coloured deserves the skidpan-t treatment. Hopefully, though, he has a spare set to change into in the phone box whilst his sullied set are being washed by dowdy Lois Lane, otherwise Lex Luther's going to have a field day. Goodie goodie gum drops.

Remember, above all, the art of pulling off a stupendous Wedgie is the element of **surprise**. So, when you've perfected and honed your skills on the above, annoyingly easy targets, you'll be ready to graduate to much more challenging and gratifying targets…

The Top Three Wedgie Targets
1. Anyone who's been run over by a bus and is lying down lazily, waiting for the ambulance: they will so *not* be expecting a Wedgie… it'll take their mind off losing their leg for a bit. You'll also be able to reveal to nosey passers-by whether or not the accident victim's wearing their good pants… this is actually the *only* reason why people rubber-neck at accident scenes.
2. The paramedics attending the above, careless idiot: they will *so not* be expecting a Wedgie either. The challenge for you is that they'll be wearing an all-in-on jumpsuit; to get round

this irritating obstacle simply snatch the scissors they're using to cut off the victim's clothes so they can resuscitate them and snip a hole in their trousers. Shame they're not crocodile scissors though. Although you could spend several hours making teeny tiny zig-zag cuttings.

3. The doctor at the hospital treating your original target: they will *truly* not be expecting a Wedgie. They'll also be the trickiest to perfom the manoeuvre on because they'll be exhausted by working a 342 hour shift and wired up on coffee, chocolate and God knows what else... consequently, they'll be flailing and stumbling all over the place, making knicker grabbing somewhat difficult. (Tip: to get to the hospital, simply hold on to the back of the ambulance and use your wheelies, or if you're not cool enough to own them, simply cover your feet in the slippy blood on the road. Woo-ooooosh).

How To Perform the Most Excruciating Wedgie Ever

Traditionally, a really sore Wedgie can be quickly and easily achieved by a simple swift and heartfelt yank of the pants. Don't stop there then...

- You can *maximise* discomfort by throwing in a *sawing* movement as you jerk.
- You can lull your victim into thinking that the Wedgie wasn't so bad by *stopping* three-quarters of the way, leading them to

prematurely sigh in relief... then, you wrench upwards a *further three feet*.
- Finally, you should complete the Wedgie by taking the knicker waistband and running 362 metres *away* before hilariously letting go. Folk in Outer Mongolia will be able to hear the resulting scream - laughs all round, you goodwill spreader, you.

WARNING: If you are seriously taller than your Wedgie Victim you may have ***too much leverage***; you'll know for sure if - after performing your Wedgie - they are sliced in two. Do a runner.

* **The Front Wedgie** is technically a similar manoeuvre to the traditional Wedgie, but it really effing hurts. All you do is face your victim. But don't do it to them if they are good at spitting.

-o-

How To Win An A.S.B.O.

Due to wonderfully high salt levels in junk food shrivelling the brain (not to mention the species-threatening decline in slug population due to them passing through saline pools of alcopop vom on pavements), not many Teenagers know that an A.S.B.O. *actually* stands for ***Anti Social Body Odour***. If you're caught with this vile, stinky-winky onion smell, you'll be awarded with a meaningless certificate by the police, then <u>shunned</u> by your local community, and deservedly so. Good... peace at last. However, catching this traumatic affliction of B.O. requires a Teenager to *break a sweat...* hmm, tricky one... So, obviously, the **only** time this is **ever** going to happen is moving, i.e. when the Teen is performing an impressive act of vandalism, committing theft, or showing off with abusive behaviour or the harassment of others more vulnerable than themselves.

Alas, though, A.S.B.O.'s are now as common as muck amongst Teenagers: it seems any old, bog-standard juvenile delinquent has one - they're now even more of a status symbol than owning a first edition 'Harry Potter'. Clearly, getting an A.S.B.O. is simply just *too easy*, which seriously diminishes the credibility of being awarded one in the first place... if you're going to win an A.S.B.O. you want it to be for doing something unusual, original and *really* shocking; after all, your heinous act of behaviour *has got to be worth* ending up stinking like a French person. Your goal is to whiff so badly that not even a phone mugger will want to come near you.

How To Be A Creative, Clever And Therefore Cooler A.S.B.O. Holder

1. Perfecting Mindless Acts Of Vandalism

a) *The Graffiti Artist*: traditionally, grown-ups *expect* a Teenager to daub crap, mis-spelt graffiti on any old surface that basically doesn't move. Therefore, copy the following passage on to your neighbour's morbidly obese child - indeed, why not show off by mimicking the italic typeface, to seriously bug your neighbours. They'll not only be annoyed because their terminally fatso offspring couldn't be arsed to move, but even more so because they won't understand the grown-up words:

Shall I compare thee to a Summer's day?

Thou are more lovely and more temperate:

Rough winds do shake the darling buds of May,

And Summer's lease hath all too short a date:

Sometime too hot the eye of heaven shines,

And often is his gold complexion dimm'd;

And every fair from fair sometime declines,

By chance or nature's changing course

untrimm'd:

But thy eternal Summer shall not fade

Nor lose possession of that fair thou ow'st;

Nor shall Death brag thou wander'st in his shade,

When in eternal lines to time thou grow'st:

So long as men can breathe, or eyes can see,

So long lives this, and this gives life to thee.

You'll probably be able to fit all this on just the fatso's double chin!

b) **Property Destruction**: historically-speaking, when Teens broke in to deserted properties and smashed them up this was merely to highlight to the local council that the targeted property was vacant and needed securing properly or bulldozing. However, there's now a huge profit to be made from remodelling these derelict buildings and flogging them to gormless first-time property buyers. Therefore, move in (you legally have squatters rights, na-na-nee-na-naaaaa), and renovate it using furniture and décor stolen from 'Harrods'*. You can then use the profits to buy yourself a JCB - this is going to be the next big trend in Teenager first cars now that the Hummer is a bit old school.

*Try wearing the Punjab as this will hide a multitude of stolen goods and no-one'll (dare) bat an eyelid. It's dead sexy too.

c) *Arson*: In the past Teenagers weren't fat like they are now, so they were forced to light fires to stay warm when they stayed out past their curfew. Nowadays, Teens *still* light fires but it's only a futile attempt to make their pasty faces have an orangey, fake tan glow. Become their saviour by smearing their pallid faces with orange squash instead... my, how c-list glamorous they'll look; plus, they'll be able to get an A.D.D. kick out of licking each other's e-numbered faces when they're getting off with each other.

2. Improving Senseless Acts Of Abuse And Harassment

a) *The Street Corner Gang Attack*: these days, people are more terrified of walking past a mob of youths than they are of creeping through a graveyard near a loony asylum at midnight; or, of even scurrying past a charity collector. This is because they expect to spat at, or worse - laughed at, verbally assaulted, or given a wedgie by the pack of undisciplined Teen scum. Die, pathetic chickens, die die die. So, if you *really* want to donate some long-lasting, quality post-traumatic stress disorder upon your passing victims, you should throw yourself at them and smother them with affection (try imagining that they've just won the lottery). They'll have panic attacks for years.

b) ***The Park Bench Ambush***: packs of Park Bench Youths are possibly *even more* feared than Teen gangs hanging on street corners. This is because these Teens *aren't* spending vast expenses of energy on standing upright on their own two feet; whilst **sitting down** on the bench they have *much* more energy to direct at passer-by fools. Now most sensible people clearly and deliberately veer across the town, or indeed country, to avoid passing a pack of tiddly Teens on a bench... the only people who don't are generally blind, your siblings (they have to prove to their friends that they're not scared of you - ha) and suicidals with a persecution complex. Instead of 'accidentally' tripping up these brave foolish souls, treat them to an acapella version of Boyz 2Men's "XXX". They'll think you've turned psycho and are about to kill them. Incidentally, you'll probably also get discovered by Simon Cowell.

c) The ***Knock and Run Attack... Well, More Like Skulk***: old people, especially, have traditionally been the target of 'Knock and Runs' by thoughtless shits just like you. So, turn cruel amusement on its head by knocking quite gently on the door (perhaps try knocking the rhythm to "We'll Meet Again" on their barricaded door - they'll love that). Then, when they finally answer (go at lunchtime - they'll think you're Meals on Wheels - especially if you tell them that you are) offer to do odd jobs for free. To make them trust you, tell them you're also from the gas-board (try flicking any old piece of cardboard in front of their cataract eyes for 'authenticity'). However, *don't* steal their lifesavings from the sugar bowl because they'll be someone else's granny or granddad just like yours and you wouldn't want to deprive some other Teenager of their pitiful inheritance... it's *much more rewarding* to imagine that Teen's horrified face when they discover they've only been left £47.37 in pennies.

3. Taking Stealing To Another Level

Clearly, you're never going to live long enough to *put back everything* you've ever stolen; for example:

- There's the thirteen thousand pounds in five and ten pieces from your Mum's purse (no brown coins though - they're stinky... apparently, they're covered in pavement poo).
- The corner shop's 4,287 toxic sherbert fizz-bombs you've downed behind the shopkeeper's back (by the way, it's your ugly mug's that's the reason why his back is always turned).

- The tonnes of chewing gum you've pinched from underneath all the desks at school…
- Your best friend's girl/boyfriend/teddy.

Ah yes, you're a veritable Robin Hood-come-Chowcheskoo.

However, now you should begin taking any items you possess (stolen or otherwise) that you've completely ruined *back to random shops* and proudly *leave them on any old shelf.* You'll be amazed and impressed at the price some people are willing to pay for your rubbish. Yet amazingly, despite your saintly acts of charity, the grumpy shop-owners won't appreciate your generosity because your reverse stealing simply highlights how their shop is full of full-price crap, and you'll be slapped with an A.S.B.O. faster than a toddler from a council estate. Ooh ooh, whilst you're in the shop, why not borrow some of that stuff you haven't got yet.

4. Perfecting Excessive Noise, Especially Late At Night

It's way too easy to just start fighting with your friends because you're all on a sugar rush, so instead, be a right little smart arse by making deafening firework noises after 11pm. Get your friends to make really loud "OOHS" and "AHHHS" too. The lack of explosions in the sky will make it hilariously hard for the fuzz to find you, too.

5. Refining The Fouling Of The Streets With Litter

This is boring and too easy... even adults do this willy-nilly (if confronted - and you love a healthy debate - they'll pretend that their litter is bio-degradable, e.g. apple cores and they don't want to fill up landfill sites). So, if you're going to *throw* litter, why not aim for people's open windows... they can then put it in their over-flowing bin, or sell it on Ebay. But what you *really* want to be doing is *crapping on the street* like a cute little doggie-woggie. In the olden days, before poo-pooing poopie-fining came along, kids had loads of fun trying to dodge the thousands of canine craps covering the pavements... it was great exercise too. Shitting on the streets will return health and physical well-being to the lazy youth of today. Plus, your poo poos don't go unattractively white like a doggie. Or do they...

6. Developing Drunken Behaviour In Public

In recent times, *teenage pools of puke* have actually, and impressively, *replaced* dog poo piles for kids to practice jumping over. The trouble with this game is that the police have begun extracting DNA from these steaming heaps to illegally gather a database of stupid Teens that they can later use when these reprobates get in proper trouble. So, any late night Special Brew and kebab-induced barfs will now have to be puked *down your girl or boyfriends mouth whilst you snog*. As a thoughtful alternative to these steaming heaps, you could instead leave little piles of useless foreign small change leftover from years of family holidays - the ensuing stampede from skint illegal immigrants will bring an alternative mayhem to city centres nationwide.

The other problem with your usual drunken behaviour is that it's often impossible to tell the difference from your everyday, sober demeanor... either way, you're staggering, unintelligible and aggressive. Therefore, you should appear unnervingly polite in public: opening doors, raising your beanie to passers-by and curtseying. You'll appear as well-behaved as a scary Nazi Youth and be duly saluted with an A.S.B.O.

7. Drugs, Man

Any old loser can become a druggie. Just look at Britney. But why would you want to give your parents a relatively valid reason for trying to throw you out; they've been secretly hoping you'd become a druggie since you turned thirteen. Besides, being a druggie is fairly boring and pointless:

- It plays havoc with your skin - and it's bad enough already.
- Whilst hardcore drugs make you skinny (whey hey), soft drugs gives you the munchies and makes you fat(ter) - trying to *juggle both* to just *maintain* your weight is simply way too much trouble.
- Pete Docherty.
- It costs money.

A far cheaper alternative is caffeine: dose up on moccachinos and you'll be wired for weeks. Plus, your breathe will be hilariously rancid and you can secretly play coffee-limbo with your friends to see who can lean furthest away falling over without whilst you're talking at them. First prize is a dead arm. And your parents' random blood tests can't prove a thing.

How To Stay Focused On Your (A.S.)B.O. Goal
It won't be easy to stomach all this tremendous physical exertion, but just remember that once you suffer from horrendous B.O. (mind you, it won't be long because basically getting out of bed makes you break into a sweat), you'll be treated as if you have leprosy... without the annoying loss of bogey-picking fingers. Once you stink, you'll be left well and truly alone, leaving you completely free to moan on and on and on and on about how well and truly alone you are. Anyhow, you'll *positively* like the smell of rancid onions - it reminds you of your late-night burger-fests.

Alternatively, if this all sounds like too much trouble and effort simply fill in the following fake document and brag this around instead.

-o-

How To Behave When You're Abducted By Aliens

Luckily, today's Teenagers stand a significantly higher chance of being abducted by aliens than of maturing into fully-rounded, emotional stable, socially productive and nice adults. In fact, the M.O.D. secretly estimates that 34,928 angst-ridden Teenagers were kidnapped in the UK last year by Extra Terrestrials - they tried to negotiate for *more* to be permanently abducted but the aliens said naff off, and that frankly, they'd rather kidnap David Guest.

So, why are *so many* Teenagers abducted by bug-eyed aliens... why not kidnap far more interesting and valuable human beings for their terrorising psychological analysis and gruesome medical experimentation, like say, your Mum and Dad? Is it because a Teenager is a super-condensed version of a human being: devastatingly rich in emotional content, and in their absolute physical prime? Nah. It's because the majority of the Teens that the aliens abduct are surly, stroppy, uncooperative and useless nightmares who end up being promptly dumped back on earth without so much as a deforming scar to prove they were abducted... the aliens can't stand the defiant Teens and have to carry on looking for specimens. Fortunately, the aliens know that no-one believes a word a Teenager says anyway.

How To "Spontaneously React" When You Come To On The Spaceship

Flipping willy-armed aliens. Abducting you in the middle of the night whilst you were having a saucy dream about David Beckham/Heidi Klum/Gordon Brown/50cent/McD's quarter-pounders/The Front Wedgie/Pinnochio (delete accordingly). Don't they know you need your ugly sleep? Agh, the aliens are almost as bad as your parents. They could have *at least* kidnapped you whilst you were in school, meeting your probation officer, or having Christmas dinn-ugh. Anyhow, when you come round from your drug-induced (bonus) abduction-sleep, why not teach the ugly E.T.s a lesson for being so inconsiderate by pretending to stay "under" as long as possible. This should be a piece of cake... you could probably pretend to be asleep for at least 146 days.

However, the aliens may grow a tad bored of waiting for you, The Sleeping Ugly to arise and decide to jettison you into space. Ordinarily, this would be well cool because you could float around space like a weightless person - and you've never been thin before; however, because you were abducted with absolutely no warning you won't have your asthma inhaler with you... and you'll need this to breathe into once the lack of oxygen in space starts to make you feel a bit giddy or dead. Consequently, if the aliens start approaching you angrily you'll need to "come round" A.S.A.P. - as a professional swearer, you won't have any trouble spotting the fact they're effing and blinding in *their* language.

How To Show The Aliens A Typical Obnoxious Teenager Waking Up

It's your moral obligation to help the aliens learn about the human race and all our idiosyncrasies; besides, if you *don't* cooperate a bit, they'll put you in a big formaldehyde jar and you'll never hold a burger again. Anyhow, you can't resist being the centre of attention, therefore, you should:

- Yawn a lot, e.g. for about 22 hours... this is also a cunning plan because you can secretly squirt out those cool sprays of spit that sometimes shoot out accidentally - this'll help you find out if the aliens are like the Evil Witch in "The Wizard of Oz" and terminally allergic to water.
- Swear a lot about it being too early. This'll help the aliens learn a lot about the very essence of homo sapien emotions through our language. Incidentally, if you're lucky (i.e. one of the mingers fancies you, and who can blame them), you could ask them to teach you how to say "F!?* off" in Alienish.
- Pull the cover over yourself, using your hands, feet and entire body to coffin yourself in, whilst muttering melodramatic, untrue statements about how rubbish your life is. But pay close

attention as to whether or not you are actually already lying on an operating table because this *significantly* reduces the amount of time you should perform this annoying part of your waking up routine... if you hear a chainsaw being revved up it's probably time to get up and start co-operating.

How To Perform Your Own Medical Experiments

Surprisingly, despite travelling the galaxies 94%* of aliens are innately and horrendously lazy. So you should get on like a school on fire. In fact, they only travel around inter-galatically because they're desperately hunting for a fizzing, crackling candy sweet that went out of manufacture in the late eighties. They actually *only* abduct humans to torture us to find out if we know if it's still in stock somewhere... so blackmail them into beaming up your cover-up stick, raz-mag, or teddy before informing them that they can still buy carcinogenic 'Spacedust' in Woolies. Alternatively, the slothful aliens will jump at the chance (though, not literally - they're bone idle; and besides, they don't really have proper legs, the mutants) if you offer to perform the "operations" *on yourself* to reveal the scientific marvels that an obnoxious Human Teenager has to offer...

1. **Show you can endure *any* physical pain -** pull a nasal and pubic hair out *simultaneously* without so much as a tear in

the eye (to avoid *actually* crying, imagine your parents are watching). If you've yet to sprout pubies (hahahahahahahahaha, you monk baby you), you can slice the scab off your childish knee with a karate chop.

2. **Demonstrate your ability to withstand *any* emotional torture** - admit to your knobheaded captors that you already secretly know that it's extremely unlikely you're ever going to be rich and famous, or even solvent and well-liked. (This is an extremely tough truth to admit, so to stop yourself blubbing like a footballer, cross your fingers behind your back to obviously stop it coming true).

3. **Reveal your physical prowess with multitasking, ambidextrous genius** - stuff a chip, a burger, a kebab, a chicken wing, a milkshake, an onion ring, and Vienetta all in your mouth at the same. *Totally* show off by successfully managing to talk really clearly with your gob completely rammed with food (you've had a lot of practise).

4. **Display your intellectual virtuosity by cracking monumental problems previously unsolved by Mankind** - show them how to get ketchup to run quickly out of a new bottle... simply smash it over your plate. Or head.

5. **Exhibit an extraordinary sense of humour/depths of depravity** - point your chewed up yellowy finger and beg to "Phone home". They won't get your hilarious "E.T." reference, however they won't be able to

stomach your appallingly unconvincing crocodile tears and they'll hand over their mobile faster than a Teenager in London. Then, call a premium rate reality TV voting phone line and cost the gullible Martians a fortune.

Why You Should Fall In Love With An Alien
It's definitely worth forcing yourself to cop off with an alien as there are many advantages to *staying on board* the spaceship:

- You won't have to go home.
- You can't understand a word they say, so even when the aliens start nagging you to stop leaving your skiddie underwear all over the place, you'll be blissfully ignorant.
- The G-force you'll experience on their space ship is hysterically funny; indeed, this'll be the first time in your life that you'll be glad you've got a fat face.
- The floors will probably be well shiny and slippy which not only makes them excellent for skidding on, but will allow you to look up their alien skirts and see what their alien "bits" actually look like.
- You can 'teach' them about our prehistoric history, for example, the ancient Egyptian art of non-oral greeting for "Hello" - this obviously involves you guffing in their mouths. Gullible idiots. Then, why not then teach your eager stupid alien students the caveman non-oral communication for "Shitface"…

How To Ignore The Fact That Your Alien Lover Is Hideously Ugly

Of course, to fall "in love" with an alien you'll have to get over the slight drawback that they're unbearably repulsive… mind you, they're probably no more disgusting than some of the Quasimodos you've previously got off with. But to help you stop chundering in their hideous mouth whilst snogging (er, is it a mouth?), you could try:

a) If you're *female*: gouging out your eyes with your cheap nail extensions (being careful to stop them pinging off)… or, why not try digging out *their* eyes as the blood/gooey stuff will instantly distract you from their unappealing mug.

b) If you're *male*, you could try rubbing your now *really* putrid socks over your eyeballs for a temporary (or maybe permanent) blinding effect.

c) If you're a trannie, just give them a traditional drag-queen makeover.

How To Make Your Alien Relationship Truly Meaningful

Who cares if your alien lover is quite a nice Martian? So what if they don't mind you occasionally giving them a Chinese Burn on their sixteen arms, or wiping your bogies behind their absolutely massive ear-ie things?! Ultimately, this relationship is doomed - you're a teenager after all. However, use your brain. For once. If you *have a baby* with your alien partner, you could make *a lot of money* in the tabloids. Or the travelling freak show. You'll fit right in too, for the first time in your life. You'll probably also be entitled to *loads* of extra welfare benefits - because the government won't want to appear un-right on... you'll receive even more privileges than if you were an illegal asylum seeker.

How To Get Sent Back To Earth
They'll come a point on board the spaceship when you feel strangely home-sick. How peculiar. You'll never have experienced this feeling before; in fact, you've yet to have *any* feeling before either. Amazingly, this isn't simply because you're missing junk food, reading "heat" magazine (well, not read exactly, more like laughing at the pictures of celebrities looking crappy), or even texting for 9 hours a day (the signal's rubbish in space), but because you're *desperate to know if your parents have noticed that you've gone.* And if they have noticed, whether or not they're glad... have they been on "Crimewatch" or at your temporary grave, dancing the night away?

Naturally, you'll have become so popular with the aliens that they'll be truly reluctant to let you go home. Yippee. Now you begin making the aliens start *hating* you... by pulling some of your best Teen moves on them:
- Sing 'Barbie Girl' (BB Twins' version) repeatedly. Or worse, 'Ground Control To Major Tom'.
- Press all the buttons manically on the control panel, whilst pretending to be

Fatboy Slim** (if it looks like the spaceship is going to crash, best stop).
* Puncture holes in the side of the spaceship by using the fattest and therefore slowest alien as a battering ram. The resulting turbulent change in air pressure won't unfortunately affect the aliens in the slightest, but it'll seriously muck your hair up and your resulting deafening shrieking will be enough to get you beamed back to earth pronto.
* Start playing the spoons.
* Or far worse, tap dance - they won't want you scuffing their shiny floors, and they won't be able to stand your fixed cheesy-psycho grin.
* Pretend to be David Guest: to achieve this simply smear poo over your hair. And face.

To guarantee that the aliens beam you back down to your lovely festering bed, and not spitefully land you in Afghanistan, Outer Mongolia or East Kilbride, you should leave the aliens your cover-up stick, raz-mag or teddie. Or the address of the only *un*-obnoxious Teenager you know (if you don't know any, I know one: Sarah Walker, 32 Ellesmere Road, Berkhamsted, Herts, HP4 2MT.)

How To Convince The Adults You Were Abducted By Aliens

Alas, as previously mentioned, you won't have any proof such as corn-circle scarring on your belly to prove to your parents and tabloid hacks that you were kidnapped by E.T.s. After all, you've been known to go walkabouts before. Plus times infinity, you're a well-known liar. The reason for you needing them to believe you is simply to get time off school/work or make money. So, the ONLY way to convince your folks that you *were* abducted is to behave EXTREMELY OUT OF CHARACTER, and therefore con them into believing you've been deeply traumatised. This, unfortunately, means appearing to have missed your parents, even *to love* your parents. In normal society that requires hugging, kissing (*not* on the lips) looking in the eye and uttering those magic three little words, "I clean room".

* The remaining 6% work in 'Planet Hollywood'.
** The author is well aware that there are far more "in" DJ's than this but she can't be arsed to go on the internet to find out who they are.

*The remaining 6% work in B&Q on a Saturday.

-o-

Printed in Great Britain
by Amazon

26181413R00208